BORROWED TIME is a collection of three novellas that together comprise the Apocalypse Trilogy.

Naming of Parts... a young Jack and his family flee the zombie plague to find his sister, but it's not only people who are rising from the dead.

Changing of Faces... were-creatures attack a beached cruise liner, the one place that Jack dares call home.

Shifting of Veils... the world has moved on. Mad, murderous wraiths haunt the overgrown towns. And Jack must embark on a final desperate journey to reunite his family.

To Pat

BORROWED TIME

Best wishes

[signature]

Fantasycon '15

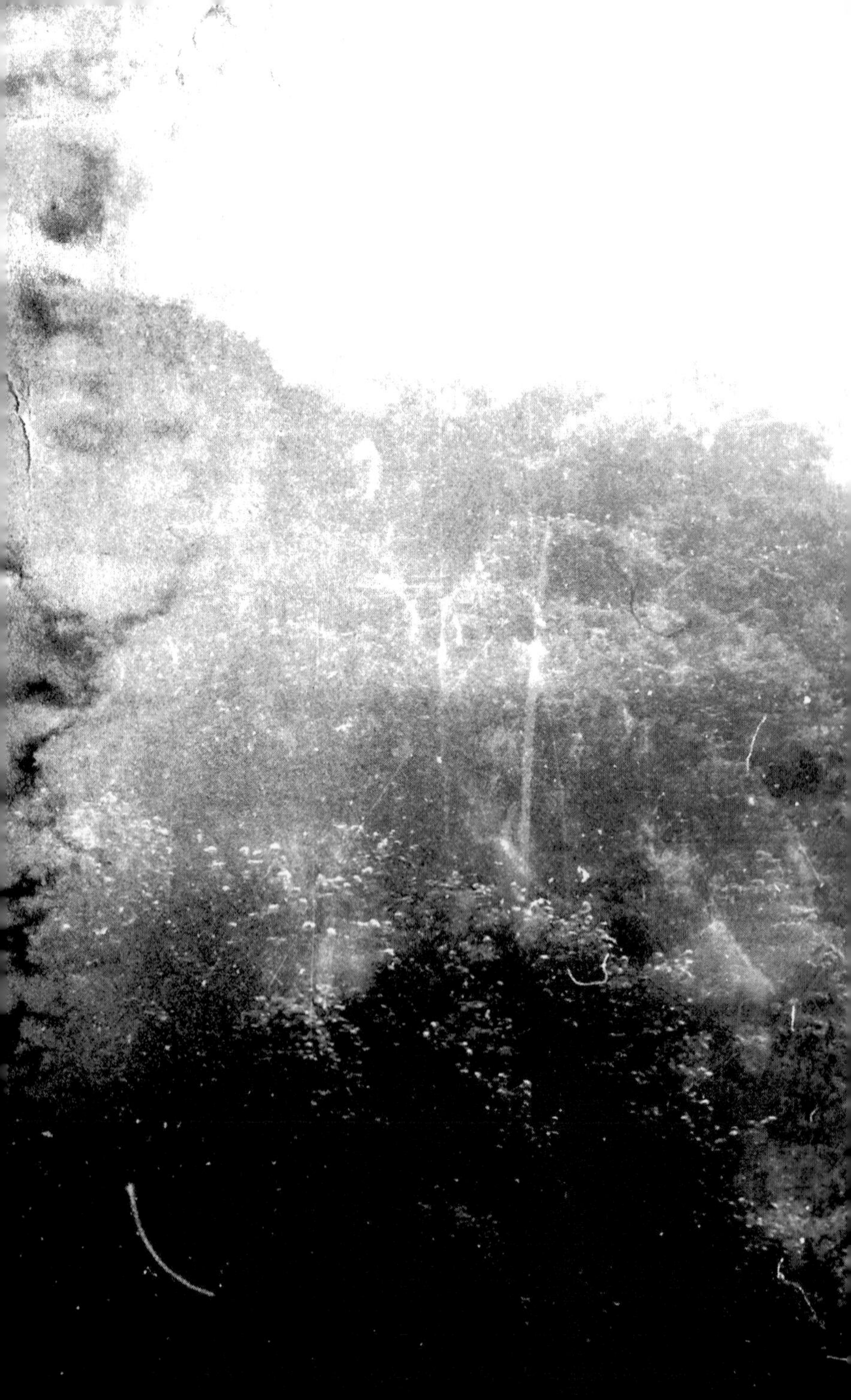

Borrowed Time

The Apocalypse Trilogy

Tim Lebbon

BORROWED TIME
THE APOCALYPSE TRILOGY
Copyright © 2015 Tim Lebbon
INTRODUCTION
Copyright © 2015 Tim Lebbon
COVER ART
Copyright © 2015 Ben Baldwin

The right of Tim Lebbon to be identified as Author of
this Work has been asserted by him in accordance with the
Copyright, Designs & Patents Act 1988.

The individual novells contained here were first published in Great
Britain in 2000 (*Naming of Parts*), 2004 (*Changing of Faces*) and 2014
(*Shifting of Veils*) This omnibus edition collecting all three books and
featuring a new Introduction and linking material by the author is first
published in October 2015 by Drugstore Indian Press, an imprint of
PS Publishing Ltd., by arrangement with the author.

This book is a work of fiction. Names, characters, places and
incidents either are products of the author's imagination or are
used fictitiously. Any resemblance to actual events or locales or
persons, living or dead, is entirely coincidental.

ISBN
978-1-848639-49-2

1 3 5 7 9 10 8 6 4 2

Design & Layout by Michael Smith
Printed and bound in England by T. J. International

Drugstore Indian Press | Grosvenor House
1 New Road Hornsea, HU18 1PG | United Kingdom

editor@pspublishing.co.uk | www.pspublishing.co.uk

CONTENTS

vii . . . . INTRODUCTION

1 . . . . NAMING OF PARTS

79 . . . . CHANGING OF FACES

169 . . . . SHIFTING OF VEILS

INTRODUCTION

NAMING OF PARTS was written right at the beginning of my career as a published writer. It was also one of PS Publishing's earliest publications in their ongoing world takeover, so you could say I'm one of PS's original authors. Considering who else was there at the time—Graham Joyce, Michael Marshall Smith, James Lovegrove, Kim Newman, Paul McAuley and Stephen Baxter—that's quite an honour.

Back then, it was *mindblowing*.

Around that time I'd had a load of short stories published in the small press, in magazines (and lots of you reading this will remember these splendid publications) with such exotic titles as Peeping Tom, Dreams from the Stranger's Cafe, Exuberance, Grotesque, Psychotrope, Sierra Heaven and Black Tears. Psychotrope was my first publication with a story called *Simon Says*, although my first acceptance was from *Peeping Tom* for a story called *First Taste*. I can still remember my mum calling the house I'd just moved into with my soon-to-be-wife Tracey and saying, "An editor just phoned for you, I gave him your number!" and me thinking, What if he gets an engaged tone and moves on to someone else! But no, Stuart Hughes rang and my first story was accepted. I've still got all those magazines somewhere, a great big pile of them. I'll get them out someday.

I'd also had my first novel, *Mesmer*, published through *Tanjen*. Not only will some of you remember them, I'll bet a few people reading this were published by them, too. *Mesmer* was shortlisted for a British Fantasy Award. I mean, bloody hell, my first FantasyCon with my first novel on the shortlist! I was probably unbearable.

After that came *White* from MOT Press, which blow me down actually *won* the British Fantasy Award, as well as being selected by Stephen Jones and Ellen Datlow for their 'Best of' anthologies and being optioned for a movie. That option lapsed, but the writer Stephen Susco (a top guy, ale lover, good beard) is still passionate about getting it made one day. It'll happen. His script is wonderful.

My next book was *Faith in the Flesh* from Razorblade Press, consisting of the two novellas *From Bad Flesh* and *The First Law*. I already knew Pete Crowther by then, and I felt cheeky enough to ask him for a blurb for *Faith in the Flesh*. I mean, come on... this was Pete Crowther!

I still remember the phone call I received from him in work. He'd read the novellas, he said, and he told me how much he loved them, and how rather than a blurb he'd like to write me an introduction. Then he said, "And I think I'd like you to write something for me."

So I did. *Naming of Parts* was the result. I'd decided to write a zombie novella, but one with a difference. So in this story it wasn't just people who died and came back to life.

Published in 2000, it also won the British Fantasy Award and was very well received. But even before publication I was thinking about Jack and his family, what they'd been through (what *I'd* put them through), and what might be waiting for them in the future. I mentioned to Pete about this being an ongoing series of three or four novellas, and he was very open to the idea. So I planned to write the next two or three novellas over the following couple of years.

Introduction

Yeah, well, that worked out well.

Changing of Faces appeared in 2004. That's not too much of a gap really, is it? I mean, in the meantime I also published my collections *As the Sun Goes Down* and *White and Other Tales of Ruin* from Night Shade Books, the novels *Face* (also Night Shade) and *The Nature of Balance* from Leisure, as well as more short stories and novellas. Things were moving in the right direction, and in around 2003 I went part time in work. Mondays, Tuesdays and Wednesday mornings were wonderful, spent making up worlds and often destroying them again. Wednesday lunchtimes ... not so good. On goes the tie and off to work I go. That's not to say I wasn't always thinking about the writing in work, of course ... and sometimes, I *might* have come home with pockets full of post-it notes with scribbled story ideas ...

Changing of Faces was also well received, and I was determined to write the next novella pretty soon after that one. But then, things happened. You know, things.

Things like more books being commissioned, giving up work to write full time, and generally starting to live the way I'd dreamed of for quite some time, making a living from my writing. Ahhh, I hear you say, if you suddenly had all that time you should have written the third novella right away.

Probably true. *Definitely* true. But it didn't happen that way.

After a while people started to ask, When are you writing the next *Naming of Parts* and *Changing of Faces* book? And my answer would always be, Soon. Because I really believed that was the case. I was determined. It was going to happen.

Fast forward ten years.

Now, PS had contracted me to write *Shifting of Veils* quite a while before I did so, at around the same time that they bought my collection *Nothing as it Seems* (I consider this my best collection, actually, so if you haven't picked it up yet drop PS a line). It was always at the back of my mind, and I have no excuse as to why it was so late.

What *should* have happened is:

Pete Crowther: Lebbon, where's that bloody novella I contracted you for years ago you useless bald git?

Lebbon: Sorry Pete, I'll get right on it.

What *actually* happened is:

Lebbon: Hi Pete, look, I know I owe you that novella but—

Pete Crowther: Honestly Tim, don't worry about it, it'll happen when it happens.

(Note to other publishers: The good cop/bad cop approach works best with me when good cop's gone for a coffee and it's just bad cop in the room).

Ten years. That's a long time to wait to read the third novella in a series, let alone write it. I'd had the title *Shifting of Veils* for some time, but the story required a longer gestation. And when the time finally came to write it, a bike ride brought it all home.

A lot has changed in my life in the years between *Naming of Parts* and *Shifting of Veils*. I wrote that first story when my daughter was just a baby, and she's now grown into a lovely young woman. My son was born in 2003, I've lost my mum, and writing has become my full-time job.

Another change is my newfound love of exercise. What, that chubby bald bloke drinking too much and smoking in the FantasyCon bar? I know, who'd have thunk it, right? It started a few years ago and it's all gone a bit mad, with me dropping 30lbs and regularly entering tough endurance events like Ironman and marathons (buy me a pint one day and I'll tell you all about it. I do still love ale). A few years ago I'd consider a 3 mile bike ride a long way, but now I do regular 40 or 50 miles bike rides at the weekend. And it was during one of these rides that I saw the church.

I'd known it was there for some time, tucked down a mile-long lane that spans between two of my regular cycling routes, one flat, the other hilly. One day I took a left on the spur of the moment, and when I pulled up outside the church, I knew it would be the setting of *Shifting of Veils*.

By the time I got home, much of the novella was already taking shape.

This introduction is, in a very waffly, beating-around-the-bush and roundabout way, an apology, not only to readers who were waiting so long for *Shifting of Veils*—I really did leave Jack and his family hanging for just too long—but also to Pete and the whole crew at PS. It took a while.

However, I hope that *Borrowed Time*, this volume of all three apocalyptic novellas, presents a satisfyingly complete story. I put Jack and his family through an awful lot of hardships. I destroyed the world (again). But I've written something of which I'm very proud, from early beginnings to an eventual end.

Tim Lebbon
Goytre
September 2015

This one's for Tim Love

Naming of Parts

"A child grows up when they realise that they will die."

—proverb

THAT NIGHT, SOMETHING tried to break into the house. Jack heard the noises as he lay awake staring at the ceiling, attempting to see sense in the shadowy cracks that scarred the paintwork. The sounds were insistent and intelligent, and before long they were fingering not only at window latches and handles, but also at the doorways of his mind.

He liked listening to the night before he went to sleep, and out here in the country there was much to hear. Sometimes he was afraid, but then he would name all the different parts that went to make up that fear and it would go away. *A sound I cannot identify. A shape I cannot see. Footsteps that may be human, but which are most likely animal. There's nothing to be afraid of, there are no monsters. Dad and Mum both say so; there are no such things as monsters.*

So he would lie there and listen to the hoots and rustles and groans and cries, content in the knowledge that there was nothing to fear. All the while the blankets would be his shield, the bedside light his protector, and the gentle grumble of the television from downstairs his guarantee.

But that night—the night all guarantees were voided—there were few noises beyond his bedroom window, and with less to hear, there was more to be afraid of. Against the silence every snapped twig sounded louder, each rustle of fur across masonry was singled out for particular attention by his galloping imagination. It meant that there was something out there to frighten everything else into muteness.

And then the careful caress of fingertips across cold glass.

Jack sat up in bed and held his breath. Weak moonlight filtered through the curtains, but other than that his room was filled with darkness. He clutched at his blankets to retain the heat. Something hooted in the distance, but the call was cut off sharply, leaving the following moments painfully empty.

Click click click. Fingernails picking at old, dried glazing putty, perhaps? It sounded like it was coming from outside and below, but it could just as easily have originated within his room, behind the flowing curtains, something frantically trying to get out rather than break in.

He tried naming his fears, this time unsuccessfully; he was not entirely sure what was scaring him.

A floorboard creaked on the landing, the one just outside the bathroom door. Three creaks down, three back up. Jack's heart beat faster and louder and he let out a gasp, waiting for more movement, listening for the subtle scratch of fingernails at his bedroom door. He could not see the handle, it was too dark, it may even be turning now—

Another creak from outside, and then he heard his mother's voice and his father hissing back at her.

"Dad!" Jack croaked. There were other sounds now: the soft thud of something tapping windows; a whispering sound, like a breeze flowing through the ivy on the side of the house, though the air was dead calm tonight.

"Dad!" He called louder this time, fear giving his voice a sharp edge to cut through the dark.

The door opened and a shadow entered, silhouetted against the landing light. It moved towards him, unseen feet creaking more boards. "It's okay, son," his father whispered, "just stay in bed. Mum will be in with you now. Won't you, Janey?"

Naming of Parts

Jack's mother edged into the room and crossed to the bed, cursing as she stumbled on something he'd left on the floor. There was always stuff on the floor in Jack's room. His dad called it *Jack debris*.

"What's going on, Dad?" he asked. "What's outside?"

"There's nothing outside," his father said. His voice was a monotone that Jack recognised, the one he used to tell fatherly untruths. And then Jack noticed, for the first time, that he was carrying his shotgun.

"Dad?" Jack said uncertainly. Cool fingers seemed to touch his neck, and they were not his mother's.

She hugged him to her. "Gray, you're scaring him."

"Janey—"

"Whatever... just be careful. Be calm."

Jack did not understand any of this. His mother hugged him and in her warmth he found the familiar comfort, though tonight it felt like a lie. He did not want this comfort, this warmth, not when there was something outside trying to get in, not when his father stood in his pyjamas, shotgun closed and aimed at the wall, not broken open over his elbow as he carried it in the woods.

The woods. Thinking of them aimed Jack's attention, and he finally noticed just how utterly silent it was out there. No voices or night-calls, true, but no trees swishing and swaying in sleep, no sounds of life, no hint of anything existing beyond the house at all.

His father moved to the window and reached out for the curtains. Jack knew what he would find when he pulled them back—nothing. Blankness, void, or infinity... and infinity scared Jack more than anything. How could something go on forever? What was there after it ended? Occasionally he thought he had some bright idea, but then sleep would come and steal it away by morning.

"Dad, don't, there's nothing out there!" he said, his voice betraying barely controlled panic.

"Shhh, shhh," his mother said, rocking him.

"I know," his father said without turning to offer him a smile. He grabbed a curtain and drew it aside.

Moonlight. The smell of night, a spicy dampness that seemed always to hide from the sun. And the noises again, tapping and scraping, tapping and scraping.

"Mum, don't let Dad open the window," Jack said, but his mother ignored him because she was hugging him, and that was usually enough. He would forget his bad dreams and go back to sleep, Mum would smile at the foolishness he'd spouted, but didn't she know? Didn't she see that they were all awake, and that what he was thinking was not foolishness because his dad really was standing in his room with a shotgun, opening the window, leaning out now, aiming the weapon before him like a torch—

There was an explosion. Like an unexpected scream in the depths of night it tore through Jack's nerves, shred his childish sense of valour and set him screaming and squirming in his mother's lap. Her arms tightened around him and she screamed too, he could smell the sudden tang of her fear, could feel the dampness between her breasts as he pressed his face to her chest.

"Gray, what the fuck—"

Her words shocked Jack but he could not lift his face to see.

"What the hell? What are you doing, what are you shooting at?"

Somewhere in the blind confusion his father came across and offered soothing words, but they were edged with his own brand of fear. Jack could not see him but he could imagine him standing there in silence, staring at a wall and avoiding his mother's eyes. It was his way of thinking about what to say next.

He said nothing. Instead, Jack felt his dad's strong hands under his arms, lifting him up out of the warmth of his mother's fear and letting the dark kiss his sweaty skin cool.

"Dad," Jack sobbed, "I'm scared!"

His dad rocked him back and forth and whispered into his ear, but Jack could barely hear what he was saying. Instead he

Naming of Parts

tried to do what he had once been told, name the parts of his fear in an attempt to identify them and set them open to view, to consideration, to understanding.

Something, outside in the dark. Dad, he saw it and shot it. The sounds, they've gone, no more picking, no more prodding at our house. Monsters, there are none of course. But if there are ... Dad scared them off.

"Gray," his mother said, and Jack looked up sharply.

"They weren't monsters, were they Dad?" His father did not say a word. He was shaking.

"Gray," his mum said again, standing and wrapping them both in her arms. "We should try the police again."

"You know the phone's dodgy, Janey."

"You shot at someone. We should try the police."

"Someone? But you saw, you—"

"Someone," Jack's Mum whispered softly. "Robbers, I expect, come to steal our Jackie's things." She ruffled his hair but Jack could not find a smile to give her.

"I heard them picking at the putty," he said. "Robbers would just smash the window. Least, they do in *The Bill*. And there's nothing else making a noise, like the fox in the woods. I always hear the fox before I go to sleep, but I haven't heard it tonight. Dad!"

His father turned and stared at him, his face unreadable.

"Did you shoot someone, Dad?"

His father shook his head. He began to smile as he pulled Jack's face into his neck, but the expression was grotesque, like one of those old gargoyles Jack had seen on churches when they were in France last year. "Of course not, Jack. I fired into the air."

But he had not fired into the air, Jack knew. He had leaned out and aimed down. Jack could not help but imagine something squirming on the ground even now, its blood running into the gravel alongside the house, screams of pain impossible because it had no jaw left to open—

"Come on," his dad said, "our room for now, son."

"Didn't you try the mobile?" Jack asked suddenly, but the look on his mother's face made him wish he hadn't.

"That's not working at all."

"I expect the batteries have run out," he said wisely.

"I expect."

His father carried him across the creaking landing and into their bedroom, a place of comfort. He dropped him gently onto the bed, and as he stood the telephone on the bedside table rang.

"I'll get it!" Jack shouted, leaping across the bed.

"Son—"

He answered in the polite manner he had been taught: "Hello, Jack Haines, how may I help you?" *It's the middle of the night*, he thought. *Who rings in the middle of the night? What am I going to hear? Do I really want to hear it, whatever it is?*

"Hey, Jackie," a voice said, masked with crackles and pauses and strange, electronic groans. "Jackie ... the town ... dangerous ... get to Tewton ... Jackie? Jackie? Ja ... ?"

"Mandy," he said, talking both to her and his parents. "It's Mandy!"

His mother took the receiver from his hand. "Mandy? You there?" She held it to her ear for a few seconds, then glanced at Jack. "No one there," she said. "Line's dead. It did that earlier." She turned to his dad and offered the receiver, but he moved to the window and shaded his eyes so he could see out.

"She said we should go to Tewton," Jack said, trying to recall her exact words, afraid that if he did he would also remember the strange way she had spoken. Mandy never called him Jackie. "She said it was safe there."

"It's safe here," his dad said without turning around. He was holding the shotgun again and Jack wanted to believe him, wanted to feel secure.

His mum stood and moved to the window. "What's that?" Jack heard her mutter.

"Fire."

Naming of Parts

"A fire?"

His father turned and tried to smile, but it seemed to hurt. "A bonfire," he said, "over on the other side of the valley."

"At night? A bonfire in the middle of the night?" Jack asked.

His parents said nothing. His mother came back to the bed and held him, and his father remained at the window.

"It *was* Mandy," Jack said.

His mother shrugged. "I didn't hear anyone."

He tried to move away from her but she held him tight, and he thought it was for her own comfort as much as his. He didn't like how his mum and dad sometimes talked about Mandy. He liked even less the way they often seemed to forget about her. He was old enough to know some stuff had happened—he could remember the shouting, the screaming, the punching on the last day Mandy had been with them—but he was not really old enough to realise exactly what.

It was so quiet, Jack could hear his father's throat clicking as he breathed.

They stayed that way until morning.

※

"There are secrets in the night," Mandy once told him. She was sitting next to his bed, looking after him because he'd been lost in the woods. He usually liked it when Mandy talked to him, told him things, but today even she could not cheer him up. She and his parents were hardly speaking, and when they did it was to exchange nothing but nastiness.

"What do you mean?"

She smiled. "You know, Jack. Secrets. You lie awake sometimes, listening for them. Don't you? I know I do."

"I just like listening," he said, but he guessed she was right. He guessed there was more going on than most people knew, and he wanted to find out what.

"If you find a secret, sometimes it's best to keep it to yourself. Not to tell Mum and Dad."

Jack was subtly shocked at her words. Why keep something from Mum and Dad? Wasn't that lying? But Mandy answered for him.

"Sometimes, grown-ups don't understand their kid's secret. And I'll tell you one now."

He sat up in bed, all wide-eyed and snotty-nosed. He wondered why Mandy was crying.

"I'm leaving home. At the weekend. Going to live in Tewton. But Jack, please, don't tell Mum and Dad until I'm gone."

Jack blinked as tears stung his eyes. Mandy hugged him and kissed his cheeks.

He didn't want his sister to go. But he listened to what she said, and he did not tell their parents the secret.

Three days later, Mandy left home.

❖

In the morning Jack went to fetch the milk, but the milkman hadn't been. His father appeared behind him in the doorway, scowling out at the sunlight and the dew steaming slowly from the ground, hands resting lightly on his son's shoulders.

Something had been playing on Jack's mind all night, ever since it happened. An image had seeded there, grown and expanded and, in the silence of his parent's bedroom where none of them had slept, it had blossomed into an all-too-plausible truth. Now, with morning providing an air of normality—though it remained quieter than usual, and stiller—he was certain of what he would find. He did not *want* to find it, that was for sure, yet he had to see.

He darted away from the back door and was already at the corner of the house before his dad called after him. The shout almost stopped him in his tracks because there was an unbridled panic there, a desperation...but then he was looking around the side of the cottage at something he had least expected.

There was no body, no blood, no disturbed flower-bed where someone had thrashed around in pain. He crunched along the

Naming of Parts

gravel path, his father with him now, standing guard above and behind.

"You *didn't* shoot anyone," Jack said, and the sense of relief was vast.

Then he saw the rosebush.

The petals had been stripped, and they lay scattered on the ground alongside other things. There were bits of clothing there, and grimy white shards of harder stuff, and clumps of something else. There was also a watch.

"Dad, whose watch is that?" Jack could not figure out what he was seeing. If that was bone, where was the blood? Why was there a watch lying in their garden, its face shattered, hands frozen at some cataclysmic hour? And those dried things, tattered and ragged around the edges, like shrivelled steak...

"Gray!" his mother called from the back door, "where are you? Gray! There's someone coming down the hill."

"Come on," Jack's dad said, grabbing his arm and pulling him to the back door.

Jack twisted around to stare up the hillside, trying to see who his mother was talking about, wondering whether it was the Judes from Berry Hill Farm. He liked Mr Jude, he had a huge Mexican moustache and he did a great impression of a *bandito*.

"We should stay in the house," his mum said as they reached the back door. "There's nothing on the radio."

If there's nothing on the radio, what is there to be worried about? Jack wondered.

"Nothing at all?" his dad said quietly.

His mother shook her head, and suddenly she looked older and greyer than Jack had ever noticed. It shocked him, frightened him. Death was something he sometimes thought about on the darkest of nights, but his mother's death... its possibility was unbearable, and it made him feel black and unreal and sick inside.

"I thought there may be some news..."

And then Jack realised what his mum had really meant... no

radio, no radio *at all*... and he saw three people clambering over a fence higher up the hill.

"Look!" he shouted. "Is that Mr Jude?"

His father darted into the cottage and emerged seconds later with the shotgun—locked and held ready in both hands—and a pair of binoculars hanging around his neck. He handed his mother the shotgun and she held it as if it were a living snake. Then he lifted the binoculars to his eyes and froze, standing there for a full thirty seconds while Jack squinted and tried to see what his dad was seeing. He pretended he had a bionic eye, but it didn't do any good.

His dad lowered the glasses, and slowly and carefully took the gun from his wife.

"Oh no," she said, "oh no, Gray, no, no, no..."

"They did warn us," he murmured.

"But why the Judes? Why not us as well?" his mum whispered.

Jack's father looked down at him, and suddenly Jack was very afraid. "What, dad?"

"We'll be leaving now, son," he said. "Go down to the car with your mum, there's a good boy."

"Can I take my books?"

"No, we can't take anything. We have to go now, because Mr Jude's coming."

"But I like Mr Jude!" A tear had spilled down his dad's cheek, that was terrible, that was a leak in the dam holding back chaos and true terror, because while his dad was here—firm and strong and unflinching—there was always someone to protect him.

His father knelt in front of him "Listen, Jackie. Mr Jude and his family have a... a disease. If we're still here when they arrive they may try to hurt us, or we may catch the disease. I don't know which, if either. So we have to go—"

"Why don't we just not let them in? We can give them tablets and water through the window, and..." He trailed off, feeling cold and unreal.

"Because they're not the only ones who have the disease. Lots of other people will have it too, by now. We may have to wait a long time for help."

Jack turned and glanced up the hill at the three people coming down. They didn't look ill. They looked odd, it was true, they looked *different*. But not ill. They were moving too quickly for that.

"Okay." Jack nodded wisely, and he wondered who else had been infected. He guessed it may be something to do with what had been on the telly yesterday, the thing his mum and dad had been all quiet and tense and pale about. An explosion, he remembered, an accident, in a place so far away he didn't even recognise the name. "Mandy said we should go to Tewton, she said it was safe there."

"We will," his father nodded, but Jack knew it was not because Mandy had said so. His parents rarely listened to her any more.

"That big bonfire's still burning," Jack said, looking out across the valley for the first time. A plume of smoke hung in the sky like a frozen tornado, spreading out at the top and dispersing in high air currents. And then he saw it was not a bonfire, not really. It was the white farm on the opposite hillside; the whole white farm, burning. He'd never met the people who lived there but he had often seen the farmer in his fields, chugging silently across the landscape in his tractor.

Jack knew where the word *bonfire* came from, and he could not help wondering whether today this was literally that.

His dad said nothing but looked down at Jack, seeing that he knew what it really was, already reaching out to pick up his son and carry him to their car.

"Dad, I'm scared!"

"I've got you, Jackie. Come on Janey. Grab the keys, the shotgun cartridges are on the worktop."

"Dad, what's happening?"

"It's okay."

"Dad..."

As they reached the car they could hear the Jude family swishing their feet through the sheen of bluebells covering the hillside. There were no voices, there was no talking or laughing. No inane *bandito* impressions this morning from Mr Jude.

His parents locked the car doors from the inside and faced forward.

Jack took a final look back at their cottage. The car left the gravelled driveway, and just before the hedge cut off the house from view, he saw Mr Jude walk around the corner. From this distance, it looked like he was in black and white.

❖

Jack kept staring from the back window so he did not have to look at his parents. Their silence scared him, and his mum's hair was all messed up.

Trees passed overhead, hedges flashed by on both sides, and seeing where they had been instead of where they were going presented so much more for his consideration.

Like the fox, standing next to a tree where the woods edged down to the road. Its coat was muddied, its eyes stared straight ahead. It did not turn to watch them pass. Jack thought it may be *his* fox—the creature he had listened to each night for what seemed like ages—and as he mourned its voice he heard its cry, faint and weak, like a baby being dragged from its mother's breast and slaughtered.

They had left the back door open. His mum had dashed inside to grab the shotgun cartridges, his dad already had the car keys in his pocket, they'd left the back door open and he was sure—he was *certain*—that his mum had put some toast under the grille before they ran away. Maybe Mr Jude was eating it now, Jack thought, but at the same time he realised that this was most unlikely. Mr Jude was sick, and from what Jack had seen of him as he peered around the corner of their cottage, toast was the last thing on his mind.

Living, perhaps, was the first thing. Surviving. Pulling through.

Naming of Parts

Jack wondered whether the rest of Mr Jude's family looked as bad.

The sense of invasion, of having his own space trespassed upon, was immense. They had left the back door open, and anyone or anything could wander into their house and root through their belongings. Not only the books and cupboards and food and fridge and dirty washing, but the private stuff. Jack had a lot of private stuff in his room, like letters from Mandy which he kept under a loose corner of carpet, his diary shoved into the tear in his mattress along with the page of a magazine he had found in the woods, a weathered flash of pink displaying what a woman *really* had between her legs.

But that sense of loss was tempered by a thought Jack was suddenly proud of, an idea that burst through the fears and the doubts and the awful possibilities this strange morning presented: that he actually had his whole life with him now. They may have left their home open to whatever chose to abuse it, but home was really with his family, wherever they may be. He was with them now.

All except Mandy.

He named his fears:

Loss, his parents disappearing into memory. Loneliness, the threat of being unloved and unloving. Death . . . that great black death . . . stealing away the ones he loved.

Stealing *him* away.

For once, the naming did not comfort him as much as usual. If anything it made him muse upon things more, and Mandy was on his mind and why she had run away, and what had happened to start all the bad stuff between the people he loved the most.

❖

Jack had come home from school early that day, driven by the headteacher because he was feeling sick. He was only eight years old. The teacher really should have seen him into the house, but instead she dropped him at the gate and drove on.

As he entered the front door he was not purposely quiet, but he made sure he did not make any unnecessary noise, either. He liked to frighten Mandy—jump out on her, or creep up from behind and smack her bum—because he loved the startled look on her face when he did so. And to be truthful, he loved the playful fight they would always have afterwards even more.

He slipped off his shoes in the hallway, glanced in the fridge to see if there were any goodies, ate half a jam tart... and then he heard the sound from the living room.

His father had only ever smacked him three times, the last time more than a year before. What Jack remembered more than the pain was the loud noise as his dad's hand connected with him. It was a sound that signified a brief failure in their relationship; it meant an early trip to bed, no supper, and a dreadful look on his mother's face which he hated even more, a sort of dried up mix of shame and guilt.

Jack despised that sound. He heard it now, not only once, not even three times. Again, and again, and again—smacking. And even worse than that, the little cries that came between each smack. And it was Mandy, he knew that, it was Mandy being hit over and over.

Their mum and dad were in work. So who was hitting Mandy?

Jack rushed to the living room door and flung it open.

His sister was kneeling on the floor in front of the settee. She had no clothes on and her face was pressed into the cushions, and the man from the bakery was kneeling behind her, grasping her bum, and he looked like he was hurting, too. Jack saw the man's willy—at least he thought that's what it was, except this was as big as one of the French bread sticks he sold—sliding in and out of his sister, and it was all wet and shiny like she was bleeding, but it wasn't red.

"Mandy?" Jack said, and in that word was everything: *Mandy what are you doing? Is he hurting you? What should I do?* "Mandy?"

Mandy turned and stared at him red-faced, and then her

mouth fell open and she shouted: "What the fuck are you doing here?"

Jack turned and ran along the hallway, forgetting his shoes, feet slapping on quarry tiles. He sprinted across the lawn, stumbling a couple of times. And then he heard Mandy call after him. He did not turn around. He did not want to see her standing at the door with the baker bouncing at her from behind. And he didn't want her to swear at him again, when he had only come home because he felt sick.

All he wished for was to un-see what he had seen.

Jack spent that night lost in the woods. He could never remember any of it, and when he was found and taken home the next day he started to whoop, coughing up clots of mucus and struggling to breathe. He was ill for two weeks, and Mandy sat with him for a couple of hours every evening to read him the fantastic tales of Narnia, or sometimes just to talk. She would always kiss him goodnight and tell him she was sorry, and Jack would tell her it was okay, he sometimes said fuck too, but only when he was on his own.

It seemed that as Jack got better, so everything else in their family got worse.

❖

It was a little over two miles to the nearest village, Tall Stennington. Jack once asked his father why they lived where they did, why didn't they live in a village or a town where there were other people, and shops, and gas in pipes under the ground instead of oil in a big green tank. His dad's reply had confused him at the time, and it still did to an extent.

You've got to go a long way nowadays before you can't hear anything of Man.

Jack thought of that now as they twisted and turned through lanes that still had grass clumps along their spines. There was no radio, his mum had said, and he wondered exactly what they would hear outside were they to stop the car now. He would talk if they did, sing, shout, just to make sure there was a sound other than the silence of last night.

The deathly silence.

"Whose watch was that in the garden, Dad?"

"I expect it belonged to one of the robbers."

Jack thought about this for a while, staring from his window at the hedges rolling by. He glanced up at the trees forming a green tunnel over the road, and he knew they were only minutes from the village. "So, what was the other stuff lying around it? The dried stuff, like meat you've left in the fridge too long?"

His dad was driving so he had an excuse, but his mum didn't turn around either. It was she who spoke, however.

"There's been some stuff on the news—"

"Janey!" his dad cut in. "Don't be so bloody stupid!"

"Gray, if it's really happening he has to know... he will know. We'll see them, lots of them, and—"

"All the trees are pale," Jack said, the watch and dried meat suddenly forgotten. He was looking from the back window at the avenue of trees they had just passed, and he had figured what had been nagging him about the hedges and the fields since they'd left the cottage: their colour; or rather, their lack of it. The springtime flush of growth had been flowering across the valley for the last several weeks, great explosions of rich greens, electric blues and splashes of colours which, as his dad was fond of saying, would put a Monet to shame. Jack didn't know what a Monet was, but he was sure there was no chance in a billion it could ever match the slow-burning firework display nature put on at the beginning of every year. Spring was his favourite season, followed by autumn. They were both times of change, beautiful in their own way, and Jack loved to watch stuff happen.

Now, something *had* happened. It was as though autumn had crept up without anyone or anything noticing, casting its pastel influence secretly across the landscape.

"See?" he said. "Mum? You see?"

Naming of Parts

His mum turned in her seat and stared past Jack. She was trying to hide the fact she had been crying; she looked embarrassed and uncertain.

"Maybe they're dusty," she said.

He knew she was lying; she didn't really think that at all. "So what was on the news?" he asked.

"We're at the village." His dad slowed the car at the hump-back bridge, which marked the outskirts of Tall Stennington.

Jack leaned on the backs of his parents' seats and strained forward to see through the windscreen. The place looked as it always had: the church dominated with a recently sand-blasted tower; stone cottages stood huddled beneath centuries-old trees; a few birds flitted here and there. A fat old Alsation trundled along the street and raised its leg in front of the Dog and Whistle, but it seemed unable to piss.

The grocer's was closed. It opened at six every morning, without fail, even Sundays. In fact, Jack could hardly recall ever seeing it closed, as if old Mrs Haswell had nothing else to do but stock shelves, serve locals and natter away about the terrible cost of running a village business.

"The shop's shut," he said.

His dad nodded. "And there's no one about."

"Yes there is," his mum burst out. "Look, over there, isn't that Gerald?"

"Gerald the Geriatric!" Jack giggled, because that's what they called him at school. He'd usually be told off for that, he knew, on any normal day. After the first couple of seconds he no longer found it all that funny himself. There was something wrong with Gerald the Geriatric.

He leaned against a wall, dragging his left shoulder along the stonework with jerky, infrequent movements of his legs. He was too far away to see his expression in full, but his jowls and the saggy bags beneath his eyes seemed that much larger and darker this morning. He also seemed to have mislaid his trademark walking stick. There were legends that he had once beaten a rat to death with that stick in the kitchen of the Dog and Whistle, and the fact that he had not frequented that pub' for a decade seemed to hint at its truth. Jack used to imagine him striking out at the darting rodent with the knotted length of oak, spittle flying from his mouth, false teeth chattering with each impact. Now, the image seemed grotesque rather than comical.

His mother reached for the door handle.

"Wait, Mum!" Jack said.

"But he's hurt!"

"Jack's right. Wait." His dad rested his hand on the stock of the shotgun wedged down beneath their seats.

Gerald paused and stood shakily away from the wall, turning his head to stare at them. He raised his hands, his mouth falling open into a toothless grin or grimace. Jack could not even begin to tell which.

"He's in pain!" Jack's mum said, and this time she actually clicked the handle and pushed her shoulder to the door, letting in cool morning air.

"Janey, remember what they said—"

"What's that?" Jack said quietly. It was the sound a big spider's legs made on his posters in the middle of the night. The fear was the same, too—unseen things.

His mum had heard it as well, and she *snicked* the door shut.

There was something under the car. Jack felt the subtle tickle of soft impacts beneath him, insistent scrapings and pickings, reminiscent of the window fumblers of last night.

"Maybe it's a dog," his mum said.

His dad slammed the car into reverse and burnt rubber. The skid was tremendous, the stench and reverberation overpowering. As soon as the tyres caught Jack knew that they were out of control. The car leapt back, throwing Jack forward so that he banged his head on his mother's headrest. As he looked up he saw what had been beneath the car... Mrs Haswell, still flipping and rolling where the chassis had scraped her along the road, her hair wild, her skirts torn to reveal pasty, pitted thighs...

Naming of Parts

His father swore as the brakes failed and the car dipped sickeningly into the ditch. Jack fell back, cracking his head on the rear window and tasting the sudden salty tang of blood as he bit his tongue. His mum screeched, his dad shouted and cursed again, the engine rose and sang and screamed until, finally, it cut out.

The sudden silence was huge. The wrecked engine ticked and dripped, Jack groaned, and through the tilted windscreen he could see Mrs Haswell hauling herself to her feet.

Steadying her tattered limbs.

Setting out for their car with slow, broken steps.

"Okay, Jackie?" his mum said. She twisted in her seat and reached back, the look in her eyes betraying her thoughts: *My son, my son!*

Jack opened his mouth to speak but only blood came out. He shuddered a huge breath and realised he'd been winded, things had receded, and only the blood on his chin felt and smelled real.

"What's wrong with her?" his dad said, holding the steering wheel and staring through the windscreen. "That's Mrs Haswell. Under our car. Did I run her over? I didn't hit her, did you see me hit her?"

"Gray, Jackie's bleeding."

Jack tried to talk again, to say he was all right, but everything went fluid. He felt queasy and sleepy, as if he'd woken up suddenly in the middle of the night.

"Gray!"

"Jack? You okay, son? Come on, out of the car. Janey, grab the binoculars. And the shells. Wait on your side, I'll get Jack out." He paused and looked along the road again. Mrs Haswell was sauntering between the fresh skidmarks, and now Gerald the Geriatric was moving their way as well. "Let's hurry up."

Jack took deep, heavy breaths, feeling blood bubble in his throat. The door beside him opened and his dad lifted him out, and as the sun touched his face he began to feel better. His mum wiped at his bloody chin with the sleeve of her jumper.

There was a sound now, a long, slow scraping, and Jack realised it was Mrs Haswell dragging her feet. She'd never done that before. She was eighty, but she'd always been active and forceful, like a wind-up toy that never ran out. She hurried through the village at lunchtime, darted around her shop as if she had wheels for feet... she had never, in all the times Jack had seen her or spoken to her, been slow.

Her arms were draped by her sides, not exactly swinging as she walked, but moving as if they were really no part of her at all. Her mouth hung open, but she did not drool.

"What's wrong with her, dad?"

"She's got the disease," his dad said quickly, dismissively, and Jack felt a pang of annoyance.

"Dad," he said, "I think I'm old enough for you to tell me the truth." It was a childish thing to say, Jack understood that straight away at some deeper level; petulant and prideful, unmindful of the panic his parents so obviously felt. But Jack was nearly a teenager—he felt he deserved some trust. "Anyway," he said, "she looks like she's dead." He'd seen lots of films where people died, but hardly any of them looked like the old woman. She seemed lessened somehow, shrunken into herself, drained. She had lost what little colour she once possessed. In his mind's eye, this was how a true, real-life dead person should look.

His dad aimed the shotgun at Mrs Haswell.

Jack gasped. For the second time in as many minutes, he found himself unable to talk.

"Gray," his mother said cautiously, quietly, hands raised in a warding-off gesture, "we should go across the fields."

Jack saw his dad's face then—tears stinging the corners of his eyes; lips pressed together tight and bloodless, the way they'd been on the day Mandy left home for the last time—and he realised what a dire situation they were in.

His dad had no idea of what to do.

"Across the fields to the motorway," his mum continued, "if there's any help, we may find it there. And I'm sure they couldn't drive." She nodded at Mrs Haswell as she spoke. "Could they? You don't think they could, do you?"

His dad was breathing heavily, just as Jack did whenever he was trying not to cry. He grabbed Jack's hand.

Jack felt the cool sweat of his father's palms... like touching a hunk of raw meat before it was cooked.

They walked quickly back the way they had come, then hopped over a stile into the field.

Jack glanced back at their car, canted at a crazy angle in the ditch, and saw that the two old people had stopped in their tracks. They stood as still as statues, and just as lifeless. This was more disturbing than ever—at least before, they had seemed to possess some purpose.

She was under our car, Jack thought. *What purpose in that?*

And then his own words sprang back at him: *She looks like she's dead.*

❖

"You know what an open mind is, Jack?" Mandy said. She had crept into his room in the middle of the night after hearing him whooping and crying. Sometimes she would sit on the edge of the bed until daybreak, just talking. Much of what she said confused him— she read all the time, and occasionally she even confused their mum and dad—but he remembered it all... and later, some of it began to make sense.

Jack had a grotesque vision of someone with a trapdoor in their skull, their brain pulsing and glowing underneath. He smiled uncertainly at this bloody train of thought.

"It's the ability to believe in the unbelievable," she continued, apparently unconcerned at his silence. "It's a free mind. Imagination. Growing up closes off so many doors. The modern world doesn't allow for miracles, so we don't see them. It's a very precious gift, an open mind, but it's not passive. You've got to nurture it like a bed of roses, otherwise it will wither and die. Make sure you don't close off your mind to things you find strange, Jack. Sometimes they may be the only truth."

They sat silently for a while, Jack croaking as he breathed past the phlegm in his throat, Mandy twirling strands of her long black hair between her fingers.

"It's something you have," she said suddenly, "and you always will. And that's another secret, to keep and tend."

"How do you know I have it?" he asked.

Mandy smiled at him and he saw a sadness behind her eyes. Maybe she still blamed herself for him being lost in the woods. Maybe she could already see how different their family was going to be.

"Hey," she said, "you're my brother." As if that was an answer.

◈

The further they moved away, the more Tall Stennington appeared normal. Halfway across the field they lost sight of the shuffling shapes in the road, the empty streets beyond, the pigeons sitting silently on the church tower. Jack found himself wishing for any sign of life. He almost called out, wanting to see windows thrust open and people he knew by name or sight lean out, wave to him, comment on what a lovely brisk spring morning it was. But his tongue hurt from the car wreck. His dad had crashed because a busy old lady had cut or torn the brake cables. And she had done that because... because...

There was nothing normal this morning. Not with Tall Stennington, not with Mr Jude, not with the fox at the edge of the woods. Not even with his parents, because they were tense and worried and hurrying across a newly-planted field, and his mum still had on her slippers. His dad carried a shotgun. His mum had her arms crossed, perhaps against the cold but more likely, Jack thought, against something else entirely.

No, nothing was normal today.

They followed the furrows ploughed into the field, stepping on green shoots and crushing them back into the earth whence they came. Jack glanced behind at his footprints, his identity stamped into the landscape only to be brushed away by the next storm. When he was younger he wanted to be an astronaut, purely for the excitement of zero-G, piloting experimental spacecraft and dodging asteroids on the way out of the Solar system. The idea still appealed to him, but his main reason now would be to walk on the moon and leave his footprints behind. He'd heard that they would be there forever, or at least near enough. When he was dead—perhaps when *everyone* was dead—some aliens might land on the moon, and see his footprints, and think, *Here was a guy willing to explore. Here was a guy with no closed doors in his head, with an open mind. Here was a guy who might have believed in us.*

Jack looked up at the ghost of the moon where it still hung in the clear morning sky. He wondered if his exact centre-line of sight were extended, would he be looking at Neil Armstrong's footprints right now?

He looked down at his feet and one of those doors in his mind flapped wide open.

Falling to his knees, he plucked at a green shoot. It felt dry and brittle between his fingers, not cool and damp as it should have. He rubbed at it and it came apart, shedding its faded outer skin and exposing powdery insides.

He picked another shoot and it was the same. The third bled a smear of greenish fluid across his fingertips, but the next was as dry as the first, and the next.

"Jack, what's up son? What are you doing?" His dad had stopped and turned, glancing nervously past Jack at the stile as if constantly expecting Mrs Haswell and Gerald the Geriatric to come stumbling after them.

Jack shook his head, not *unable* to understand—he understood perfectly well, even for a twelve year old—but *unwilling*. The doors were open but he was stubbornly grasping the frames, not wanting to enter the strange rooms presenting themselves to him now.

"This crop's dead," he said. "It looks fresh, Dad. Mum? Doesn't it all look so fresh?" His mum nodded, cupping her elbows in her hands and shivering. Jack held up a palm full of crushed shoot. "But look. It's all dead. It's still green, but it's not growing any more."

He looked back at the village. Their footprints stood out in the young crop, three wavering lines of bent and snapped shoots. And the hedge containing the stile they had hopped over... its colours like those of a faded photograph, not lush and vibrant with the new growth of spring ... He'd once read a book called *The Death of Grass*. Now, he might be living it.

To his left the hillsides, speckled with sheep so still they looked like pustules on the face of the land.

To his right the edge of a stretch of woodland, at the other end of which stood their house, doors open, toast burnt in the grille, perhaps still burning.

"Everything's dying."

His dad sighed. "Not everything," he said.

Jack began to shake, his stomach twisted into a knot and he was sure he was going to puke. Another terrible admission from his father, another fearful idea implanted when really, he should be saying, *There, there, Jackie boy, nothing's changed, it's all in your imagination.*

What could he name? How could he lay all this out to understanding, to comprehension, to acceptance, all as he had been told? He tried, even though he thought it was useless: *The villagers, like walking dead, perhaps they are. The plants, dry and brittle even though it's springtime. Mum and dad, scared to death...* He thought at first there was nothing there that would work, but then he named another part of this terrible day and a sliver of hope kept the light shining: *Mandy, in the town, saying it's safe.*

"Not everything, Jack," his dad said again, perhaps trying to jolt his son back to reality.

"Let's go," his mum said. "Come on, Jack, we'll tell you while we're walking... it's only two or three fields away... and there'll be help there." She smiled but it could not reach her eyes.

The motorway was not three fields away, it was six. His parents told Jack all they knew by the time they'd reached the end of the second field. He believed what they said because he could smell death in the third field, and he mentioned it, but his mum and dad lied to themselves by not even answering. Jack was sure as hell he knew what death smelled like; he'd found a dead badger in the woods a year ago, after all, and turned it over with a stick, and run home puking. This was similar only richer, stronger, as if coming from a lot more bodies. Some of them smelled cooked.

They saw the stationary cars on the motorway from two fields away. Wisps of smoke still rose here and there. Several vehicles were twisted on their backs like dead beetles.

From the edge of the field abutting the motorway they saw the shapes sitting around the ruined cars—the grey people in their colourful clothes—and although they could not tell for sure what they were eating, it was mostly red.

Jack's dad raised his binoculars. Then he turned, grabbed Jack's and his mother's hand and ran back they way they had come.

※

"Were they eating the people from the cars?" Jack asked, disgusted but fascinated.

His father—white-faced, frowning, shaking his head slightly as if trying to dislodge a memory—did not answer.

They walked quickly across another field, their path taking them away from the woods and between Tall Stennington and the motorway. Neither was in view any longer—the landscape here dipped and rose, and all they could see around them was countryside. Nothing to give any indication of humankind's presence; no chimney smoke or aircraft trails; no skyscrapers or whitewashed farm buildings.

No traffic noise. None at all.

Jack realised that he only noticed noise when it was no longer there.

"Dad, tell me!" Jack said. "The dead people—were they eating the people from the cars?"

"No," his father said.

Jack saw straight through the lie.

He had taken it all in, everything his parents had told him, every snippet of information gleaned from the panicked newscasts yesterday, the confused reports from overseas. He had listened and taken it all in, but he did not really understand. He had already seen it for himself—Mr Jude and the people in the village did not have a disease at all, and the young crop really was dead—but he could not believe. It was too terrifying, too unreal. Too crazy.

He whispered as they walked, naming the parts that scared him the most: *Dead people, dead things, still moving and walking. Dumb and aimless, but dangerous just the same.*

Those fingers last night had not sounded aimless, those probings and proddings at their locked up, safe cottage. They had sounded anything *but* aimless.

He carried on naming. *Those of you who are immune, stay at home.* The broadcasts his parents had listen to had told of certain blood groups succumbing slower than others, and some being completely immune. In a way, these positive elements to the broadcasts—the mentions of immunity—scared Jack more. They made him feel increasingly isolated, one of the few survivors, and what was left? What was there that they could use now, where would they go when dead people could cut your brake cables (and that sure as shit wasn't aimless, either), when they caused crashes on the motorway so they could ...they could...

Jack stumbled, dug his toes into a furrow and hit the dirt. His face pressed into the ground and he felt dry dead things scurrying across his cheeks. He wanted to cry but he could not, neither could he shout nor scream, and then he realised that what he wanted most was comfort. His mother's arms around him, his father sitting on the side of his bed stroking his brow as he did when Jack had the occasional nightmare, a cup of tea before bed, half an hour reading before he turned out his light and lay back to listen to the night.

Hands did touch him, voices did try to soothe, but all Jack could hear was the silence. All he could smell was the undercurrent of death in the motionless spring air.

Before the world receded into a strange flat brightness, Jack saw in sharp detail a line of ants marching along a furrow. They were moving strangely—too slowly, much slower than he'd ever seen one moving before, as if they were in water—and he passed out wondering how aimless these red ants really were.

❖

He was not unconscious for long. He opened his eyes to sunlight and sky and fluffy clouds, and he suddenly knew that his parents had left him. They'd walked on, leaving him behind like an injured commando on a raid into enemy territory, afraid that he would slow them down and give the dead things a chance—

And then his mother's face appeared above his and her tears dropped onto his cheeks. "Jackie," she said, smiling, and Jack could hear the love in her voice. He did not know how—it did not sound any different from usual—but out here, lost in a dying landscape, he knew that she loved him totally. She would never leave him behind. She would rather die.

"I want to go home," Jack said, his own tears mixing with his mother's on his face. He thought of the cottage and all the good times he had spent there. It would be cold inside by now, maybe there were birds...dead birds, arrogantly roosting on plate racks and picture frames. "Mum, I want to go home, I want none of this to happen." He held up his arms and she grabbed him, hugging him so tightly that his face was pressed into her hair, his breath squeezed out. He could smell her, a warm musk of sweat and stale perfume, and he took solace in the familiar.

"We can't stay here too long," his father said, but he sat down in the dirt next to his wife and son. "We've got to get on to Tewton."

"To find Mandy?"

"To find safety," his dad said. He saw Jack's crestfallen expression and averted his eyes. "And to find Mandy."

"She never hurt me, you know," Jack muttered.

"She scared you, made you run away!"

"I ran away myself! Mandy didn't make me, she only ever hurt herself!" Once more, he tried to recall his time in the woods, but the effort conjured only sensations of cold, damp and dark. Ironically, he could remember what happened afterwards with ease—the coughing, the fevers, the nightmares, Mandy by his bed, his shouting parents, Mandy running down their driveway, leaving her home behind—but still a day and a night were missing from his life.

It was a pointless argument, a dead topic, an aimless one. So nothing more was said.

They were silent for a while, catching their breath and all thinking their own thoughts. His mother continued to rock him in her lap but Jack knew she was elsewhere, thinking other things. His dad had broken open the shotgun and was making sure the two cartridges in there were new.

"How do you kill a dead thing, Dad?" Jack asked. A perfectly simple question, he thought. Logical. Reasonable.

His dad looked across the fields. "Tewton should be a few miles that way," he said. He looked at his watch, then up at the sun where it hung low over the hills. "We could make it by tonight if we really push it."

Jack's mum began to cry. She pulled a great clod of mud from one of her slippers and threw it at the ground. "We can't go that far alone," she said. "Not on foot. Gray, we don't know what's happened, not really. They'll come and help us, cure everyone, send us home."

"'They'?"

"You know what I mean."

"There was a film called *Them* once," Jack said. "About giant ants, and nuclear bombs. It was nothing like this, though." Even as he spoke it, he thought maybe he was mistaken. He thought maybe the film was *very much* like this, a monstrous horror

Naming of Parts

of humankind's abuse of nature, and the harvest of grief it reaps.

"It's all so sudden," his dad said then. Jack actually saw his shoulders droop, his head dip down, as if he was being shrunken and reduced by what had happened. "I don't think there's much help around, not out here. Not yet."

"It'll be all right in Tewton," Jack said quietly. "Mandy said it was safe there, she phoned us because she was worried, so we've got to go. I don't want to stay out in the dark. Not after last night, Mum. Remember the noises?"

His mother nodded and tightened her lips.

"I don't want to know what made those noises." Jack felt close to tears once more but he could not let them come, he would not.

A breeze came up and rustled through the dead young crop.

Jack jerked upright, eyes wide, mouth hanging open.

There was something around the corner of the L-shaped field, out of sight behind a clump of trees. He could not hear it, nor smell it exactly, but he knew it was dead, and he knew it was moving this way.

"Mum," he said, "Dad. There's something coming."

They looked around and listened hard, his dad tightening his grip on the shotgun. "I can't—"

"There!" Jack said, pointing across the field a second before something walked into view.

His mother gasped. "Oh, no."

His dad stood and looked behind them, judging how far it was to the hedge.

Eight people emerged from the hidden leg of the field, one after another. There were men and women, and one child. All of them moved strangely, as if they only just learnt how to walk, and most of them wore night clothes. The exceptions were a policeman—his uniform torn and muddied—and someone dressed in thick sweater, ripped jeans and a bobble hat. He had something dangling from his left hand; it could have been a leash, but there was no dog.

One of the women had fresh blood splattered across the front of her night-gown.

The child was chewing something bloody. Flies buzzed his head, but none seemed to be landing.

Perhaps, Jack thought, the flies were dead as well.

The people did not pause. They walked straight at Jack and his parents, arms swinging by their sides from simple motion, not habit.

"I doubt they can run that fast," Jack's dad said.

"I'm scared," his mother whispered.

"But can they get through the hedge, Dad? Once we're through, will they follow us?"

Jack looked from the people to the hedge, and back again. He knew what was wrong with them—they were dead and they craved live food, his parents had learned all that from the news yesterday—but still he did not want to *believe*.

Their nostrils did not flare, their mouths hung open but did not drool, their feet plodded insistently... but not aimlessly. These dead things had a purpose, it seemed, and that purpose would be in their eyes, were they moist enough to throw back reflections.

"They're looking at us," Jack said quietly.

They walked slowly, coming on like wind-up toys with broken innards; no life in their movements at all.

Seconds later, they charged.

Whatever preconceptions Jack had about the ability of dead things to move were slaughtered here and now. The dead folk did not run, they rampaged, churning up the earth with heavy footfalls, shattering the strange peace with the suddenness of their movement. Yet their faces barely changed, other than the slack movement of their jaws snapping shut each time their feet struck mud. They did not shout or pant because, Jack guessed, they had no breath.

His dad fired the shotgun and then they all ran towards the hedge. Jack did not see what effect the shot had, he did not want to. He could sense the distance rapidly closing between them. The hedge seemed a hundred steps away, a thousands miles, and then he saw his father slowly dropping behind.

"Dad, come one!"

"Run Jackie!"

"Dad!" He was fumbling with the shotgun, Jack saw, plucking out the spent cartridges and trying to load fresh ones. "Dad, don't bother, just run!"

"Gray, Gray," he heard his mother panting under her breath, but she did not turn around. She reached the hedge first and launched herself at what she thought was an easy gap to squeeze through. She squealed, and then screamed, when she became impaled on barbed wire and sharp sticks.

Jack was seconds from the hedge but his dad was now out of sight, behind him and to the left. Jack was watching his feet so he did not trip, but in his mind's eye he saw something else: his father caught, then trampled, then gnawed into, eaten alive while he lay there broken-backed and defenceless...

He reached the hedge but did not slow down. Instead he jumped, scrabbling with his hands and feet even before he struck the tangled growth, hauling himself up and through the sharp thorns, the biting branches, the crisp spring foliage. Bloody tears sprang from cuts on his hands and arms.

"Mum!" he shouted as he tumbled over the other side. The breath was knocked from him as he landed, and he crawled back to the hedge in a kind of silent, airless void.

As he found his breath, he heard the blast of the shotgun once more. Something hit the ground.

His mum was struggling in the heart of the hedge and Jack went to her aid. She was already cut and bleeding, the splashes of blood vivid against withered leaves and rotting buds. "Stop struggling!" he shouted.

The shotgun again.

"Dad!"

He could see glimpses of frantic movement through the hedge—

And then he knew it was going to be all right. Not for ever—

in the long term everything was dark and lonely and different—but for now they would all pull through. He saw his bloodied parents hugging each other, felt the coolness of blood on his neck, smelled the scent of death receding as they left the mindless dead behind to feed on other things. He also saw a place where everything would be fine, but he had no idea how to get there.

"Jack, help me!" his mother shouted, and everything rushed back. He reached out and grabbed her arms, and although she screamed, still he pulled.

The hedge moved and shuddered as bodies crashed into it on the other side. He could not see his dad but he did not worry, there was nothing to worry about

(*yet*, nothing to worry about *yet*)

and then he came scrambling over, throwing the shotgun to the ground and following close behind.

His mother came free with a final harsh scream. Jack saw the wounds on her arms and shoulders where the barbed wire had slashed in and torn out, and he began to cry.

"Oh Janey," his dad said, hugging his wife and letting his tears dilute her blood. Jack closed his eyes because his mum was bleeding... she was hurt and she was bleeding... But then she was hugging him and her blood cooled on his skin.

"Come on, I don't want to stay here a minute longer," his father said. "And maybe they'll find a way through. Maybe."

They hurried along the perimeter of the new field, keeping a wary look out in case this place, too, had occupants ready to chase them into the ground.

Jack looked back only once. Shapes were silhouetted on and in the hedge like grotesque fruits, their arms twitching uselessly, clothes and skin stretched and torn on barbed wire and dead wood

He did not look again, but he heard their struggles for a long while. By the time he and his family reached the gate that led out into a little country lane, their stench had been carried away on the breeze.

Naming of Parts

The lane looked unused, but at least it was a sign of humanity. Jack was so glad to see it.

❖

They turned east. Jack wondered at his conviction that there was something dangerous approaching, moments before the crowd had rounded the corner in the field. He had smelled them, of course, that was it. Or perhaps he had heard them, he had a good sense of hearing, his mother always said so.

Or perhaps he had simply known that they were there.

His mother and father were walking close together behind him, almost rubbing shoulders. Almost, but not quite, because his mum's arm was a mess, there was blood dripping from her fingertips as they walked, and Jack had seen her shoulder where a flap of skin hung down across her armpit, and he'd seen the *meat* of her there where the barbed wire had torn her open.

It didn't hurt, she said, it was numb but it didn't hurt. Jack knew the numbness would not last. Once the shock had worn off and the adrenaline drained from her system, the slow fire would ignite and the pain would come in surges. For his mother, the future was a terrifying place promising nothing but worse to come.

Total silence surrounded them. The landscape had taken on an eerie appearance, one normally reserved for the strangest of autumn evenings, when the sun was sinking behind wispy clouds and the moon had already revealed itself. The hills in the distance were smothered in mist, only occasional smudges of green showing through like old bruises. Nearer by, clumps of trees sprouted on ancient hillocks. The trees were all old, Jack knew, otherwise the farmers would have cut them down; but today they looked positively ancient. Today they looked fossilised, petrified like the wood his friend Jamie had brought back from his holiday in the Dominican Republic the year before, wood so old it was like stone.

What would those trees feel like now, Jack wondered? Would their trunks be cold and dry as rock, or was there still that electric dampness of something alive? Were their leaves as green and fresh and vibrant as they should be in the spring... or were they as dead inside as the young harvest across the fields?

If I cut them, Jack thought, *will they bleed?*

"Hang on," his mum said, and he knew that the pain had begun. He turned back and saw her sink slowly to her knees in the lane, his dad standing over her, one hand reaching out but not touching her shoulder because he did not know what to do. It was always Jack's mum who did the comforting, the molly-coddling when Dad had a cold, the reassuring when Jack woke from nightmares and became frustrated when he just could not explain exactly what they were about. And now that she needed comforting, his dad was standing there like he was balancing a teacup on the back of his hand, unable to help his wife where she knelt bleeding and crying into the muck.

"Mum," Jack said, "my teacher said that pain is transitory."

"Big words, Jackie," she said, trying to smile for him.

"It's what he said, though. He was telling us because Jamie was going to the dentist for a filling, and he was scared of the needle. Mr Travis said pain is transitory, you feel it when it happens but afterwards you can't remember exactly what it was like. You can't recreate pain in your memories because your body won't let you, otherwise it'll only hurt again."

His dad handed her a handkerchief and she lifted her sleeve slowly, revealing some of the smaller cuts and dabbing at them as if that would take her attention from the gaping wound in her shoulder. "The point being?" she said, sharply but not unkindly. Jack could see that she was grateful for the distraction.

"Well, if you're hurting just cast your mind into the future. When you're all better, you won't even remember what the hurting was like. And pain doesn't actually *hurt* you, anyway. It's only in your head. Your cuts will heal, Mum. In a few days it won't matter."

"In a few days..." she said, smiling and sighing and opening her mouth as if to finish the sentence. But she left it at that.

"It's almost midday," his dad said.

"I should be in school."

"School's off, kiddo!" Tears were cascading past his mum's smiling mouth.

"We should get moving, if we can. Janey, you think you can move, honey? If we're going to get to Tewton—"

"Where are we now?" Jack's mum asked suddenly.

His dad frowned but did not answer.

"Gray? Don't tell me that. Don't say we're lost."

"Well," he said, "Tall Stennington is maybe three miles back thataway." He turned and pointed the way they had come, though Jack thought he was probably off by about a sixth of a circle anyway. "So we must be nearing the river by now. You think, Jackie?"

You think, Jackie? His dad, asking him for advice in something so important. He tried to see himself from his father's eyes. Short, skinny, into books instead of his dad's beloved football, intelligent in his own right but academically average... a kid. Just a kid. However much Jack thought about things, used big words, had a hard-on when he watched bikini-clad women on holiday programmes... he was just a kid to his dad.

"No," Jack said. "I think you're a bit out there, Dad. I reckon we're closer to Peter's Acre than anything, so we really need to head more that way, if we can." He pointed off across the fields to where the landscape rose in the distance, lifting towards a heavily wooded hillside. "Tewton is over that hill, through the woods. If you drive you go that way, yes," he said, indicating the direction his father had suggested. "But if I was a crow, I'd go there."

"So by the time we get that far," his mum said, "what I'm feeling now I'd have forgotten."

Jack nodded, but he was frowning.

"Ok, Jackie. Let's hit it." And up she stood, careful not to look down at the strip of her husband's T-shirt wrapped around her shoulder, already stained a deep, wet red.

They left the lane and moved off across the fields towards the tree-covered hillside in the distance. Between them and the woods lay several fields, a veiny network of hedges, hints of other lanes snaking from here to there and a farmstead. It looked quiet and deserted; no smoke rose from its chimneys; its yard seemed, from this distance, empty and still. Yet for the first time, Jack was glad that his dad was carrying the gun.

Something had changed, Jack thought, since before their flight from the dead people and his mother being tangled and wounded in the hedge. It was her attitude to things—the nervousness had been swept aside by the pain, so that now she seemed to accept things more as they came than as she expected them to be. But this change in his mother had also moved down the line to his father and himself, altering the subtle hierarchy of the family, shifting emphases around so that none of them were quite the people they had been that morning.

Jack suddenly wanted to see Mandy. In the four years since her leaving home she had become something of a stranger. They still saw her on occasion—though it was always she who came to visit them—but she changed so much every time that Jack would see a different person walking in the door. She and Jack were still very close and there was an easy atmosphere between them that his parents seemed to resent, but she was not the Mandy he remembered.

Sometimes Jack would imagine that his sister was still living at home. He would go into her bedroom, and although it had been cleared out by his parents and left sterile and bland—forever awaiting a visitor to abuse its neatness—he could sense her and hear her and smell her. Only his memories placed her there, of course, but he would sit and chat with her for hours.

Sometimes, when he next spoke to her on the phone, they would carry on their conversation.

"When can we go to see Mandy?" he asked, realising as he spoke that he sounded like a whiner. They were going, that was that, and they certainly could not move any faster.

"We'll be there by tonight, Jackie," his mother said comfortingly.

"You do love her, don't you?" he asked.

"Of course we do! She's our daughter—your sister—so of course we love her!"

"So why don't we go to see her any more?"

His mother was silent for a while, his father offering no help. There was only the crunch of their feet crushing new grass into crisp green fragments in the dirt. It sounded to Jack as though they were walking on thin ice.

"Sometimes people fall out," his mother said. "There was that time she made you run away—"

"She didn't make me, I told you, I did it myself!"

His mother winced in pain as she turned to him and Jack felt ashamed, ashamed that he was putting her through this soon after she had been dragged through a wire fence and torn to shreds. But then, he thought, maybe there was no better time. Her defences were down, the pain was filtering her thoughts and letting only essential ones through, holding back the ballast and, maybe, discarding it altogether.

"Mandy scared you," she said. "She was doing something she shouldn't have been doing and she scared you and you ran away. We didn't find you until the next day, and you don't..." She looked up at the sky, but Jack could still see the tears. "You don't know what that night did to your Dad and me."

"But you still love her?"

His mother nodded. "Of course we do."

Jack thought about this for a while, wondering whether easy talk and being together were really the most important things there were. "That's okay then," he said finally. "I'm hungry."

Mum dying, because she's hurt, he thought, naming his fears automatically. *Things changing, it's all still changing. Dead people. I'm afraid of the dead people.*

"We'll eat when we get to Tewton," his dad said from up ahead.

"And I'm thirsty." *No food, no drink... no people at all. Death; we could die out here.*

"When we get to Tewton, Jackie," his dad said, more forcefully than before. He turned around and Jack could see how much he had changed, even over the last hour. The extraordinary had been presented to him, thrust in his face in the form of a gang of dead people, denying disbelief. Unimaginable, impossible, true.

"I expect those people just wanted help, Dad." He knew it was crazy even as he said it—he *knew* they'd wanted more than that; he had seen the fresh blood—but maybe the idea would drain some of the strain from his dad's face. And maybe a lie could hide the truth, and help hold back his mother's pain, and bring Mandy back to them where she belonged, and perhaps they were only on a quiet walk in the country...

"Come on, son," his father said, and Jack did not know whether he meant *move along*, or *give me a break*. Whatever, he hated the air of defeat in his voice.

My dad, failing, he thought. *Pulling away from things already, falling down into himself. What about Mum? What about me?*

Who's going to protect us?

They had crossed one field and were nearing the edge of another when Jack suddenly recognised with their surroundings. To the left stood an old barn, doors rotted away and ivy making its home between the stones. The ivy was dead now, but still it clotted the building's openings, as if holding something precious inside. To the right, at the far corner of the field, an old metal plough rusted down into the ground. He remembered playing war here, diving behind the plough while Jamie threw mud grenades his way, *ack—ack—acking* a stream of machine-gun fire across the field, crawling through the rape crop and ploughing their own paths towards and away from each other. Good times, and lost times, never to be revisited; he felt that now more than ever. Lost times.

Naming of Parts

"I know this place!" he said. "There's a pond over there behind that hedge, with an island in the middle and everything!" He ran to the edge of the field, aiming for the gate where it stood half-open.

"Jack, wait!" his dad shouted, but Jack was away, cool breeze ruffling his hair and lifting some of the nervous sweat from his skin. The crinkle of shoots beneath his feet suddenly seemed louder and Jack wanted nothing more than to get out onto the road, leave these dead things behind, find a car or thumb a lift into Tewton where there would be help, where there had to be help, because if there wasn't then where the hell *would* there be help?

Nowhere. There's no help anywhere. The thought chilled him but he knew it was true, just as he had known that there were dead people around the corner of the field—

—just as he knew that there was something very, very wrong here as well. He could smell it already, a rich, warm tang to the air instead of the musty smell of death they had been living with all morning. A *fresh* smell. But he kept on running because he could not do anything else, even though he knew he should stay in the field, knew he *had* to stay in the field for his own good. He had played here with Jamie, they had shared good times here so it must be a good place.

Jack darted through the gate and out onto the pitted road.

The colours struck him first. Bright colours in a landscape so dull with death.

The car was a blazing yellow, a metal banana his mum would have called it, never lose that in a car park she would say. Inside the car sat a woman in a red dress, and inside the woman moved something else, a squirrel, its tail limp and heavy with her blood. The dress was not all red, he could see a white sleeve and a torn white flap hanging from the open door, touching the road.

Her face had been ripped off, her eyes torn out, her throat chewed away.

There was something else on the road next to the car, a mass of meat torn apart and spread across the Tarmac. Jack saw the flash of bone and an eyeless head and a leg, still attached to the bulky torso by strands of stuff, but they did not truly register. What he did see and understand were the dozen small rodents chewing at the remnants of whatever it had been. Their tails were long and hairless, their bodies black and slick with the blood they wallowed in. They chewed slowly, but not thoughtfully, because there could not have been a single thought in their little dead minds.

"Dad," Jack gasped, trying to shout but unable to find a breath.

More things lay further towards the pond, and for a terrible moment Jack thought it was another body that had been taken apart (because that's what he saw, he knew that now, his mind had permitted understanding on the strict proviso that he—)

He turned and puked and fell to his knees in his own vomit, looking up to see his father standing at the gate and staring past him at the car.

Jack looked again, and he realised that although the thing further along the road had once been a person—he could see their head, like a shop dummy's that had been stepped on and covered in shit and set on fire so the eyes melted and rolled out to leave black pits—there was no blood at all, no wetness there. Nothing chewed on these sad remains.

Dead already when the car ran them over. Standing there in the road, dead already, letting themselves be hit so that the driver—he had been tall, good looking, the girl in his passenger seat small and mouse-like and scared into a gibbering, snotty wreck—would get out and go to see what he had done. Opening himself up to attack from the side, things darting from the ditches and downing him and falling on him quickly... and quietly. No sound apart from the girl's screams as she saw what was happening, and then her scream had changed in tone.

When they'd had their fill, they dragged themselves away to leave the remains to smaller dead things.

"Oh God, Dad!" Jack said, because he did not want to know

Naming of Parts

any more. Why the hell should he? How the hell did he know what he knew already?

His dad reached down and scooped him up into his arms, pressing his son's face into his shoulder so he did not have to look any more. Jack raised his eyes and saw his mother walk slowly from the field, and she was trying not to look as well. She stared straight at Jack's face, her gaze unwavering, her lips tensed with the effort of not succumbing to human curiosity and subjecting herself to a sight that would live with her forever.

But of course she looked, and her liquid scream hurt Jack as much as anything ever had. He loved his mum because she loved him, he knew how much she loved him. His parents had bought him a microscope for Christmas and she'd pricked her finger with a needle so that he could look at her blood, that's how much she loved him. He hated to hear her scared, hated to see her in pain. Her fear and agony were all his own.

His father turned and ushered his mum down the road, away from the open banana car with its bright red mess, away from the bloody dead things eating up what was left. Jack, facing back over his dad's shoulder, watched the scene until it disappeared around a bend in the road. He listened to his father's laboured breathing and his mother's panicked gasps. He looked at the pale green hedges, where even now hints of rot were showing through. And he wanted to go home.

❖

"Are you scared, Jack?" Mandy had asked.

"No," he said truthfully.

"Not of me," she smiled. "Not of Mum and Dad and what's happening, that'll sort itself out. I mean ever. Are you ever scared, of things. The dark, spiders, death, war, clowns? Ever, ever, ever?"

Jack went to shake his head, but then he thought of things that did frighten him a little. Not outright petrified, just disturbed, that's how he sometimes felt. Maybe that's what Mandy meant.

"Well," he said, "there's this thing on telly. It's Planet of the Apes, the TV show, not the film. There's a bit at the beginning with the gorilla army man, Urko, his face is on the screen and sometimes it looks so big that it's bigger than the screen, it's really in the room, you know? Well . . . I hide behind my hands."

"But do you peek?"

"No!"

"I've seen that programme," Mandy said, even though Jack was pretty sure she had not. "I've seen it, and you know what? There's nothing at all to be scared of. I'll tell you why: the bit that scares you is made up of a whole bunch of bits that won't. A man in a suit; a camera trick; an actor; a nasty voice. And that man in the suit goes home at night, has a cup of tea, picks his nose and goes to the toilet. Now that's not very scary, is it?"

Even though he felt ill Jack giggled and shook his head. "No!" He wondered whether the next time he watched that opening sequence, he'd be as scared as before. He figured maybe he would, but in a subtly different way. A grown-up way.

"Fear's made up of a load of things," she said, "and if you know those things . . . if you can name them . . . you're most of the way to accepting your fear."

"But what if you don't know what it is? What if you can't say what's scaring you?"

His sister looked up at the ceiling and tried to smile, but she could not. "I've tried it, over the last few days," she whispered. "I've named you, and Mum, and Dad, and the woods, and what happened, and you . . . out there in the woods, alone . . . and loneliness itself. But it doesn't work." She looked down at Jack again, looked straight into his eyes. "If that happens then it should be scaring you. Real fear is like intense pain. It's there to warn you something's truly wrong."

I hope I always know, Jack thought. *I hope I always know what I'm afraid of.*

Mandy began singing softly. Jack slept.

◈

Naming of Parts

"Oh no! Dad, it's on fire!"

They had left the scene of devastation and towards the farm they'd spotted earlier, intending to find something to eat. It went unspoken that they did not expect to discover anyone alive at the farm. Jack only hoped they would not find anyone dead, either.

They paused in the lane, which was so infrequently used that grass and dock leaves grew in profusion along its central hump. Insipid green grass and yellowed dock now, though here and there tufts of rebellious life still poked through. The puddled wheel ruts held the occasional dead thing swimming feebly.

Jack's dad raised his binoculars, took a long look at the farm and lowered them again. "It's not burning. Something is, but it's not the farm. A bonfire, I think. I think the farmer's there, and he's started a bonfire in his yard."

"I wonder what he could be burning," Jack's mother said. She was pale and tired, her left arm tucked between the buttons of her shirt to try to ease the blood loss. Jack wanted to cry every time he looked at her, but he could see tears in her eyes as well, and he did not want to give her cause to shed any more.

"We'll go and find out."

"Dad, it might be dangerous. There might be.... those people there. Those things." *Dead things*, Jack thought, but the idea of dead things walking still seemed too ridiculous to voice.

"We need food, Jack," his dad said, glancing at his mother as he said it. "And a drink. And some bandages for your mum, if we can find some. We need help."

"I'm scared, why can't we just go on to Tewton?"

"And when we get there, and there are people moving around in the streets, will you want to hold back then? In case they're the dead things we've seen?"

Jack did not answer but he shook his head, because he knew his dad was right.

"I'll go on ahead slightly," his dad said, "I've got the gun. That'll stop anything that comes at us. Jack, you help your mum."

Didn't stop the other people, Jack thought. *And you couldn't shoot at Mrs Haswell, could you Dad? Couldn't shoot at someone you knew.*

"Don't go too fast," his mum said quietly. "Gray, I can't walk too fast. I feel faint, but if I walk slowly I can keep my head clear."

He nodded then started off, holding the shotgun across his stomach now instead of dipped over his elbow. Jack and his mother held back for a while and watched him go, Jack thinking how small and scared he looked against the frightening landscape.

"You alright, Mum?"

She nodded but did not turn her head. "Come on, let's follow your Dad. In ten minutes we'll be having a nice warm cup of tea and some bread in the farmer's kitchen."

"But what's he burning? Why the bonfire?"

His mother did not answer, or could not. Perhaps she was using all her energy to walk. Jack did the only thing he could and stayed along beside her.

The lane crossed a B-road and then curved around to the farmyard, bounded on both sides by high hedges. There was no sign of any traffic, no hint that anyone had come this way recently. Jack looked to his left where the road rose slowly up out of the valley. In the distance he saw something walk from one side to the other, slowly, as if unafraid of being run down. It may have been a deer, but Jack could not be sure.

"Look," his mum said quietly. "Oh Jackie, look."

There was an area of tended plants at the entrance to the farm lane, rose bushes pointing skeletal thorns skyward and clematis smothered in pink buds turning brown. But it was not this his mother was pointing at with a finger covered in blood; it was the birds. There were maybe thirty of them, sparrows from what Jack could make out, though they could just as easily have been siskins that had lost their colour. They flapped uselessly at the air, heads jerking with the effort, eyes like small black stones. They did not make a sound, and that is perhaps why his father had not seen them as he walked by. Or maybe he

Naming of Parts

had seen them and chosen to ignore the sight. Their wings were obviously weak, their muscles wasting. They did not give in. Even as Jack and his mother passed by they continued to flap uselessly at air that no longer wished to support them.

Jack kept his eyes on them in case they followed.

They could smell the bonfire now, and tendrils of smoke wafted across the lane and into the fields on either side. "That's not a bonfire," Jack said. "I can't smell any wood." His mother began to sob as she walked. Jack did not know whether it was from her pain, or something else entirely.

A gunshot coughed at the silence. Jack's father crouched down low, twenty paces ahead of them. He brought his gun up but there was no smoke coming from the barrel. "Wait—!" he shouted, and another shot rang out. Jack actually saw the hedge next to his dad flicker as pellets tore through.

"Get away!" a voice said from a distance. "Get out of here! Get away!"

His dad backed down the lane, still in a crouch, signalling for Jack and his mum to back up as well. "Wait, we're all right, we're normal, we just want some help."

There was silence for a few seconds, then another two aimless shots in quick succession. "I'll kill you!" the voice shouted again, and Jack could tell its owner was crying. "You killed my Janice, you made me kill her again, and I'll kill you!"

Jack's dad turned and ran to them, keeping his head tucked down as if his shoulders would protect it against a shotgun blast. "Back to the road," he said.

"But we could reason with him."

"Janey, back to the road. The guy's burning his own cattle and some of them are still moving. Back to the road."

"Some of them are still moving," Jack repeated, fascination and disgust—two emotions which, as a young boy, he was used to experiencing in tandem—blurring his words.

"Left here," his father said as they reached the B-road. "We'll skirt around the farm and head up towards the woods. Tewton is on the other side of the forest."

"There's a big hill first, isn't there?" his mum said. "A steep hill?"

"It's not that steep."

"However steep it is..." But his mum trailed off, and when Jack looked at her he saw tears on her cheeks. A second glance revealed the moisture to be sweat, not tears. It was not hot, hardly even warm. He wished she was crying instead of sweating.

His father hurried them along the road until the farm was out of sight. The smell of the fire faded into the background scent of the countryside, passing over from lush and alive, to wan and dead. Jack could still not come to terms with what he was seeing. It was as if his eyes were slowly losing their ability to discern colours and vitality in things, the whole of his vision turning into one of those sepia-tinted photographs he'd seen in his grandmother's house, where people never smiled and the edges were eaten away by time and too many thumbs and fingers. Except the bright red of his mother's blood was still there, even though the hedges were pastel instead of vibrant. His dad's face was pale, yes, but the burning spots on his cheeks—they flared when he was angry or upset, or both— were as bright as ever. Some colours, it seemed, could not be subsumed so easily.

"We won't all fade away, will we Dad? You won't let me and Mum and Mandy fade away, will you?"

His dad frowned, then ruffled his hair and squeezed the back of his neck. "Don't worry son. We'll get to Tewton and everything will be all right. They'll be doing something to help, they're bound to. They have to."

"Who are 'they', Dad?" Jack said, echoing his mum's question from that morning.

His dad shook his head. "Well, the government. The services, you know, the police and fire brigade."

Maybe they've faded away too, Jack thought. He did not say anything. It seemed he was keeping a lot of his thoughts to himself lately, making secrets. Instead, he tried naming some of his fears—they seemed more expansive and numerous every time he thought about them—but there was far too much he did not know. Fear is like pain, Mandy had told him. Maybe that's why his mum was hurting so much now. Maybe that's why *he* felt so much like crying. Underneath all the running around and the weirdness of today, perhaps he was truly in pain.

They followed the twisting road for ten minutes before hearing the sound of approaching vehicles.

"Stand back," Jack's dad said, stretching out and ushering Jack and his mum up against the hedge. Jack hated the feel of the dead leaves and buds against the back of his neck. They felt like long fingernails, and if he felt them move... if he felt them twitch and begin to scratch...

The hedges were high and overgrown here, though stark and sharp in death, and they did not see the cars until they were almost upon them. They were both battered almost beyond recognition, paint scoured off to reveal rusting metal beneath. *It's as if even the cars are dying*, Jack thought, and though it was a foolish notion it chilled him and made him hug his dad.

His dad brought up the gun. Jack could feel him shaking. He could feel the fear there, the tension in his legs, the effort it was taking for him to breathe.

"Dad?" he said, and he was going to ask what was wrong. He was going to ask why was he pointing a gun at people who could help them, maybe give them a lift to Tewton.

"Oh dear God," his mum said, and Jack heard the crackle as she leant back against the hedge.

There were bodies tied across the bonnets of each car. He'd seen pictures of hunters in America, returning to town with deer strapped across the front of their cars, parading through the streets with kills they had made. This was not the same, because these bodies were not kills. They were dead, yes, but not kills, because their heads rolled on their necks, their hands twisted at the wrist, their legs shook and their heels banged on the hot metal beneath them.

Jack's father kept his gun raised. The cars slowed and Jack

saw the faces inside, young for the most part, eyes wide and mouths open in sneers of rage or fear or mockery, whatever it was Jack could not tell. Living faces, but mad as well.

"Wanna lift?" one of the youths shouted through the Ital's smashed windscreen.

"I think we'll walk," Jack's dad said.

"It's not safe." The cars drifted to a standstill. "These fuckers are everywhere. Saw them eating a fucking bunch of people on the motorway. Ran them over." He leaned through the windscreen and patted the dead woman's head. She stirred, her eyes blank and black, skin ripped in so many places it looked to Jack like she was shedding. "So, you wanna lift?"

"Where are you going?" Jack asked.

The boy shrugged. He had a bleeding cut on his face; Jack was glad. The dead don't bleed. "Dunno. Somewhere where they can figure out what these fuckers are about."

"Who are 'they'?" Jack's dad asked.

The youth shrugged again, his bravado diluted by doubt. His eyes glittered and Jack thought he was going to cry, and suddenly he wished the youth would curse again, shout and be big and brave and defiant.

"We'll walk. We're going to Tewton."

"Yes, Mandy rang and said it's safe there!" Jack said excitedly.

"Best of luck to you then, little man," the driver said. Then he accelerated away. The second car followed, frightened faces staring out. The cars—the dead and the living—soon passed out of sight along the road.

"Into the fields again," Jack's dad said. "Up the hill to the woods. It's safer there."

Safer among dead things than among the living, Jack thought. Again, he kept his thought to himself. Again, they started across the fields.

They saw several cows standing very still in the distance, not chewing, not snorting, not flicking their tails. Their udders hung slack and empty, teats already black. They seemed to be looking in their direction. None of them moved. They looked like photos Jack had seen of the concrete cows in Milton Keynes, though those looked more lifelike.

It took an hour to reach the edge of the woods. Flies buzzed them but did not bite, the skies were empty of birds, things crawled along at the edges of fields, where dead crops met dead hedges.

The thought of entering the woods terrified Jack, though he could not say why. Perhaps it was a subconscious memory of the time he had been lost in the woods. That time had been followed by a mountain of heartache. Maybe he was anticipating the same now.

Instead, as they passed under the first stretch of dipping trees, they found a house, and a garden, and more bright colours than Jack had names for.

❖

"Look at that! Janey, look at that! Jack, see, I told you, it's not all bad!"

The cottage was small, its roof slumped in the middle and its woodwork was painted a bright, cheery yellow. The garden was a blazing attack of colour, and for a while Jack thought he was seeing something from a fairytale. Roses were only this red in stories, beans this green, grass so pure, ivy so darkly gorgeous across two sides of the house. Only in fairytales did potted plants stand in windowsill ranks so perfectly, their petals kissing each other but never stealing or leeching colour from their neighbour. Greens and reds and blues and violets and yellows, all stood out against the backdrop of the house and the limp, dying woods behind it. In the woods there were still colours, true, vague echoes of past glories clinging to branches or leaves or fronds. But this garden, Jack thought, must be where all the colour in the world had fled, a Noah's Ark for every known shade and tint and perhaps a few still to be discovered. There was magic in this place.

"Oh, wow," his mum said. She was smiling, and Jack was glad.

But his father, who had walked to the garden gate and pulled an overhanging rose stem to his nose, was no longer smiling. His expression was as far away from a smile as could be.

"It's not real," his dad said.

"What?"

"This rose isn't real. It's...synthetic. It's silk, or something."

"But the grass, Dad..."

Jack ran to the gate as his father pushed through it, and they hit the lawns together.

"Astroturf. Like they use on football pitches, sometimes. Looks pretty real, doesn't it, son?"

"The beans. The fruit trees, over there next to the cottage."

"Beans and fruit? In spring?"

Jack's mum was through the gate now, using her one good hand to caress the plants, squeeze them and watch them spring back into shape, bend them and hear the tiny snap as a plastic stem broke. Against the fake colours of the fake plants, she looked very pale indeed.

Jack ran to the fruit bushes and tried to pluck one of the red berries hanging there in abundance. It was difficult parting it from its stem, but it eventually popped free and he threw it straight into his mouth. He was not really expecting a burst of fruity flesh, and he was not proved wrong. It tasted like the inside of a yoghurt carton: plastic and false.

"It's not fair!" Jack ran to the front door of the cottage and hammered on the old wood, ignoring his father's hissed words of caution from behind him. His mum was poorly, they needed some food and drink, there were dead things—*dead* things, for fucking hell's sake—walking around and chasing them and eating people. Saw them eating a fucking bunch of people on the motorway, the man in the car had said.

All that, and now this, and none of it was fair.

The door drifted open. There were good smells from within, but old smells as well: the echoes of fresh bread; the memory of pastries; a vague idea that chicken had been roasted here recently, though surely not today, and probably not yesterday.

Naming of Parts

"There's no one here!" Jack called over his shoulder.

"They might be upstairs."

Jack shook his head. No, he knew this place was empty. He'd known the people in the field were coming and he'd seen what the dead folk in the banana car were like before... before he saw them for real. And he knew that this cottage was empty.

He went inside.

His parents dashed in after him, even his poorly mum. He felt bad about making her rush, but once they were inside and his dad had looked around, they knew they had the place to themselves.

❖

"It's just not fair," Jack said once again, elbows resting on a windowsill in the kitchen, chin cradled in cupped hands. "All those colours..."

There was a little bird in the garden, another survivor drawn by the colours. It was darting here and there, working at the fruit, pecking at invisible insects, fluttering from branch to plastic branch in a state of increasing agitation.

"Why would someone do this?" his mum asked. She was sitting at the pitted wooden table with a glass of orange juice and a slice of cake. Real juice, real cake. "Why construct a garden so false?"

"I feel bad about just eating their stuff," his dad said. "I mean, who knows who lives here? Maybe it's a little old lady and she has her garden like this because she's too frail to tend it herself. We'll leave some money when we go." He tapped his pockets, sighed. "You got any cash, Janey?"

She shook her head. "I didn't think to bring any when we left this morning. It was all so... rushed."

"Maybe everything's turning plastic and this is just where it begins," Jack mused. Neither of his parents replied. "I read a book once where everything turned to glass."

"I'll try the TV," his dad said after a long pause.

Jack followed him through the stuffy hallway and into the living room, a small room adorned with faded tapestries, brass ornaments and family portraits of what seemed like a hundred children. Faces smiled from the walls, hair shone in forgotten summer sunshine, and Jack wondered where all these people were now. If they were still children, were they in school? If they were grown up, were they doing what he and his parents were doing, stumbling their way through something so strange and *unexpected* that it forbore comprehension?

Or perhaps they were all dead. Sitting at home. Staring at their own photographs on their own walls, seeing how things used to be.

"There it is," his dad said. "Christ, what a relic." He never swore in front of Jack, not even damn or Christ or shit. He did not seem to notice his own standards slipping.

The television was an old wooden cabinet type, buttons and dials running down one side of the screen, no remote control, years of mugs and plates having left their ghostly impressions on the veneered top. His dad plugged it in and switched it on, and they heard an electrical buzz as it wound itself up. As the picture coalesced from the soupy screen Jack's dad glanced at his watch. "Almost six o'clock, news should be on any time now."

"I expect they'll have a news flash, anyway," Jack said confidently.

His dad did something then that both warmed his heart and disconcerted him. He laughed gently and gave him a hug, and Jack felt tears cool and shameless on his cheek. "Of course they will, son," he said, "I'm sure they will."

"Anything?" called his mum.

"Nearly," Jack shouted back.

There was no sound. The screen was stark and bland, and the bottom half stated: 'This is a Government Announcement'. The top half of the screen contained scrolling words: 'Stay calm...Remain indoors...Help is at hand...Please await further news.'

And that was it.

Naming of Parts

"What's on the other side, Dad?"

Buttons clicked in, the picture fizzled and changed, BBC1, BBC2, ITV, Channel 4, Channel 5, there were no others. But if there were, they would probably have all contained the same image. The Government notice, the scrolling words that should have brought comfort but which, in actual fact, terrified Jack. "I wonder how long it's been like that," he said, unable to prevent a shiver in his voice. "Dad, what if it isn't changing."

"It says 'Please await further news'. They wouldn't say that unless they were going to put something else up soon. Information on where to go, or something."

"Yeah, but that's like a sign on a shop door saying 'Be back soon'. It could have been there for months."

His dad looked down at him, frowning, chewing his lower lip. "There's bound to be something on the radio. Come on, I think I saw one in the kitchen."

His mum glanced up as they entered and Jack told her what they had seen. The radio was on a shelf above the cooker. It looked like the sort of antique people spent lots of money to own nowadays, but it was battered and yellowed, and its back cover was taped on. It crackled into instant life. A sombre brass band sprang from the speakers.

"Try 1215 medium wave," Jack said. "Virgin."

His dad tuned; the same brass band.

In six more places across the wavelengths, the same brass band.

"I'll leave it on. Maybe there'll be some news after this bit of music. I'll leave it on."

They tried the telephone as well, but every number was engaged. 999, the operator, the local police station, family and friends, random numbers. It was as if everyone in the world was trying to talk to someone else.

Twenty minutes later Jack's dad turned the radio off. They went to check the television and he switched that off as well. His mum laid down on the settee and Jack washed the cuts on her arms and the horrible wound on her shoulder, crying and gagging at the same time. He was brave, he kept it down. His mum was braver.

Later, after they had eaten some more food from the fridge and shared a huge pot of tea, his dad suggested they go to bed. No point trying to travel at night, he said, they'd only get lost. Besides, better to rest now and do the final part of the trip tomorrow than to travel all night, exhausted.

And there were those things out there as well, Jack thought, though his dad did not mention them. Dead things. *These fuckers are everywhere.* Dead cows, dead birds, dead insects, dead grass, dead crops, dead trees, dead hedges... dead people. Dead things everywhere with one thing in mind—to keep on moving. To find life.

How long before they rot away?
Or maybe the bugs that make things rot are dead as well.

❖

There were two bedrooms. Jack said he was happy sleeping alone in one, so long as both doors were kept open. He heard his mother groan as she lowered herself onto their bed, his father bustling in the bathroom, the toilet flushing... and it was all so normal.

Then he saw a spider in the corner of his room and there was no way of telling whether it was alive or dead—even when it moved—and he realised that 'normal' was going to have to change its coat.

Night fell unnaturally quickly, but when he glanced at his watch in the moonlight he saw that several hours had passed. Maybe he had been drifting in and out of sleep, daydreaming, though he could not recall what these fancies were about. He could hear his father's light snoring, his mother's breathing pained and uncomfortable. What if something tries to get in now? he thought. What if I hear fingers picking at window latches and tapping at the glass, nails scratching wood to dig out the frames? He looked up at the misshapen ceiling and thought he saw tiny dark things scurrying in and out of cracks, but it may have been fluid shapes on the surfaces of his eyes.

Then he heard the noises beginning outside. They may be the sounds of dead things crawling through undergrowth, but so long as he did not hear them shoving between plastic stems and false flowers, everything would be fine. The dark seemed to allow sounds to travel further, ring clearer, as if light could dampen noise. Perhaps it could; perhaps it would lessen the sound of dead things walking.

The night was full of furtive movements, clawed feet on hard ground, sagging bellies dragging through stiff grasses. There were no grunts or cries or shouts, no hooting owls or barking foxes screaming like tortured babies, because dead things can't talk. Dead things, Jack discovered that night, can only wander from one pointless place to another, taking other dead things with them and perhaps leaving parts of themselves behind. Whether he closed his eyes or kept them open he saw the same image, his own idea of what the scene was like out there tonight: no rhyme; no reason; no competition to survive; no feeding (unless there were a few unlucky living things still abroad); no point, no use, no ultimate aim...

...aimless.

He opened and closed his eyes, opened and closed them, stood and walked quietly to the window. The moon was almost full and it cast its silvery glare across a sickly landscape. He thought there was movement here and there, but when he looked he saw nothing. It was his poor night vision, he knew that, but it was also possible that the things didn't want to be seen moving. There was something secretive in that. Something intentional.

He went back to bed. When he was much younger it had always felt safe, and the feeling persisted now in some small measure. He pulled the stale blankets up over his nose.

His parents slept on. Jack remained awake. Perhaps he was seeking another secret in the night, and that thought conjured Mandy again. All those nights she had sat next to his bed talking to him, telling him adult things she'd never spoken of before, things about fear and imagination and how growing up closes doors in your mind. He had thought she'd been talking about herself, but she'd really been talking about him as well. She'd been talking about both of them because they were so alike, even if she was twice his age. And because they loved each other just as a brother and sister always should, and whatever had happened in the past could never, ever change that.

Because of Mandy he could name his fears, dissect and identify them, come to know them if not actually come to terms with them. He would never have figured that for himself, he was sure.

What she said had always seemed so right.

He closed his eyes to rest, and the dead had their hands on him.

They were grabbing at his arms, moving to his legs, pinching and piercing with rotten nails. One of them slapped his face and it was Mandy, she was standing at the bedside smiling down at him, her eyes shrivelled prunes in her grey face, and you should always name your fears..

Jack opened his mouth to scream but realised he was not breathing. It's safe here, he heard Mandy say. She was still smiling, welcoming, but there was a sadness behind that smile—even behind the slab of meat she had become—that Jack did not understand.

He had not seen Mandy for several months. She should be pleased to see him.

Then he noticed that the hands on his arms and legs were her own and her nails were digging in, promising never, ever to let him go, they were together now, it was safe here, safe...

"Jack!"

Still shaking, still slapped.

"Jack! For fuck's sake!"

Jack opened his eyes and Mandy disappeared. His dad was there instead, and for a split second Jack was confused. Mandy and his Dad looked so alike.

Naming of Parts

"Jackie, come with me," his dad said quietly. "Come on, we're leaving now."

"Is it morning?"

"Yes. Morning."

"Where's Mum?"

"Come on, son, we're going to go now. We're going to find Mandy."

Her name chilled him briefly, but then Jack remembered that even though she had been dead in his dream, still she'd been smiling. She had never hurt him, she *would* never hurt him. She would never hurt any of them.

"I need a pee."

"You can do that outside."

"What about food, Dad? We can't walk all that way without eating."

His dad turned his back and his voice sounded strange, as if forced through lips sewn shut. "I'll get some food together when we're downstairs, now come on."

"Mum!" Jack shouted.

"Jackie—"

"Mum! Is she awake yet, Dad?"

His father turned back to him, his eyes wide and wet and overflowing with grief and shock. Jack should have been shocked as well, but he was not, not really that shocked at all.

"Mum..." he whispered.

He darted past his father's outstretched hands and into the bedroom his parents had shared.

"Mum!" he said, relief sagging him against the wall. She was sitting up in bed, hands in her lap, staring at the doorway because she knew Jack would come running in as soon as he woke up. "I thought... Dad made me think..." *that you were dead.*

Nobody moved for what seemed like hours.

"She was cold when I woke up," his dad sobbed behind him. "Cold. So cold. And sitting like that. She hasn't moved, Jackie. Not even when I touched her. I felt for her pulse and she just looked at me... I felt for her heart, she just stared... she just keeps staring..."

"Mum," Jack gasped. Her expression did not change, because there was no expression. Her face was like a child's painting: two eyes, a nose, a mouth, no life there at all, no heart, no love or personality or soul. "Oh Mum..."

She was looking at him. Her eyes were dry so he could not see himself reflected there. Her breasts sagged in death, her open shoulder was a pale bloodless mass, like over-cooked meat. Her hands were crossed, and the finger she had pricked so that he could study her swarming blood under his microscope was pasty grey.

"We'll take her," Jack said. "When we get to Tewton they'll have a cure, we'll take her and—"

"Jack!" His father grabbed him under the arms and hauled him back towards the stairs. Jack began to kick and shout, trying to give life to his mother by pleading with her to help him, promising they would save her. "Jack we're leaving now, because Mum's dead. And Mandy is all we have left, Jackie. Listen to me!"

Jack continued to scream and his father dragged him downstairs, through the hallway and into the kitchen. He shouted and struggled, even though he knew his dad was right. They had to go on, they couldn't take his dead Mum with them, they had to go on. They'd seen dead people yesterday, and the results of dead people eating living people. He knew his dad was right but he was only a terrified boy, verging on his teens, full of fight and power and rage. The doors in his mind were as wide as they'd ever been, but grief makes so many unconscious choices that control becomes an unknown quantity.

Jack sat at the kitchen table and cried as his father filled a bag with food and bread. He wanted comfort, he wanted a cuddle, but he watched his dad work and saw the tears on his face too. He looked a hundred years old.

At last Jack looked up at the ceiling—he thought he'd heard

Naming of Parts

movement from up there, bedsprings flexing and settling—and he told his dad he was sorry.

"Jack, you and Mandy... I have to help you. We've got to get to Mandy, you see that? All the silly stuff, all that shit that happened... if only we knew how petty it all was. Oh God, if only I could un-say so much, son. Now, with all this... Mandy and Mum can never make up now." Bitter tears were pouring from his eyes, no matter how much he tried to keep them in. "But Mandy and I can. Come on, it's time to go."

"Is there any news, Dad?" Jack wanted him to say yes, to hear they'd found a cure.

His dad shrugged. "TV's the same this morning. Just like that 'Be back soon' sign."

"You checked it already?"

"And the phone, and the radio. All the same. When I found your Mum, I thought... I wanted help."

They opened the front door together. Jack went first and as he turned to watch the door close, he was sure he saw his mother's feet appear at the top of the stairs. Ready to follow them out.

It was only as they came to the edge of the grotesquely cheerful garden that Jack saw just how much things had changed overnight.

Looking down the hillside he could recognise little. Yesterday had come along to kill everything, and last night had leeched any remnants of colour or life from those sad corpses. Everything was dull. Branches dipped at the ground as if trying to find their way back to seed, grasses lay flat against the earth, hedgerows snaked blandly across the land, their dividing purpose now moot. Jack's eye was drawn to the occasional hints of colour in clumps of trees or hedges, where a lone survivor stood proudly against the background of its dead cousins. A survivor much like them.

Nothing was moving. The sky was devoid of birds, and for as far as they could see the landscape was utterly still.

"Through the woods. Back of the house. Come on son, one hour and we'll be there." Jack thought it would be more like two hours, maybe three, but he was grateful for his dad's efforts on his behalf.

They skirted the garden. Jack tried desperately not to look at the cottage in case he saw a familiar face pressed against a window.

Ten minutes later they were deep in the woods, still heading generally upward towards the summit of the hill. The ground was coated with dead leaves—autumn in spring—and in places they were knee-deep. Jack had used to enjoy kicking through dried leaves piled along pavements in the autumn, his mother told him it was an indication of the rebirth soon to come, but today he did not enjoy it. His mum was not here to talk to him... and he was unsure of what sort of rebirth could ever come of this. He saw a squirrel at the base of one tree, greyer than grey, stiff in death but its limbs still twitching intermittently. It was like a wind-up toy whose key was on its final revolution. Some branches were lined with dead birds, and only a few of them were moving. There was an occasional rustle of leaves as something fell to the ground.

Grief was blurring Jack's vision, but even without tears the unreality of what was on view would have done the same. Where trees dipped down and tapped him on the shoulder, he thought they were skeletal fingers reaching from above. Where dead things lay twitching, he thought he could see some hidden hand moving them. There had to be something hidden, Jack thought, something causing and controlling all of this, otherwise what was the point? He believed strongly in reasons, cause and effect. Coincidence and randomness were just too terrifyingly cold to even consider. Without reason, his mum's death was pointless.

His dad kept reaching out to touch him on the head, or the shoulder, or the arm, perhaps to make sure he was still there, or maybe simply to ensure that he was real. Occasionally he would mumble incoherently, but mostly he was silent. The only other sound was the swish of dead leaves, and the intermittent impact of things hitting the ground for the final time.

Jack looked back once. After thinking of doing so, it took him several minutes to work up the courage. They had found an old track that led deep into the woods, always erring upwards, and they were following that path now, the going easier than ploughing across the forest floor. He knew that if he turned he would see his mother following them, a grey echo of the wonderful woman she had been yesterday, her blood dried black on her clothes, smile caused by stretched skin rather than love. She had pricked her finger for him that Christmas, and to the young boy he'd been then, that was the ultimate sign of love—the willingness to inflict pain upon herself for him. But now, now that she was gone, Jack knew that his mother's true love was something else entirely. It was the proud smile every time she saw him go out to explore and experience. It was the hint of sadness in that smile, because *every single time* she said goodbye, somewhere deep inside she knew it could be the last. And it was the hug and kiss at the end of the day, when once again he came home safe and sound.

So Jack turned around, knowing he would see this false shadow of all the wonderful things his mother had been.

There was nothing following them, no one, and Jack was pleased. But still fresh tears came.

They paused and tried to eat, but neither was hungry. Jack sat on a fallen tree and put his face in his hands.

"Be brave, Jack." His dad sat next to him and hugged him close. "Be brave. Your mum would want that, wouldn't she?"

"But what about you, Dad?" Jack asked helplessly. "Won't you be lonely?"

His dad lowered his head and Jack saw the diamond rain of tears. "Of course I will, son. But I've got you, and I've got Mandy. And your mum would want me to be brave as well, don't you think?"

Jack nodded and they sat that way for a while, alternately crying and smiling into the trees when unbidden memories came. Jack did not want to relive good memories, not now, because here they would be polluted by all the dead things around them. But they came anyway and he guessed they always would, and at the most unexpected and surprising times. They were sad but comforting. He could not bear to drive them away.

They started walking again. Here and there were signs of life, but they were few and far between: a bluebell still bright amongst its million dead cousins; a woodpecker burrowing into rotting wood; a squirrel, jumping from tree to tree as if following them, then disappearing altogether.

Jack began to wonder how long the survivors would survive. How long would it be before whatever had killed everything else killed them, like it had his mum? He was going to ask his dad, but decided against it. He must be thinking the same thing.

In Tewton it would be safe. Mandy had said so, Mandy was there, and now she and Dad could make up for good. At least then, there would still be something of a family about them.

❖

They walked through the woods and nothing changed. Jack's dad held the shotgun in both hands but he had no cause to use it. Things were greyer today, blander, slower. It seemed also that things were deader. They found three dead people beneath a tree, not one of them showing any signs of movement. They looked as though they had been dead for weeks, but they still had blood on their chins. Their stomachs were bloated and torn open.

Just before midday they emerged suddenly from the woods and found themselves at the top of the hill, looking down into a wide, gentle valley. The colours here had gone as well; it looked like a fine film of ash had smothered everything in sight, from the nearest tree to the farthest hillside. In the distance, hunkered down behind a roll in the land as if hiding itself away, they could just make out the uppermost spires and roofs of Tewton. From this far away it was difficult to see whether there

Naming of Parts

were any signs of life. Jack thought not, but he tried not to look too hard in case he was right.

"Let's take a rest here, Jackie," his dad said. "Let's sit and look." Jack's mum had once used that saying when they were on holiday, the atmosphere and excitement driving Jack and Mandy into a frenzy, his dad eager to find a pub, an eternity of footpaths and sight-seeing stretched out before them. *Let's just sit and look*, she had said, and they had heeded her words and simply enjoyed the views and surroundings for what they were. Here and now there was nothing he wanted to sit and look at. The place smelled bad, there were no sounds other than their own laboured breathing, the landscape was a corpse laid out on a slab, perhaps awaiting identification, begging burial. There was nothing here he wanted to see.

But they sat and looked, and when Jack's heartbeat settled back to normal, he realised that he could no longer hear his father's breathing.

He held his breath. Stared down at the ground between his legs, saw the scattered dead beetles and ants, and the ladybirds without any flame in their wings. He had never experienced such stillness, such silence. He did not want to look up, did not want events to move on to whatever he would find next. *Dad dead*, he named. *Me on my own. Me, burying Dad.*

Slowly, he raised his head.

His father was asleep. His breathing was long and slow and shallow, a contented slumber or the first signs of his body running down, following his wife to that strange place which had recently become even stranger. He remained sitting upright and his hands still clasped the gun, but his chin was resting on his chest, his shoulders rising and falling, rising and falling, so slightly that Jack had to watch for a couple of minutes to make sure.

He could not bear to think of his father not waking up. He went to touch him on the shoulder, but wondered what the shock would do.

They had to get to Tewton. They were here—hell, he could

even *see* it—but still they found no safety. If there was help to be had, it must be where Mandy had said it would be.

Jack stood, stepped from foot to foot, looked around as if expecting help to come galloping across the funereal landscape on a white charger. Then he gently lifted the binoculars from his dad's neck, negotiated the strap under his arms, and set off along the hillside. Ten minutes, he figured, if he walked for ten minutes he would be able to see what was happening down in Tewton. See the hundreds of people rushing hither and tither, helping the folks who had come in from the dead countryside, providing food and shelter and some scrap of normality amongst the insanity. There would be soldiers there, and doctors, and tents in the streets because there were too many survivors to house in the buildings. There would be food as well, tons of it ferried in by helicopter, blankets and medicines... maybe a vaccine... or a cure.

But there were no helicopters. And there were no sounds of life.

He saw more dead things on the way, but he had nothing to fear from them. Yesterday dead had been dangerous, an insane, impossible threat; now it was simply no more. Today, the living were unique.

❖

Jack looked down on the edge of the town. A scattering of houses and garages and gardens spewed out into the landscape from between the low hills. There was a church there as well, and a row of shops with smashed windows, and several cars parked badly along the two streets he could see.

He lowered the binoculars and oriented himself from a distance, then looked again. A road wound into town from this side, trailing back along the floor of the valley before splitting in two, one of these arteries climbing towards the woods he and his father had just exited. Jack frowned, moved back to where the road passed between two rows of houses into the town, the

Naming of Parts

blurred vision setting him swaying like a sunflower in the breeze.

He was shaking. The vibration knocked him out of focus. There was a cool hand twisting his insides and drawing him back the way he had come, not only to his father, but to his dead mother as well. It was as if she were calling him across the empty miles that now separated them, pleading that he not leave her alone in that strange colour-splashed cottage, singing her love to tunes of guilt and with a chorus of childlike desperation so strong that it made him feel sick. However grown up Jack liked to think he was, all he wanted at that moment was his mother. And in a way he *was* older than his years, because he knew he would feel like that whatever his age.

Tears gave him a fluid outlook. He wiped his eyes roughly with his sleeve and looked again, breathing in deeply and letting his breath out in a long, slow sigh.

There were people down there. A barricade of some sort had been thrown across the road just where houses gave way to countryside—there was a car, and some furniture, and what looked like fridges and cookers—and behind this obstruction heads bobbed, shapes moved. Jack gasped and smiled and began to shake again, this time with excitement.

Mandy must be down there somewhere, waiting for them to come in. When she saw it was just Jack and his dad she would know the truth, they would not need to tell her, but as a family they could surely pull through, help each other and hold each other and love each other as they always should have.

Jack began to run back to his dad. He would wake him and together they would go the final mile.

The binoculars banged against his hip and he fell, crunching dry grass, skidding down the slope and coming to rest against a hedge. A shower of dead things pattered down on his face, leaves and twigs and petrified insects. His mum would wipe them away. She would spit on her handkerchief and dab at the cuts on his face, scold him for running when he should walk, tell him to read a book instead of watching the television.

He stood and started off again, but then he heard a voice.
"Jack."

It came from afar, faint, androgynous with distance and panic. He could hear that well enough; he could hear the panic.

"Jack."

He looked uphill towards the forest, expecting to see the limp figure of his mother edge out from beneath the trees' shadows, coming at him from the woods.

"Jack!"

The voice was louder now and accompanied by something else—the rhythmic *slap slap slap* of running feet.

Jack looked down the hill and made out something behind a hedge denuded of leaves. Lifting the binoculars he saw his father running along the road, hands pumping at the air, feet kicking up dust.

"Dad!" he called, but his father obviously did not hear. He disappeared behind a line of brown evergreens.

Jack tracked the road through the binoculars, all the way to Tewton. His dad must have woken up, found him missing and assumed he'd already made his way to the town, eager to see Mandy, or just too grief-stricken to wait any longer. Now he was on his way into town on his own, and when he arrived he would find Jack absent. He would panic. He would think himself alone, alone but for Mandy. How would two losses in one day affect him?

His dad emerged farther down the hillside, little more than a smudge against the landscape now, still running and still calling.

Jack ran as well. He figured if he moved as the crow flies they would reach the barricade at the same time. Panic over. Then they would find Mandy.

He tripped again, cursed, hauled the binoculars from his shoulder and threw them away. As he stood and ran on down the hill, he wondered whether they would ever be found. He guessed not. He guessed they'd stay here forever, and one day they would be a fossil. There were lots of future fossils being made today.

He could no longer see his dad, but he could see the hedgerow hiding the road that led into Tewton. His feet were carrying him away, moving too fast, and at some point Jack lost control. He was no longer running, he was falling, plummeting down the hillside in a reckless dash that would doubtless result in a broken leg—at least—should he lose his footing again. He concentrated on the ground just ahead of him, tempted to look down the hillside at the road but knowing he should not, he should watch out for himself, if he broke a limb now and there were no doctors in Tewton...

As the slope of the hill lessened so he brought his dash under control. His lungs were burning with exertion and he craved a drink. He did not stop running, though, because the hedge was close now, a tangled, bramble-infested maze of dead twigs and crumbling branches.

Tewton was close too. He could see rooftops to his right, but little else. He'd be at the barricade in a matter of minutes.

He hoped, how he hoped that Mandy was there to greet them. She and their father would have made up already, arms around each other, smiling sad smiles. *I've named my fears* Jack would tell her, and though their father would not understand they would smile at each other and hug, and he would tell her how what she had told him had saved him from going mad.

He reached the hedge and ran along it until he found a gate. His knees were flaring with pain, his chest tight and fit to burst, but he could see the road. He climbed the gate—there was a dead badger on the other side; not roadkill, just dead, and thankfully unmoving—and jumped into the lane.

It headed around a bend, and he was sure he heard pounding footsteps for a few seconds. It may have been his heart; it was thumping at his chest, urging him on, encouraging him to safety. He listened to it and hurried along the lane, moving at a shuffle now, more than a run.

As he rounded the bend everything came into view.

The people first of all, a couple of them still dragging themselves from the drainage reens either side of the road, several more converging on his father. He stood several steps from the barricade, glancing frantically around, obviously searching for Jack but seeing only dead people circling him, staring at him.

"Dad!" Jack shouted, at least he tried to. It came out as a gasp, fear and dread and defeat all rolled into one exhalation. Tewton... hope.... help, all given way to these dead things. For a fleeting instant he thought the barricade was a dividing line behind which hope may still exist, but then he saw that it wasn't really a barricade at all. It may have been once, maybe only hours ago, but now it was broken down and breached. Little more than another pile of rubbish that would never be cleared.

"Dad!" This time it *was* a shout. His dad spun around, and it almost broke Jack's heart to see the relief on his face. But then fear regained its hold and his dad began to shout.

"Jack, stay away, they're here, look! Stay away, Jack!"

"But Dad—"

His father fired the shotgun and one of the dead people hit the road. It—Jack could not even discern its sex—squirmed and slithered, unable to regain its feet.

Mandy, he thought, *where's Mandy, what of Mandy?*

Mandy dead, Mandy gone, only me and Dad left—

But the naming of his fears did him no good, because he was right to be afraid. He knew that when he heard the sounds behind him. He knew it when he turned and saw Mandy scrabbling out from the ditch, her long black hair clotted with dried leaves, her grace hobbled by death.

"Mandy," he whispered, and he thought she paused.

There was another gunshot behind him and the sound of metal hitting something soft. Then running feet coming his way. He hoped they were his father's. He remembered the dead people in the field yesterday, how fast they had moved, how quickly they had charged.

Mandy was grey and pale and thin. Her eyes showed none of his sister, her expression was not there, he could not *sense* her

Naming of Parts

at all. Her silver rings rattled loose on long stick fingers. She was walking towards him.

"Mandy, Mandy, it's me, Jack—"

"Jack! Move!" His father's words were slurred because he was running, it *was* his footsteps Jack could hear. And then he heard a shout, a curse.

He risked a glance over his shoulder. His father had tripped and slid across the lane on his hands and knees, the shotgun clattering into the ditch, three of the dead folk closing on him from behind. "Dad, behind you!" Jack shouted.

His father looked up at Jack, his eyes widened, his mouth hung open, his hands bled. "Behind you!" he shouted back.

A weight struck Jack and he went sprawling. He half turned as he fell so that he landed on his side, and he looked up and back in time to see Mandy toppling over on top of him. The wind was knocked from him and for a few seconds his chest felt tight, useless, dead.

Perhaps this is what it's like, he thought. *To be like them.*

At last he drew a shuddering breath, and the stench of Mandy hit him at the same time. The worst thing... the worst thing of all... was that he could detect a subtle hint of *Obsession* beneath the dead animal smell of her. His mum and dad always bought *Obsession* for Mandy at the airport when they went on holiday, and Jack had had a big box of jelly-fruits.

He felt her hands clawing at him, fingers seeking his throat, bony knees jarring into his stomach, his crotch. He screamed and struggled but could not move, Mandy had always beaten him at wrestling, she was just so strong—

"Get off!" his dad shouted. Jack could not see what was happening—he had landed so that he looked along the lane away from Tewton—but he could hear. "Get the fuck off, get away!" A thump as something soft hit the ground, then other sounds less easily identifiable, like an apple being stepped on or a leg torn from a cooked chicken. Then the unmistakable metallic snap of the shotgun being broken, reloaded, closed.

Two shots in rapid succession.

"Oh God, oh God, oh ... Jack, it's not Mandy Jack, you know that don't you!"

Jack struggled onto his back and looked up at the thing atop him.

You can name your fears, Mandy had said, and Jack could not bear to look, this bastard thing resembling his beautiful sister was a travesty, a crime against everything natural and everything right.

Jack closed his eyes. "I still love you Mandy," he said, but he was not talking to the thing on top of him now.

There was another blast from the shotgun. A weight landed on his chest, something sprinkled down across his face. He kept his eyes closed. The weight twisted for a while, squirmed and scratched at Jack with nails and something else, exposed bones perhaps—

A hand closed around his upper arm and pulled.

Jack screamed, shouted until his throat hurt. Maybe he could scare it off.

"It's alright, Jackie," a voice whispered into his ear. Mandy had never called him Jackie, so why now, why when—

Then he realised it was his father's voice. Jack opened his eyes as he stood and looked straight into his dad's face. They stared at each other because they both knew to stare elsewhere—to stare *down*—would invite images they could never, ever live with.

They held hands as they ran along the lane, away from Tewton. For a while there were sounds of possible pursuit behind them, but they came from a distance and Jack simply could not bring himself to look.

They ran for a very long time. For a while Jack felt like he was going mad, or perhaps it was clarity in a world gone mad itself. In his mind's eye he saw the dead people of Tewton waiting in their little town, waiting for the survivors to flee there from the countryside, slaughtering and eating them, taking feeble strength from cooling blood and giving themselves a few more hours before true death took them at last. The image gave him a strange sense of hope because he saw it could not go on forever. Hope in the death of the dead. A strange place to take comfort.

At last they could run no more. They found a petrol station and collapsed in the little shop, drinking warm cola because the electricity was off, eating chocolate and crisps. They rested until mid-afternoon. Then, because they did not know what else to do, they moved on once more.

❖

Jack held his father's hand. They walked along a main road, but there was no traffic. At one junction they saw a person nailed high up on an old telegraph pole. Jack began to wonder why but then gave in, because he knew he would never know.

The countryside began to flatten out. A few miles from where they were was the coast, an aim as good as any now, a place where help may have landed.

"You okay to keep going, son?"

Jack nodded. He squeezed his dad's hand as well. But he could not bring himself to speak. He had said nothing since they'd left the petrol station. He could not. He was too busy trying to remember what Mandy looked like, imprint her features on his mind so that he would never, ever forget.

There were shapes wandering the fields of dead crops. Jack and his dad increased their pace but the dead people were hardly moving, and they seemed to pose no threat. He kept glancing back as they fell behind. It looked like they were harvesting what they had sown.

As the sun hit the hillsides behind them they saw something startling in the distance. It looked like a flash of green, small but so out of place amongst this blandness that it stood out like an emerald in ash. They could not run because they were exhausted, but they increased their pace until they drew level with the field.

In the centre of the field stood a scarecrow, very lifelike, straw hands hidden by gloves and face painted with a soppy sideways grin. Spread out around its stand was an uneven circle of green shoots. The green was surrounded by the rest of the dead crop, but it was alive, it had survived.

"Something in the soil, maybe?" Jack said.

"Farming chemicals?"

Jack shrugged. "Maybe we could go and see."

"Look," his dad said, pointing out towards the scarecrow.

Jack frowned, saw what his dad had seen, then saw the trail leading to it. It headed from the road, a path of crushed shoots aiming directly out towards the scarecrow. It did not quite reach it, however, and at the end of the trail something was slumped down in the mud, just at the boundary of living and dead crop. Jack thought he saw hair shifting in the breeze, the hem of a jacket lifting, dropping, lifting again, as if waving.

They decided not to investigate.

They passed several more bodies over the next couple of hours, all of them still, all of them lying in grotesque contortions in the road or the ditches. Their hands were clawed, as if they'd been trying to grasp a hold of something before coming to rest.

Father and son still held hands, and as the sun began to bleed across the hillsides they squeezed every now and then to reassure each other that they were alright. As alright as they could be, anyhow.

Jack closed his eyes every now and then to remember what Mandy and his mum had looked like. Each time he opened them again, a tear or two escaped.

He thought he knew what they would find when they reached the coast. He squeezed his father's hand once more, but he did not tell him. Best to wait until they arrived.

For now, it would remain his secret.

THE END

J ACK AND HIS FATHER reach the coast, and there is nothing resembling hope. It has taken them four days of walking by day and hiding by night. During the days they saw some walkers, but far fewer than before, and they stumbled more than walked, aimless and without purpose. It is as if the dead have gone blind. At night they hid in deserted homes, checking them first for bodies. In each home, Jack made sure he looked at family photographs by the light of a candle, silently asking them for permission to stay.

The dunes are high, the coast barren, the sea as grey and forbidding as the skin of the dead.

Jack's father drops to his knees, then forward onto his hands, which he fists in the sand as if he's trying to grab onto the world, hold it still, prevent it from sliding even more into chaos and catastrophe. But Jack knows that it's far too late for that.

He kneels beside his father and holds him tight. They both take comfort from the contact.

"Come on," Jack says. "It'll be dark soon." He doesn't need to say anymore. Darkness is falling, and it has always been the place where dangers lay. That is the case now more than ever before.

They find an old wooden bungalow just inland from the dunes. It has been deserted for some time—years, not just since the dead started walking—its façade scored by sand carried on the wind and bleached by the sun. The walls are bare wood. Crabs scuttle inside, but the smooth floor provides a comfortable surface to sleep away from the weather.

Jack makes a small fire from dried wood. It gives them heat and light, and he watches his father staring into the flames, eyes lifeless, the tears on his cheeks catching the fire, red as blood.

❖

Next morning it's Jack who decides which way to go.

His father is quiet, hardly there. Sometimes he mumbles, but when Jack asks what he's saying, he shakes his head and holds his son's shoulder, squeezing. Jack doesn't like what that implies: *You're too young to know.*

He doesn't feel young. He feels like he's grown up far too quickly.

They walk along the hard sand halfway down the beach, beneath the high tide mark signified by piles of seaweed, crab and fish corpses, and a few pieces of driftwood that remind Jack of the bungalow they stayed in. He wonders if everything becomes smoothed by time.

They walk all day. A few times they have to go inland and find the coastal path, moving slowly and cautiously, but they're alone. They don't see one zombie, and Jack thinks it's the first day that's happened since this all began. As soon as they can, they find their way back to the beach.

Once, there are footprints in the sand, prints of bare feet with spatters of blood alongside them every few steps. They disappear into the waves, and as the tide comes in those closer to the sea have already started to fall away at the edges. Soon they will be gone.

Close to evening, they see movement in the distance.

Jack's father drops to the sand and pulls him down. "Shhh!"

"It's okay, Dad," he says. "That's not a zombie."

"I know that," his father says. "But we don't know *who* it is."

If it's not a zombie, it must be a person, so that can only be good! Jack thinks. But he understands his father's caution. It's a different world now, and they have to be careful.

They follow the person along the edge of the beach, hiding behind a row of old beach huts close to a little seaside town. They try to move quickly past the town. Jack can smell rotting things, and from somewhere far off comes the heavy, steady drone of a million flies.

When the figure passes over a small rise and disappears down the other side, Jack and his father start to run. Jack tries to imagine what they'll see over the rise. Most of what he imagines is terrifying, and several times he wants to stop, hold back, turn and go the other way. Maybe it should just be him and his dad out here. With Mandy and his mum gone, maybe that's how it should be forever.

But his father is faster than him, and Jack sees him freeze as he reaches the top of the small rise and looks beyond.

"Dad," Jack says, scurrying to catch up, grabbing onto long grasses to help him up the slope. "Dad, what is it?" Finally, he looks down onto the next long, wide beach and sees the beached ship.

"It's hope," his father says.

CHANGING OF FACES

"God hath given you one face and you make yourselves another."
—William Shakespeare, Hamlet

A FULL MOON brought the first tide of death.
They saw them in the distance, loping along the beach, crawling through the sand, ducking and diving in the air, leaping from the sea where waves dashed whitely against the shore. The curved bay was wide, the approaching shadows at least a mile distant, and this far out the threat could only exist in the minds of the observers. But after all they had been through they were attuned to dangers, both apparent and potential. They had come to expect the worst.

"We haven't seen any walking dead since you got here," Janine said, looking accusingly at Jack and his father. "But no walking living, either..." She trailed off with the same note of subdued panic that Jack had come to recognise amongst the adults. Nothing they could do, no one they could turn to, no one in charge.

"This looks different," Oscar said. He was a tall man, middle-aged, physically and mentally strong, and he'd quickly become the leader of their group. They stood on the slanting deck of the beached ferry and Oscar was the calmest. He hadn't lost anyone, he told them, because he'd had no one to lose.

"I can hear them," Jack said. The sea hushed onto the beach, a sound he had already become so used to that it became background. But now between each surge there was something else, a distant whisper like a storm approaching in the night. He held his breath and closed his eyes, trying to make it out.

"I can't hear a thing," a man said. Jack thought his name was Steve, although he rarely spoke.

"Whatever it is, I think we should get inside," Oscar said. "Lock all the doors and windows. Batten down like we've discussed."

"But I thought it was all over," Janine said. "I thought it was just a case of waiting!"

Jack took a final look across the bay at the advancing threat. In the night, lit only by moonlight, it looked like waves of shadow twisting and flipping towards them, one end splashing in the sea and breaking its natural rhythm, the top edge grasping at the sky and blocking out the stars. There was a definite sound now. Splashes, a rhythmic flapping at the air, the dull impacts of feet on sand, running. And behind it all, something else. Jack strained, hoping for voices. He heard growls and grunts instead.

"Its them," he whispered, grasping his dad's hand, needing to feel safe. Safe was somewhere he had known once, safe with his family, but with half of them gone the word had lost meaning. Safe was a fantasy place now, like Narnia or Never-Never Land or Middle Earth.

"It might not be," his dad said, still so full of doubt and dread.

"Inside!" Oscar hissed. Nobody argued.

There were noises now, strange cries in the night. Jack listened as he hurried along in front of his father. Sometimes, beneath those screams, he could hear voices.

The ten people filed across the uneven deck and through the open door. Oscar slammed it behind them, shutting out the hush of the sea and the violence in the noise slowly drowning it.

"We need to lock as many doors and windows as we can," he said. "Then we'll meet in the bar and shut it up. We've got the

Changing of Faces

guns. We've got the gas canisters. If it is them, we can hold them off—"

"It isn't," Jack said. He was panting with fear, sweat tickled his sides and his father's hand squeezed his shoulder. "Not them, not the walking dead. Something different." He closed his eyes and wished he could scream. The dark behind his eyelids bulged and swam with threat, and his spine seemed to stretch with an awful promise of pain. "Something worse," he said. And then they heard the first of the long, dreadful screams from outside.

"What the fuck was that?" Nathan said. He was a young lad, little more than sixteen, but to Jack he seemed all grown up. He smoked and swore, and swore he'd screwed Janine.

"Doors!" Oscar said, trying to control the panic that buzzed around them. "And windows!."

"Come on," Jack's dad said. He held onto Jack's arm as he moved away. "We'll close up this way. Meet you all in the bar."

"I think we may have three or four minutes," Oscar said, and then another scream came, closer, higher, already victorious. He looked at them all where they stood silent and cold, and whispered: "Let's hurry."

Jack and his dad dashed away and turned the first corner in the wide corridor, checking windows, slamming and locking them where necessary.

"How do you know they're not the walking dead?" his dad said as they hurried from window to window.

Jack checked a catch and moved on to the next one. "Just do. It's ... obvious."

"To you."

He nodded. "Yeah, to me."

His father had reached a door that hung half-open. He pulled it shut and twisted the catches at the head and foot, kicking it once to make sure it was secure. "Your mum always said you had a touch of your grandmother's insight."

"It's nothing like that!" Jack said, surprised at the anger in his voice. The last thing he would do, could ever do, was to hurt his dad. Even disagreeing with him felt bad since his mother and sister had died. But this... Jack was scared. He felt things, knew things he didn't want to know, and he had no idea how.

His dad looked at him and smiled in the weak light. "Down to the next floor. Then the bar."

"Will we hold them off in there?" Jack asked. When he'd closed his eyes earlier he'd sensed something out there, a raw power born of desperation and hunger. He wondered how determined something would have to be to get in. As he glanced at the door his father had just bolted, the thin metal handles of the locking plates, Jack thought of those fluid shadows they had seen rolling along the beach.

Another cry from outside, as if in answer to Jack's thought. It was a scream in the dead of night, too loud and powerful to belong here. Jack shivered, coolness flooded his spine and for a brief, awful moment he thought he was going to piss himself.

"How far away—?" his dad said quietly, but when the thing struck the metal bulkhead outside, they knew.

"Dad!"

"Keep still!" Something solid scraped across metal, screeching in places, scoring, testing. They heard a snort or a heavy breath. Then, nearer and louder than ever, another screech.

Something began smashing against one of the small windows they had just locked.

They heard shouts back along the corridor—Oscar or one of the others. Jack couldn't tell what they were saying, if anything at all.

"The bar!" his dad said. "Quick!"

The window obscured and the next impact drove something through... something long and ridged, solid as stone, fresh scrapes along its length a muddy golden colour.

"A beak..." Jack said. And then his father picked him up and ran.

Fear gives strength, Jack had heard, and his father must have been terrified. It took only a few short seconds, barely more that a dozen flustered heartbeats, but by the time they stopped

Changing of Faces 85

and his dad set him down there was a closed door between them and the outside corridor. It had glass viewing panels, but they were small and wire-reinforced. And the thing back there must have been too big to actually fit into the corridor. The thing with a beak...

Jack wondered at its wing span and tried to think about something else.

"Thought it was...all over!" his dad gasped. Jack could see the utter, unnameable fear in his father's eyes. For him, probably. For his young son, the last thing he had left in the world. "Thought we might be...safe here."

"Let's get to the bar," Jack said. "It'll be safe there." But he knew that it was a lie. He knew, however he sometimes knew these things, that safe was a long, long way from here. Maybe too far away to ever see again. "Safe's what you make it," he mumbled, and although his dad must have heard he said nothing.

The bar was down a wide set of stairs at the end of the corridor. And the whole boat, until now so silent and peaceful with only the nine of them living here, was filled with noise. Some of the sounds were familiar—the receding echo of running footsteps; a calling voice, androgynous with distance, only panic evident behind the indistinguishable words—and others were mysterious, and terrifying. A regular thud, thud from the depths of the ferry, like something trying to penetrate the thick base-plates; a long, low whistle through the air conditioning vents; a sudden scream, perhaps human, perhaps not.

Jack thought the noises were loud until they were drowned out by the sudden explosion behind them.

He spun around in time to see the door shatter from its hinges. Sparks flew as metal tore, starring the air along with shards of the frame.

"Come on!" his dad shouted. He shoved Jack ahead of him. A sound filled the corridor like the roar of a jet engine, so loud that it hurt, so powerful that it seemed to give them an extra nudge, push them on toward the stairwell a dozen paces ahead. There was a smell, too; rotten, decayed, bad meat.

It is one of the dead! Jack thought, but as the thing screeched again and launched itself at them he wondered whether they were merely smelling its insides, the aroma of its unfortunate last meal.

They reached the stairwell and, at the head of the first flight, Jack tripped over his own foot. His heart thudded, time slowed, and a sick not-happening-to-me feeling rose in his stomach as he tipped forward. He would break his wrists and fingers, he knew, and most likely his neck as the rest of his body rolled after him, but there was nothing he could do. The thing with the beak—too big for a bird, too not real—was charging them, leathery wings scoring the walls as if made of metal, not flesh and bone. Overhead lights smashed out as the creature's head knocked them aside. The air became full of the smell of rot and the sound of its cry, and as Jack opened his mouth to scream he could taste something beyond the tang of his own fear: death. He could taste death. The same dusty, musty sheen on his tongue that had followed the deaths of his mother and sister.

It would get his dad first.

And then he felt his shirt grabbed and his father was tugging him back, balancing the risk of the fall against the danger from the thing halfway along the corridor. Jack grabbed hold of the handrail and stumbled down the first few steps, shouting incoherently in an effort to ward off the things' screeches. His dad followed. On the half-landing they turned to the second flight . . . and Jack could not help but look up.

The thing had reached the head of the stairs. It stood there now, crying down at them, head jerking forward in grotesque pecking motions. And it was a bird. And it was—as Jack saw but could not believe, really, how could this be—a crow. Huge, misshapen, its eyes a deep royal blue, not black, much of its body leathery and unfeathered . . . but a crow.

Big birds, Jack thought, come to kill us, come from nowhere. But naming his fear did not help, not when it was standing there facing him, beak only feet away, wings tucking in to allow access down the stairwell.

"Down!" his dad said.

Jack jumped down the first few stairs without taking his eyes off the huge bird. There was a mark near the bare root of one wing, something pressed blackly into the skin, a smudged shaped like a skull. Below it, unreadable but definitely there, a word. Jack couldn't make out what it said, but he knew precisely what it meant. He'd seen tattoos before.

"Now I'm seeing things!" he shouted.

"Me too," his dad said, and Jack wondered what he meant.

"It's a bird, Dad! It's a bird with a—"

"Just keep going, Jackie," his dad said.

Jack's mum had called him Jackie, when she was tucking him into bed for the night or guiding him along the pavement on his new stabilised bike, forgetting to tell him that she'd let go and that he was actually riding on his own, then calling when he was twenty feet away, saying Jackie, you're doing it Jackie. Jack felt tears welling but he glanced at the shape trying to force itself down the staircase, and the unreality of the situation truly took him for the first time.

Two weeks ago, they had been fleeing the living dead countryside, dodging dead folk and seeing cattle and grass and trees die and then live again, a perverted existence that could not last for long. Cattle and family, dying and living again... Even now, Jack was half convinced that it had all been some dreadful dream. Perhaps his mother and sister really were dead and it had driven him mad. He didn't hear voices like people in books or on TV—at least he hadn't yet—but he did seem to know things. And the only way he could know them was in dreams.

Now, a tattooed crow was trying to eat him.

They reached the next level, and Jack immediately wished he could change his dreams. He shouted out, fear and disgust and a horrible sense of dread slurring his voice.

The thing was still calling out behind them. Jack could hear its hide and feathers scraping along the walls as it forced its way down the staircase.

He could also hear the other thing in front of him eating Janine.

"Dad..."

"Keep going, Jack, just keep..." Jack did not need to turn around to know that his dad had seen it as well. Hands clasped onto his shoulders, hurting him but making him glad for the pain. Janine could not feel pain. She had, only recently, and it must have been awful. But not now. Not any more.

"Is that a...?" his dad said, unable to finish.

Jack finished for him. "A weasel, Dad. Me and Mandy saw one once in the woods. After I got lost in there, before I could go in there on my own again. She took me for a walk. She found me a stick. We saw a weasel."

"It's huge."

Jack nodded. Understatement, he wanted to say, but he suddenly felt the crow behind them, looming at the bottom of the staircase, as if its presence had altered gravity and lifted Jack's hair on end.

His dad half-pushed, half-carried him past Janine and the weasel. It took them three long strides to pass the chewing rodent. It was the size of an Alsatian. Jack tried not to see which part of Janine it was eating.

There was a bee there as well, a bumble bee as big as his head, harvesting blood like pollen. It had something through one wing, a silvery flash that was barely still enough to see. It looked like jewellery, but of course that was plain stupid.

Just crazy.

"Dad, what the fuck is going on?" Jack hissed. He wanted to shout and scream and cry, have his dad hold him tight as he raged and cried himself out.

"Keep going," his dad said. "The bar. Oscar will be there with the guns."

The bird called out behind them. The bird with the tattoo.

The weasel hissed wetly.

The bee buzzed. The bee with the jewellery.

Jack started to run and his dad kept up with him. The corridor opened up and the décor became more aesthetically pleasing. They were approaching the heart of the ferry, the restaurant and bar area, and the walls suddenly splashed out a dozen murals of idyllic holiday scenes. The vinyl flooring gave way to carpet, the ceiling rose and lighting became more comforting. Bigger, wider... Jack wondered how big the space would need to be before...

And then he knew. He heard the sound and knew what it was, like a heavy sheet snapping out straight in the wind. The crow came at them, flying, its wingtips slicing the walls up and down, bursting doors, smashing pictures from their hooks.

"Ahead and to the left!" his dad shouted, pushing Jack so hard that he almost stumbled and fell, almost, and Jack knew just what would happen then. He ran into the fall until he had regained his balance. And he was suddenly certain that those were the last words he'd ever hear his father say. Ahead and to the left would be his passing testimony, not I love you son, or This is how things should be, Jack.

And then Jack saw Oscar standing there, ahead and to the left, a shotgun braced against his shoulder, one side of his face bloodied and tatty and just hanging off... and the gun was pointing straight at Jack.

What if he can't see right? Jack thought, but then the explosion blasted all thought away. That was it. He was either saved or dead. He fell.

His dad landed on top of him. Something wet hit the back of Jack's neck and ran down his shirt, wet and horribly warm. It tickled like a spider seeking refuge from all the impossibilities happening right then.

The bird screamed. It was a horrible sound because it resembled a child in pain, a totally out-of-control cry like Jack had seen on television once, watching a lady giving birth with his mum and sister, wondering why his mum was crying...

"Stay still, Jack," his dad said.

"You alright Dad?"

His father must have heard Jack's desperation. "Yes, I am. Two seconds then we run to Oscar. Got it?" The bird screamed again. "One..." Then it cried, a huge sob filled with regret as well as pain. Jack almost turned around. "Two!" His dad heaved him to his feet and they ran the final few steps, ducking past Oscar and rolling to the floor as the door was slammed shut behind them.

"That's everyone but Janine," Jack heard Nathan say. When he looked up he saw that the boy had shut the door and locked it, propping chairs beneath the handles.

"That was a giant crow," Jack's dad said matter-of-factly.

Oscar stood above them and held out a hand to Jack. "I saw a cat," he said. "Biggest fucking thing I've ever seen. Remember the one that used to live at Paddington Station, big old fat thing that became a bit of a tourist attraction? Kitten."

"We saw a weasel..." Jack's dad said, then he trailed off and glanced at Nathan.

"It was eating Janine," Jack said. He realised the cruelty of his statement straight away, but he did not feel in control. And he was disgusted and terrified and shocked and fascinated. And he was still, really, just a kid.

Nathan's eyes went wide and his face slackened. All the bluster seemed to seep away, and Jack saw tears in his eyes.

"Damn!" Oscar winced and put a hand to his face, holding it millimetres from his wound as if its proximity could help. He could not bear to touch it. Blood flowed, slashed skin hung tattered and loose.

One of the women was standing at the row of scenic windows facing out to sea. She pressed her face to the glass and shielded her eyes from the dimmed lighting in the bar. "There are things out there," she said. "Flying. Circling us."

"We should have hidden somewhere deep inside the boat," Steve said. "Those windows won't stand up to much."

"They're triple-glazed," Oscar said, voice slightly distorted by his injury. He was trying to talk from one corner of his mouth, Jack saw. Trying to convince himself, perhaps, that it would all get better. "It'll withstand the worst storms the sea can throw at it. It'll... it would hold back anything living dead."

"What about giant crows and bees?" Jack's dad asked.

Oscar shook his head, sat slowly into a plastic bucket seat, rested the shotgun against a table. "I just don't have a clue...." he said, trailing off. He pressed a handkerchief to his face and hissed. It soaked red immediately.

We should be helping him, Jack thought. Should be rushing to his aid, looking for towels and bandages and stuff to clean the wound with. They were in a bar after all, there was plenty of whiskey there, that's what they used in films. They'd give him a few swigs first to numb him, then put a wooden spoon in his mouth for him to bite down on while they poured whiskey across raw flesh, cleaning it out.

But today people were more concerned with helping themselves, trying to discover what was happening. Trying to believe. They were standing in a confused tangle, panting, looking around the bar, searching for a weapon or a way out. Lucy, the teenaged girl, pretty and utterly silent since he'd first seen her sixteen days earlier, went to the bar and climbed over. She walked along the display shelves, running her fingers from bottle to bottle until she appeared to find what she wanted.

"Come on," Jack's dad said. "Lucy, that won't help." She set the bottle down, unscrewed the top and filled a half pint glass with the golden fluid. Jack wondered just what she'd seen over the past few weeks.

She took several huge gulps from the glass, winced, rested her forehead on the bartop.

"They're circling us," the woman at the window said. "All flying the same way."

"They'll easily see you there," Nathan said.

"See us all." Steve picked up Oscar's shotgun slowly, watching the big man for any reaction. He was struggling to remain conscious as he pressed his hand to his wound, trying to stop the bleeding. "They're out in the dark, we're behind bare glass in the light. Like pies in a display cabinet."

"Nice way of putting it," Nathan said.

"And you're the mystery pie," Steve quipped, unable to raise even a smile.

There was a sudden flurry of noise from the double doors leading into the bar. There were three entrances, two of them small single doors, one a double. The singles were piled high with furniture already, but the doubles had only just been slammed shut behind Jack and his dad. A couple of bolts held them locked, the chairs propped there barely any help.

Jack remembered that huge crow smashing in the window, bursting the doors and shredding the metal hinges.

"Where are the rest of the guns?" his dad asked.

Steve broke the shotgun and replaced the spent cartridges from a box on the table. "Didn't have time to get them. Oscar was here first. I think they're under the bar."

"Lucy?" Jack's dad called, but the silent girl was busy finishing off another half-pint of her poison. He turned to Jack. "Stay with Steve. I'm going to get the other guns."

Jack went to stand next to Steve, who hardly seemed to notice him. He watched his dad wind between tables and chairs to the bar, feeling alone, vulnerable and lost. It wasn't an ocean away, but it seemed that the space between them grew massively with every step his dad took, and if the doors burst open now they wouldn't have time to reach each other, they'd be apart, and whatever came in would have a choice between the two of them instead of having to choose both.

"Dad," Jack whispered.

Steve glanced down, eyes red, skin pale, stubble speckled with bits of food from the ferry's huge larders. "It's alright, mate," he said quietly, smiling, clicking the shotgun shut. And the assault began.

Up until then the things outside must have been probing, looking for weaknesses, sending in a few of their number here and there to test the waters. Now, with Janine dead and Oscar

Changing of Faces

slumped forward as his blood continued to flow, the testing was over.

Jack screamed, but the attack was so sudden and loud that he barely heard himself. The noise came from behind him, where the furniture piled against the single doors shook and shimmied as something repeatedly struck the other side, the timber already splintering. It came from ahead of him too; the flying things had stopped circling and were now dashing themselves against the glass, illuminated by the weak artificial light for a split second before they struck. Birds, some of them big and clumsy but some, like a wren the size of a small dog, elegant and almost graceful in the instant before it hit the glass, fluttering in pain and fury as it slid out of sight below. And more than birds. Bats, bees, insects...

...and something that could only have been an angel.

It hovered slightly away from the window, stretching its legs and scoring the surface of the glass with its metal-sharp toes, slowly, patiently, the scraping sound audible above the impacts and cries and panicked shouting of those in the bar.

"A moth!" Steve shouted. "A fucking huge moth!"

More noise, closer, more dangerous. The double doors.

They bowed inward at the first assault, opening down the centre so that they could all see the outline of the thing outside. It was as tall as the doors. Its speckled black and brown fur was punctuated at the top where knife-long teeth were bared, dripping and scraping at the door even as it struck again.

"Dad!" Jack shouted. "Daddy!" *They're going to die suffering, those things. They're not natural, they're hurting, and they'll die in agony.* He knew that, even though he knew it wouldn't be now. Wherever the thought came from he tried to shove it away.

"Jack, here, now!" His dad was standing behind the bar, struggling to load a sawn-off shotgun with shaking hands. Lucy stood next to him, watching events with a bemused expression. Jack wished he felt as peaceful as she appeared. The bottle next to her was almost empty. Her eyes were glazed and there was a faint, sad smile on her face, as though she were watching something else entirely.

Steve fired his shotgun.

It was so close to Jack that he thought he'd been shot. The pain was so great, the sound like a solid punch, that for a few seconds he heard and sensed nothing. It felt similar to when he'd been hit in the face with a basketball in school, only worse, harder, louder. Dazed, he went to his knees, tears fleeing his eyes, and when he looked again he saw a ragged hole in one of the double doors.

The thing trying to get in had barely paused in its assault. Shot or not, it wanted in.

"Jack!" The voice came in from the distance like a bomb, exploding in his head when his ears popped.

"Dad!" he said, scrambling across the carpeted floor, wondering how many other people had walked this way in more pleasant circumstances. Wondering too how many of those people were still alive today.

Better off dead, he thought. And even after all he had seen over the past few weeks, somehow the idea held true. Perhaps because death itself had become so meaningless, both in its implications—not always, it seemed, the end—and its prolificacy.

"Come on!" his dad called, leaning over the bar and motioning with one hand. The other held the shotgun, resting on the timber surface and pointing over Jack's head at the double doors. There was another crunch behind Jack, and he saw from the look on his dad's face that they had almost caved in that time. One more attack, one more charge, and whatever was outside would be in.

Jack crawled.

Huge flying things crashed at the windows, the glass starring with each impact.

His dad called, waving to him as if he could haul him in on some invisible line.

And from somewhere Jack had an overwhelming sense of

utter excitement, hunger and rage. They'll die in agony, but for now.... this is just the best there is. The thought was like a whispering collage of voices in his head, voices which were not human but should be.

He paused and looked over his shoulder as the doors gave way. And when he saw what stood there he knew how right he was.

It let out a joyous howl even as two shotguns emptied into it.

Tall as a man, wide as a bear, its auburn pelt holed and bleeding, the fox dropped onto all-four and darted into the room. For something so large it was surprisingly quick.

Steve backed away as fast as he could, but it took only seconds for him to stumble against a table, drop the shotgun and tumble onto his back. The fox advanced, leaving splashes of blood on the carpet from its various wounds, huge teeth bared, its eyes... its eyes...

They were wrong. Jack saw that through his fear, sensed it above the cacophony of chaos and panic that filled the bar. Its eyes were wrong because they were so very intelligent. And even through the pain of its wounds, it was enjoying this far too much.

"Steve," his dad was muttering, trying to break open the gun.

The woman at the window screamed as the battering intensified, and several of the panes turned obscure as a prelude to shattering. Jack could see big shadows dancing beyond the windows, the shapes flying back and forth, silhouetted against silvery moonlight. They'll be in soon, he thought, can't go on like this forever. They'll be in, and they can't wait because they're hungry. They're starving. Haven't eaten, ever.

"Jack, the shells!" his father hissed, and Jack felt the shotgun cartridges dropping on his toes. His dad had knocked the box over.

Lucy watched them. Her eyes were wide but empty, glazed by alcohol and madness.

Jack glanced at Steve—the fox was standing over him now, it had knocked a table aside with its head and its jaws were inches from his chest—and then ducked down for the cartridges. It was dark behind the bar and he had to feel around on the floor.

He'd used to do this in his room at home when he heard a sound in the night. The woods were filled with things hunting and mating and calling out, and although he could usually identify them there were always one or two which eluded him. So he'd scramble around on the floor, searching for his pen-light torch so that he could open the window and lean out, hold his breath, feel the cool night air take him to itself. Strange how removing a shield of glass could make him feel so much more a part of the night, while now... here, huddled behind the bar, glass was all that kept them safe.

For now.

His fingers touched some cartridges—

"Jack! Hurry!"

—and he snatched them up, handing them up to his dad as things changed once again.

It was a sound; or rather, a lack of it. Steve no longer screamed. The fox had ceased growling. Something replaced both, and Jack did not want to see what was causing it. Behind the battering at the windows and the various shouts and cries from those around the bar, the unmistakable sound of eating.

Jack stood as his father locked the gun and brought it to his shoulder.

"I'll hit Steve," he said. The shotgun was sawn off. The shot would spread.

The huge fox was trying to chew into its victim's mouth. Steve had managed to bring up his arm to protect himself, and now it was crushed between him and the creature, the thing's long teeth piercing all the way through, jaws working, Steve's hand flapping uselessly...

Jack shook with terror, but it was a clearing sensation, well levelled, flushing his mind of confusion. Being eaten, he thought, the thing coming at me, eating me. Eating Dad. His fear was controlled. Maybe it was shock.

"He'll definitely die if you don't, Dad."

"Shoot the fucking thing!" Nathan shouted. He was hiding behind one of the big settees across the bar, only his head and two hands visible.

Lucy laughed. It was a grotesque sound amongst the chaos, so out of place below the growls and screams and crashes of things hitting the window. For a second they all looked at her—even the fox, Steve's arm a tangled mess in its mouth—and then Jack's dad fired.

As Steve's screams were silenced and the fox fell to its side, Lucy laughed again.

"Oh God . . ." Jack's father dropped the shotgun onto the bar and leaned forward, resting his forehead on the wood.

For a second or two there was total silence. The assault paused, the shouting and crying stopped, even Lucy was quiet. Then the fox growled at the silence and launched itself back at Steve's body.

If the shot had not killed him, what the fox did to his head did.

Jack tried not to see. "That thing killed him," Jack said, standing and putting his arm around his father's shoulders. His dad felt shrunken and weak. Jack hated that, he was there to help and protect him, not to fall apart and submit. Sometimes Jack felt much stronger—he knew more, there was that—but most of the time he was just a kid, and his dad was his guardian and shouldn't be weak..

He glanced across at the fox. It was shaking, ravaging poor Steve's body, a focal point for everyone else. For the first time Jack took stock of what was happening, calmly and dispassionately. He felt weird because he knew he should be crying, cowering . . . but for that instant he did not feel in danger. Removed, perhaps. Set aside. But not under threat.

It was as if he'd died ages ago and was watching this from above. Maybe the crow killed me straight away, he thought. Maybe the zombies did. Maybe I died that first night in my bedroom.

He looked around the bar lounge. Oscar was slumped across

a table, a pool of blood spreading around his face. Jack could not tell whether he was conscious or passed out, alive or dead. Lucy was behind the bar with him and his dad, opening another bottle and sending the lid tapping across the bar and onto the floor. Her eyes seemed to move independently of one another, as if catching up. Nathan was still down behind the settee across the other side, peeking above now and then to watch the fox. Jack tried to catch his eye but the boy was petrified, his stare looking so far into panic that there was no communicating with him, not from this distance. Next to him a man and a woman, a couple so they claimed, Elizabeth and Peter in their fifties. And by the window the woman whose name Jack had never known, still standing there even though the glass was now starred with impacts and the moth...or angel...hung directly outside, scraping at the glass with its sharp claws, scoring, fluttering back and allowing another shape to crash at it again.

Be in soon, Jack thought, and as well as that awful fear of the unknown, he felt an intense excitement as well. He looked back at the fox and what it was doing to Steve, and the feeling faded. The creature was shaking now, spasms vibrating through its body, claws scraping on the carpet, teeth snagging bones.

Another smash at the window. The woman screamed and Nathan shouted, and there was a clear, sharp sound of glass cracking. Jack's dad looked up, deliberately avoiding Steve and the huge dying fox. He held on tightly to Jack's hand, hurting him, but Jack didn't mind.

"Stand away from there," he shouted to the woman, but she seemed not to hear. The full moon was refracted a hundred times through the cracked glass, bathing her in its weak silvery glow.

"It's nearly dead, Dad," Jack said. He nudged his father and pointed at the fox. "Look, it's bleeding loads." The creature was slumped down over Steve, virtually obscuring his body with its own, and even though its jaws still worked they chewed only fresh air.

Changing of Faces

Jack's dad picked up the shotgun from the bartop, broke it, reloaded, clicked it together, braced its stock against his shoulder and fired in one continuous movement. No pause to breathe or look or think.

The shot hit the fox's flank and shoved it six inches across Steve's wet remains. It squealed, a sound that faded quickly into a cry and a sob. It sounded like a baby in distress. Then it was still, silent, dead.

And changing.

"They're coming in," the woman at the window said. A big, dark shape struck the window in front of her and kept coming.

"Dad, its fur's going, it's just ... going!" The fox seemed to be shrinking as its fur faded away into the carpet.

The shape at the window burst through the smashed glass, shards falling around it like rain.

The fox was on its side now, and Jack saw that it was not nearly as big as Steve. And it was getting smaller still, paws retracting, wounds in its side pursing and blowing bloody bubbles like the bright red lips of a kissing starlet.

The woman at the window didn't even scream. She stood and accepted her fate as the huge bat—larger than her with a wingspan of eight feet—pierced her chest and shoulders with its ebony claws and dragged her back to the smashed window. It had a necklace on, Jack saw. Pearls, probably fake, glinting in the artificial light like a string of boils.

The fox was not a fox anymore. Its wounds had shrunk, but they still looked vicious in the chest and stomach of the corpse it had become. Jack had seen a naked woman before—there was that time when he saw his sister and the village baker—but never like this. Never with teeth so long. Never so dead.

The woman at the window cried out at last, a scream that could have meant anything. Then the bat pulled her into the night and took flight. Before it left the range of the bar lighting the woman fell from its claws, her arms and legs waving, and something bigger swooped by and plucked her from the air.

"Bye," Lucy said, the first thing anyone had heard her say that night, and then she laughed again and took another drink.

"Nathan!" Jack's dad shouted. "Those doors! Shut them! That crow's still out there, and we saw a bee, and a weasel... Peter, Elizabeth, help him, shift some tables to block it off."

"Dad...?"

"Jack, pick up the rest of those cartridges and follow me." His dad climbed over the bar, knocking Lucy's bottle of brandy out of the way. She did not react.

"Peter, Elizabeth... please!" Nathan, terrified and dribbling snot, was already up and heaving at furniture. He'd kicked the double doors shut and was now throwing chairs and tables against them, trying not to get too close.

Peter and Elizabeth stood together and went to help.

Jack knew that they were all avoiding looking at the dead naked woman lying in Steve's remains. Because two minutes ago she hadn't been a woman. Two minutes ago she had been a fox.

A shadow flitted at the window and added its darkness to the gap.

"Dad!" Jack had a handful of shells but he dropped them. He'd never liked spiders. Living in the country he'd seen some big ones, and his parents used to keep one in their garden shed, catching flies and dropping them in its web. It had become something of a pet. They'd called it Fred. It had grown big, furry, fat on easy prey... and some nights Jack had thought he could hear the shed door opening, something crossing the gravelled path below his window. He'd only been seven then, of course. But still...

How can a woman be a fox?

The spider in the window was as big as the Labradors their neighbour Mr Jude had used to keep. Its body was fat and misshapen, bristling with crazily curled fur, the hair on its back ginger and... dreadlocks. Jack had seen them before, a boy in his school had them...

Dreadlocks.

Changing of Faces

If a woman can be a fox, can a man be a spider?

They couldn't let it in. It was crouched and ready to jump, Jack had never actually seen a spider jump, and if they let it in they'd never catch it. It would run around, dodge and duck, choosing its victim in its own good time.

He could throw a cartridge to his dad... but he might miss, and the sudden movement could startle the thing

(dreadlocks, it had dreadlocks!)

into motion.

"Dad!" he hissed, but his father did not turn. Instead, keeping his eye on the black spider in the dark window, he backed up until his heel nudged Steve's leg.

The spider sat there, like a black boil on the glass just waiting to burst.

Jack looked down and saw what his father was thinking. But he wondered sickly, shockingly, if his dad knew just how bad this was going to be.

Before Jack had a chance to whisper a warning his dad had squatted, dropped the sawn-off and reached around, feeling through the mess on the floor for Steve's shotgun. The spider leapt as he brought the gun around, firing both barrels. It came apart and was forced back against the shattered window. Bits slid slowly down the glass. Jack saw the dreadlocks drowning in the mess, like baby spiders themselves.

"Jack", his dad said softly, "best bring me those cartridges now." He dropped the gun and started wiping his hands on his shirt. He had bits of Steve on him, and Jack thought he'd faint or vomit or both. But he knelt down again and picked up the sawn-off, and by the time Jack reached him he'd broken the gun open and pulled out the spent cartridges.

"You alright, son?"

"Yes!" Jack's answer was loud and sharp, edged with panic. An hour ago we thought we were safe, he thought, looking at the dead woman, unable to avoid glancing between her legs where they were splayed across Steve's corpse. Her hair there was rusty auburn like a fox.

"Jackie?"

Jack looked up at his dad, into his eyes, and he saw the love there and the knowledge of shared experience, something strong and powerful and there forever. "You sure you're alright?"

"I don't know what's happening Dad," he said, glancing back down at the dead woman. "But... she was a fox. Now she's just dead. Like nothing ever happened to her."

His dad touched his face and gently turned his head so that they were staring into each others eyes once more. "I'm sure much more happened to her than we can ever know."

It may be that we know sooner than you think, he thought, but he had no idea where the words had come from. He certainly didn't want to speak them. His dad seemed quite calm at the moment, but Jack knew how suddenly that could change. He'd seen it, he'd known it forever, and in a very adult way he thought that he could handle all this with more composure than his father. Maybe it was something to do with being a kid.

Elizabeth, Peter and Nathan were still piling furniture against the double doors, and now that they were effectively barricaded in Nathan was becoming more daring. He scrambled on top of the tables and chairs and peered through the crack between the double doors.

"Lights are still on out there," he said. "No sign of the crow. Nothing moving."

"Don't get too near!" Jack said, his voice sounding even more frightened that he felt. He didn't know Nathan that well, didn't like what he did know, but he'd seen enough dead people. He didn't want to see any more. Seen far too much, he thought, Mum and Mandy, and too much more. At the same time he knew that he still had a way to go before he would have seen his own share of death.

Maybe even as far as his own.

Nathan turned around. The bravado and bluster were back. "Don't worry about me, squirt. I can take care of myself." He

Changing of Faces 103

put his face back to the crack in the doors and did a good impression of standing guard.

"There are big animals," Jack's dad said. "And... the fox changed back when I killed her."

"Changed back?" Peter said. Elizabeth was clasping his arm, her cardigan torn and tattered but still held together down the front by three mismatched buttons. Peter himself wore sports shoes, trousers and a shirt open at the neck. Jack was amazed he didn't wear a tie. If ever he should have chosen two people unlikely to survive all this, he would have closed his eyes and imagined Elizabeth and Peter. They reminded him of his grandparents, now long dead.

"Back to the woman it was."

Peter looked down at the dead woman. Elizabeth closed her eyes. Over behind the bar, just for a change, Lucy laughed. It ended with a cough, a cry and then she vomited, dropping a bottle and following it behind the bar.

"I'll go," Jack said, wondering just what he could do. "Dad..." He nodded to the smashed window and his father pointed the shotgun there, edging back slightly until he was leaning against a fixed table.

Jack reached the bar and leaned over, looking for Lucy.

"What happened to you a couple of weeks ago?" his father said behind him. "Did you see the living dead? I did. They chased me and my family from my home, they killed... my wife and daughter died because of them."

Lucy was lying there, liquid puke speckling her face. She stank of whiskey.

"What caused it?" Peter asked exasperated. They'd held this discussion a hundred times in the two weeks they'd been together on the beached ferry. None of them ever deviated from the stories they had, nor offered anything other than the tales they knew in their hearts to be true.

She was out cold. Her skirt had ridden up to show her knees, a loose ankle bracelet, the underside of her thighs. Jack felt a guilty thrill. He could have climbed over and tried to wake her, he supposed, but what would be the point? She'd be no use, probably couldn't even walk. And she might even be safe back there. Safe. Whatever that was.

"Oscar put it down to pollution of some kind. I heard something on the radio about some explosion overseas, but why should I believe that? Janine... she put it down to God and Satan fighting the final fight, Satan's soldiers fleeing to Earth. Why shouldn't I believe that?"

Jack slid back off the bar and went to stand next to his dad. He watched the hole in the window while the adults talked. So why wasn't anything attacking now? Because they're out there eating, Jack thought, but that just didn't sound right. Too many of them for a start. Too many to feast on only one woman.

"Claptrap, that's why," Peter said. Elizabeth closed her eyes as if in silent disagreement. "Religious claptrap. Mind control. Mind pollution. Maybe Oscar had a point there somehow."

Jack glanced over at Oscar and wondered if he was dead. It was a horrible thought. Oscar had walked him around the ferry on his first day here, shown him the cabins full of unpacked suitcases, the car decks where vehicles stood in disturbed ranks, having already made their final journey. He couldn't be dead.

Jack glanced down at the fox-woman and felt a sting in his chest, wanted to cry for her pain as well.

"Claptrap?" Jack's dad said. "What, like were-creatures attacking a beached car ferry for the living food inside?"

"What-creatures?" Peter was already scoffing, but Elizabeth had opened her eyes and Nathan slithered down from the pile of furniture to listen.

"Were. Like wolves."

"Oh for-" Peter began, but he never finished. Not that night at least. Because that was when the massed creatures chose to attack again.

The sudden noise was deafening, and it jarred them all from the brief respite they had been enjoying. Jack hid behind his dad and peered around his shoulder at the ragged gap where the window had been smashed. Just as he did so something big and black came in, clumsily folding its wings to squeeze through the gap, allowing Jack's dad a precious few seconds to make sure the first shot counted well.

It did. The creature's head flipped back, spraying blood at the ceiling, and it fell out from the window. Jack heard a splash from down below, and then more splashes as something fought over the body.

Nathan was at their side then with the other shotgun, breaking and reloading it, handing it to Jack's dad as something else rode in on the light spewing from the window. Robin Redbreast, Jack thought, and then its head took on a similar colour as a blast shattered its skull. It fell through the window, one long wing flipping at the glass-speckled carpet as something else tried to force in behind it. By then Nathan had reloaded the sawn-off, Jack's dad fired, handed the gun back... again, again... and within a few seconds the hole in the glass was filled with dead or dying things.

Things changing, shedding feathers, taking on flesh, blood thinning, flesh twisting and deforming, not in life but in transformation, other creatures trying to claw of push or bite their way through these dead things turning slowly from animal to human, whatever magic or taint was within them fleeing with their lives, perhaps chasing their souls into the beyond to harass and abuse them there as it had in this life. Because these bodies were tortured and twisted, Jack saw, not just by the recent gunshot wounds but by whatever strangeness had overtaken them. Bones were snapped, eyes popped from sockets, limbs distorted and skin stretched or rucked up.

They attacked that single breach in the window instead of forming more. They attacked for three more hours. By that time there were so many dead stuck in the window opening that the living things had to try to eat their way through... and perhaps they took their fill that way, because the assault eventually calmed down and the violence lessened.

Jack thought it was something else coming for them then,

something much larger and more powerful, glowing with its own strange hunger as it came in over the horizon and raced across the sea. But then he realised that he was seeing the sunrise, and the creatures had gone, and he was so, so tired.

He fell asleep in his father's comforting arms, dreaming fractured dreams of his dead mother.

※

Jack did not sleep for very long.

A bird was serenading the dawn. Jack jerked awake, his dream pursuing him. He looked around, certain he would see giant birds eating Peter's head, perhaps a seagull burying its red-tipped beak into Lucy's skull as her hangover kept her under...

There was a blackbird sitting on the floor next to Steve's body. For a few seconds, as dream and reality sparred in Jack's mind, his sight distorted and the bird was huge. Its yellow beak was blood-tinged, its feathers sparse, its skin shadowed with ambiguous tattoos. Then he heard someone groaning behind him as they too stirred, and the bird was its normal size.

He sat up slowly, trying not to frighten the bird away. It looked at him, down, up again. Something was clasped in its claws. The bird pecked at it. After each peck it looked up as if to check that Jack was still watching.

"Get out of it!" someone shouted. An empty shotgun cartridge spun across the room and bounced from the floor several feet from the bird, but it was enough to scare it out through the smashed window and into the red sky.

Red sky in the morning, sailor's warning, his mother used to say. It was one of her many saying which Jack had always loved, but never got around to asking his mum what it really meant. Maybe now it had more relevance than ever.

"It's been there for ten minutes," Peter said. Jack looked over and saw where he and Elizabeth were sitting at a table in the far corner of the bar. They were holding hands across the table. Elizabeth had been crying, and the tears still looked fresh.

Changing of Faces

"Didn't want to scare it away. It seemed normal. It was nice to see it."

"Well, it was eating." Jack stood and his dad got up from the chair, stretching his arms, twisting his back to try to get rid of the aches and pains that had set in there. Jack thought he looked old and worn and weary, but the last couple of weeks had hardened him up as well. He looked fit, like his friend Jamie's dad, who played rugby a lot and worked as a fireman. Used to, Jack silently corrected himself. Bet he's not that fit now.

"We should clean it up. Bury Steve." Peter was still looking at the mess on the floor.

"Not much left to bury," Nathan said.

"That's not the point." Elizabeth spoke up now, trying to squeeze her husband's hand to steer his attention back to her. "He needs some sort of a ... service."

"And Oscar?" Jack's dad said.

Jack gasped. No. He'd fallen asleep, his dad too, and as if that wasn't stupid enough when those things might still be out there, they'd done it while Oscar was badly wounded, unconscious, perhaps dying. The others ... the others had just left him where he was slumped, head resting on the table. Blood had dried in his hair. He did not appear to have moved since the beginning of the attack.

"No," Jack said, "he's not dead, he can't be!"

"It's alright son—"

"Dad, no, he can't be dead, we can't have let him die!"

"Oh Jesus Christ ... " Elizabeth muttered.

"Him? Lot of fucking good he's been over the last few weeks." Nathan's shouting made him seem even more like a kid to Jack. The swearing, too. A scared little kid trying to impress his friends.

"Elizabeth's right," Jack's dad said. "It's not fair leaving them there. Especially Steve, next to that."

Jack looked from Oscar—his head rested on the round table like a sleeping drunk—to Steve. He didn't want to, certainly didn't need to, but he looked. Steve was a mess on the floor, the blood darker now it had dried, his open wounds less fresh. The dead woman lying next to him—the fox woman—was peppered with shotgun wounds. He couldn't help but look at that place between her legs. It was supposed to be a secret place, Jack knew, and any other time his dad would have turned him away and covered his eyes. But this wasn't any other time, this was a weird time.

More shocked at the sight of her fanny than her seeping wounds... that's how weird this was!

"Cover her up, dad!" Jack said. "Please, cover her up."

"Oh Christ, Jackie." His dad sounded almost as if he'd forgotten that his young son was here, bearing witness to atrocity. He held Jack and shuffled him towards the bar. Lucy still lay behind it, smothered in her own puke and stinking and maybe even dead, but there was really nowhere else for them to go. One way lay the mess of Steve and the woman, and towards the back of the room, Oscar. The other way, towards the window...

More dead. Stuck in the jagged opening in the panoramic windows. Blood dried into dark sheens across the glass. Dead people whom none of them knew, dead people who had not been there before they were shot last night. Last night, before the lead poisoned them with death, they had been bats and rats and spiders.

"What about them?" Jack asked, but his dad did not reply and he supposed that was right. Steve and Oscar were people they had known, if only vaguely. They should deal with them first.

"So what?" Nathan piped up. "What the hell happened? Look at those, those things."

"They're people, Nathan," Peter said.

"Not last night they weren't."

"Were," Jack's dad said, pronouncing it weir.

"Well I'm not bloody touching them!" Nathan had not moved from his station at the double doors. He sat on one of the tables they'd pushed there, the smashed door at his back, the rest of the room all in his sight. He was trying to exude attitude, but to Jack he simply looked scared.

"What do we do?" Elizabeth asked. "They've gone for now, but maybe they'll be back. Maybe..."

"Don't even know what they were," Jack's dad said, "not really. I mean, they're dead people now. But they weren't people last night. Were they?"

"Not people, no," Peter agreed.

Jack remained next to his dad, close in so that they kept contact, and he sensed that his dad took as much comfort from this as he.

Things felt paused, like a breath held between screams. The bar was a chaos of blood and bodies, and even those people left alive were frightening in different ways. There was Nathan, the teenager acting up like an adult, his bluster and arrogance drawing his face into a mask of barely-withheld terror. He tried not to catch anyone's eye, but when he and Jack locked gazes Nathan's eyes went slightly wider, his face slackened, and Jack really thought that he was going to cry. He switched his attention to Peter and Elizabeth, the older couple trying to remain calm, sensible and normal throughout. They still sat either side of a round table, hands held across its surface. Jack noticed for the first time that Elizabeth was clutching something in her other hand, something she would not let go of—it was creased and crumpled—and it looked like a photograph. Someone who is dead, Jack thought. She's holding onto someone who is dead. But then, weren't they all.

Lucy, behind the bar, still covered in puke. She'd stirred a couple of times, muttered something unintelligible and drifted off back into her coma. Lucky, Jack thought, even though nobody seemed particularly bothered about her. Strange; they'd be concerned if she had been attacked. Maybe adult values still existed here, even now. He'd seen Mandy drunk a couple of times and it had scared him, but what had frightened him more had been the reaction of his parents—she'd been poorly, but they could only manage anger.

He had grown up since then.

"Lucy's ill," he said to his dad, moving behind the bar.

"She'll come around in her own time," his dad said.

Jack nodded and smiled, and wet a rag in the grubby water in the sink to wash the puke away from Lucy's mouth. The girl mumbled as he wiped at her, moving her head from side to side, frowning, tears squeezing from her eyes... and Jack wondered just what she was seeing in there. He probably did not want to know. He'd probably seen much the same.

"I think one of those is still alive," Peter said quietly.

Still alive. Oscar! Jack jumped up behind the bar, but his dad and the others were all looking in the wrong direction, away from Oscar and towards the breached glass wall.

"I'm sure I saw a movement there," Peter said. He stood from the table and let go of Elizabeth's hand. She gave it grudgingly. "Maybe it was a bird, or some carrion thing."

"Out of the way!" Nathan said. He slipped from the table by the double doors and advanced, picking up the dropped shotgun on the way.

"Wait!" Jack's dad said. "If one of them is still alive it'll be too hurt to harm us."

Jack was staring at the slew of dead people laying in an untidy mess beneath the window. One of them moved.

"Get back!" Nathan shouted, trying to barge past Jack's dad and bring the shotgun to bear. He looked like a clumsy kid playing at war, but fear gave his expression a mad glow.

In one movement, Jack's dad snatched the shotgun from his hands and clasped him around the neck.

"I'll have that," he said, tucking the gun under his left arm. His right hand squeezed until Nathan flinched. "Now calm down, boy. Take a look. If that poor sod is a threat to us now, then I'll kill him myself."

"It's... it's not a person!" Nathan squealed.

"Whatever is it," Peter said, "it might tell us what's going on."

Jack's dad nodded, let go of Nathan and advanced the final few steps to where the bodies began.

Some were still caught in the hole in the window. These were obviously dead, dreadful wounds on display from where their cousins had tried to eat a passage through them. Others had managed to get inside, only to fall victim to the shotgun. Jack didn't want to look too closely, but he was fascinated. What he was seeing, his reaction to it, the very fact that he was allowed to see, all meant that his dad's attitude toward him had changed quite drastically. The world had altered, slipped quickly into a very different state, and old values must have slipped with it.

His dad glanced back and Jack saw something in his eyes that he found curiously comforting: fear. Stay afraid, Dad, he thought. Stay afraid and you stay safe. Safe is what you make it. He smiled. His dad smiled back, then knelt beside the twitching body, resting the shotgun barrel under its chin before he spoke.

"I'll shoot you if you try anything stupid," he said. "Don't know if you can understand me, don't know what you are, don't care. Try anything and you lose your head. Got it?"

There was no sign that the wounded body had heard.

"You should get back from there," Nathan said. "Shoot the thing and get away. Don't know what it'll do. Maybe it's infected."

"Much as I hate to agree, I think maybe the lad has a point," Peter said.

Jack's dad suddenly leaned closer as the person raised a hand and clasped his knee. It was a man, Jack could see now. He was naked, he had black hair, fair skin and a hole in his stomach the size of a small cat. Dad did that, he thought, but he did not wish to dwell on it. The man raised his head slightly, Jack's dad lowered his, and a whisper added itself to the sounds of the sea outside.

He did not speak for long. His body gave a huge convulsion and Jack's dad stood quickly, backing away. The man screeched—it sounded like a crow being strangled—and thudded one bare foot on the floor. And then he was still. Blood bubbled in his stomach wound, black as ink.

Jack's father turned around and walked back to his son, looking down at his feet, frowning, shaking his head, keeping a firm hold on the shotgun. He held Jack's head and kissed his cheek.

"You okay, son?"

"Yes, Dad." Jack felt very brave. He was not okay at all.

"So what did he say?" Peter asked, looking from the corpse to Jack's dad, back again.

"Well, it's not easy. It's . . . difficult. To really believe."

Nobody spoke. Jack was thinking about the walking dead, and he guessed everyone else was as well.

"At least I think we'll be safe until tonight," his dad continued. "Even then they may not attack again, not for a while. It all depends."

"On what?" Peter asked.

"The moon."

❖

They decided not to stay in the bar; it was dirty and exposed and full of death. So they moved the furniture away from the double doors, opened them carefully—there were splashes of blood on the walls, floor and ceiling of the corridor beyond, but no dead things—and left. Jack and his Dad first, then Peter and Elizabeth, then Nathan helping Lucy hobble along, her head hanging, feet dragging.

"Where should we go?" Elizabeth asked. "Surely not back to the cabins we've been using. They've got balconies. Windows."

"The car hold," Peter said. "Get in there, shut all the doors—"

"And then?" Nathan said. "Sit and wait? For what? And for how long? We sit there, those things will get everywhere in the boat apart from there. And then it won't take long for them to find their way in to us."

"We go there, barricade ourselves in with plenty of food and water, wait for help." Peter's tone was hopeless, not hopeful, and nobody said anything in response.

Changing of Faces

"Somewhere with small windows, that's what we need." Jack's dad spoke quietly, as if talking to himself, and Jack realised with a jolt that he'd somehow become their leader. "So we can see out, but they can't get in. Not the big ones, anyway."

"We need to run." They all paused in the corridor, shocked at the fact that Lucy had spoken. She still hung from Nathan's shoulder, head down, hair matted with vomit. But Jack noticed that she seemed more there than before. Her shoulders were not so slumped, her legs were straighter. And although she was young and hungover and in a mess, her words held a peculiar weight. She sounded, Jack thought, as though she knew what she was talking about.

"Run where?" Jack's dad asked, but the girl seemed not to hear.

"Give them some sport," she said, still looking at her feet. "Run, let them come after us, sport, 'cos old foxy lady used to like sport. Sporting plays for at the town's eligible bachelors and married guys alike."

Foxy lady, she'd said. Jack thought of the woman splayed across the remains of Steve, the auburn hair between her legs.

"You're still drunk," Elizabeth said.

"Just a bit tipsy by now, old lady," Lucy said, and this time she did look up.

Jack gasped. She looked tired, ill and drawn, and yet she seemed totally in control. He realised straight away why this was: Lucy was smiling. She saw humour, found something to tickle her in all of this, and in a very basic way that made her their superior. She was surviving.

"You're mad," Elizabeth said, and Lucy did not argue or agree, and Jack thought no, that isn't it at all.

"We need to find somewhere safe," Jack's dad said. All but Lucy agreed. She simply looked at him, blinking.

"The crew's quarters," Peter said suddenly. "Low down to the beach on one side. The portholes are small. And if we pick the right rooms, we'll be close to the exit out onto a small foot ladder."

"Perfect," Lucy said, smiling. "For the next four weeks, at least. Then it'll make a very lovely dining room."

"Let's just get there and see," Jack's dad said. "Then we can get some food together, blankets, try out the radio... And Peter, if you'll help me, I'd like to sort out something decent for Steve and Oscar."

"And Janine," Nathan said.

"And Janine."

If there's anything left of her, Jack thought, but it was not something that should be said. He was young and sometimes so confused by adult-speak that he thought they used some weird code to communicate. But here, now, he could feel the tension as well as anyone. Instead of pulling the survivors together, last night's attack seemed to have driven them further apart. They'd barely had time to get to know each other over the past three weeks, but now Nathan was more aggressive than ever, Peter was confused, Elizabeth was superior and aloof, almost like the clichéd Rich Old Woman in the crappy disaster films Jack's mum loved... used to love...

Lucy, all but silent until just now, and now spouting weirdness and stuff that scared Jack more than it seemed to worry the adults because it was so knowing.

And then there was his dad. Unsure, guilt-stricken, depressed, and their leader by default. Oscar had been more controlled and accepting, Steve had been younger and fitter and willing to listen... but they were dead.

Jack's dad. The leader of the pack. Mum would have been amused and proud.

"What then, Dad?"

His father glanced down at Jack, smiling. "Then I think we should find time to properly discuss our options. But right now, I think we just need to batten down the hatches and take stock."

"Survival supersedes disbelief," Elizabeth said.

"I believe anything now," Lucy said. "I've seen it all." She looked at Jack and smiled. He didn't like that one little bit.

They found two cabins on the crew decks, one each side of an exit leading out onto a small balcony. The platform was only about eight feet above the beach, and the ladder had survived the ferry's grounding. Nathan shut the door after peering outside, twisting the two locks securely. It was a way out if they desperately needed it, but if there was something terrible to escape from in here, to flee outside would be...

"Hopeless," Lucy said. It was a word she had started using a lot. She seemed to like the reaction it provoked.

◈

He and his father were alone in their cabin. Jack was standing on a bench, staring through the round porthole across the beach at the dunes, tumbled fence and dilapidated beach huts that marked its inland extreme. His dad sat on the bed, head resting against the wall. His eyes were closed. Jack wanted to ask what he was thinking, but his dad had the expression of someone who didn't wish to be disturbed.

In a world of his own, Jack thought.

Since they'd arrived here they had seen hardly any wildlife. It was the commonly held belief amongst the small group of survivors that most of it was dead, just as most of the people seemed to be dead. Really dead now, finally dead, not that shambling, pathetic mockery of existence that had plagued the landscape for a few terrible days. As such it was always pleasing for Jack when he saw a bird or something else flit by. And now, looking across the beach, he watched happily as a pair of wrens darted in and out of the dune undergrowth. Whether they found any food in there he did not know. Insect corpses perhaps. Mummified worms. The small creatures had been affected as much as the large. The food chain he'd learned about in school was now a much altered affair. Still the birds fluttered in, disappeared for a few moments and came out again, alighting on a thick stem or one of the rotten fence posts, head flicking from left to right as they kept guard.

We're all God's survivors, Elizabeth had said a couple of weeks ago. He's preserved all he wants to preserve, and cast the rest into damnation. It had started Jack thinking of the Noah's Ark story, and the fact that they'd been living and surviving on a boat made it resonate all the more. God was something Jack had been taught to believe in and fear in school, but as he grew up and his mind became more his own, he'd started to ask questions. Firstly, the use of that word fear, and why someone who loved all His creations could cast the bulk of them into Hell simply for not believing. And this... if Elizabeth was right and they were all God's survivors, surely He would have chosen someone different from Nathan and Lucy to preserve?

And what god could have ever even allowed this?

Lucy knows something, Jack thought. That's why she got so drunk. She knows, and it's terrible.

Jack had always loved nature. It was not a conscious effort on his part, he had simply grown up in the country, with a fine respect for the world around him and an affection for the wilds. He was at home in the woods, running and playing and building dens, avoiding poison ivy, picking blackberries and staining his hands with their juice, taking them home for his mum to bake into a pie, watching the sun rise through the early morning mist and fall behind the hills at the rear of their house, spreading its red remnants through the woods as if spewing flame, trawling the pond for frog spawn and watching it every day until the tadpoles appeared, thousands of them...

His sister Mandy would join in for a time. But then she'd grown up and discovered boys.

Argued. Left.

For the thousandth time Jack told himself that it would do no good to think like this. But that never stopped him. He'd seen his sister dead and yet coming for him, and that was not something that he could ever forget.

Every time he closed his eyes...

"So they're werewolves?" Jack said

"Hmm?"

"Those things. The fox lady. The others."

His dad nodded, but kept his eyes shut. "Werewolves. Except . . . bats. And the weasel. And the fox."

"Everything," Jack said.

His dad looked at him, frowning.

"Everything. We saw all those things, and more. And did you hear the splashing in the sea? Everything was living dead a few weeks ago, Dad, and now everything's . . . changed."

"What about us?"

Jack shrugged, looked back out at the wrens. But they had gone. "Don't know. We didn't catch living dead, neither did Peter or Lucy or Oscar. Maybe we won't catch this either. Maybe we can't."

"Come here son," his dad said. Jack thought he had moisture in his eyes as he went to him, so he ducked into his embrace so that he didn't have to see the tears start to flow. His father smelled warm and musty and familiar, and underlying this were the scents of new clothes and fresh aftershave. The ferry had shops that they had all made good use of. Before arriving at the coast, even after everything that had happened, Jack would have never considered breaking and entering, taking some-thing without paying. But once here, realising how few survivors there were and trying to come to terms with the fact that there was no help—no officials, no army, no government drive to protect the survivors—they had all become comfortable with using what they could. Better than leaving it to fossilise when we're gone, Oscar had said. Jack had thought about that: people from other countries or continents, coming here in a couple of centuries when they judged it safe, finding the ferry with the smashed panoramic window, searching its corridors and the shops with clothing rotted stiff, and discovering a couple of rooms that may have been lived in for a while after the Apocalypse. No sign of the tenants, though. Nothing to show how long they had been here or what had driven them on.

"We won't be here forever, will we Dad?"

"I'm not sure we can stay here at all," Jack's dad said, but his voice did not invite further discussion. Jack could feel intimate tears falling on his head.

"Thanks for looking after me," he said. His dad did not respond, but the tears hitting Jack's skin felt different.

He thought back to the attack. The fear, the sheer terror at what was happening and what those things would do if and when they got in, smashed through the doors and windows from outside, looking for tender, fresh food. A shiver passed through him as he recalled the fox eating into Steve's exposed throat... and the woman it had become after being shot. The naked woman, the tawny hair between her legs, pathetic, dead.

Imagine being a bat, he thought. Or a sparrow hawk! Wonder what it's like to fly? Must be safe up there, safe as houses as Nan would have said, and safe is what you make it.

They had come along the beach.

Jack closed his eyes and someone spoke to him, but it was not his father. The words were blurred, the distance great. It was probably Mandy speaking from his memory, telling him how to confront his fears, confiding in him before she ran away. Or his mother perhaps, comforting him even though she would end up dead in a strange house, watching him, watching him leave her there to rot away.

But as Jack drifted off he realised who it really was he could hear.

Lucy.

❖

"Mad cow's gone," Nathan said as he burst in a few minutes later. "I just got back with Peter and went next door into their room, Elizabeth said the silly bitch vanished while she was having a wash."

"She can't have gone far," Jack said. He had heard her speak to him, but he did not add that. He hadn't heard her, as such.

Not with his ears. He was sure of that, as sure as he was of anything right now. "She's probably just wandering around the ferry. She'll come back soon."

Nathan shook his head. He looks dangerous, Jack thought. He's not much older than me, but he's terrified. And he looks dangerous.

"There's something about her," Nathan said. "Always has been. She freaks me out. I don't like her where we can't see her, that's all."

Jack's dad stood and stretched. "It's a free boat," he said. "Did you get much food?"

"Me and Peter hauled a few boxes down. Tinned stuff, loads of drink. Not alcoholic. I figure Miss Piss-Head will track that down for herself. And we found some bandages and plasters and stuff."

"Let's get in with Peter and Elizabeth," Jack's dad said. "We need to talk."

Peter was sitting on their bed while Elizabeth unpacked the boxes of food. She inspected every tin or bottle, as if ready to criticise if her husband had not brought the correct brand.

"Nathan says Lucy's gone," Jack's father said.

Elizabeth nodded. "She slipped out while I was in the bathroom. Glad to see the back of her, to be honest. Weird girl. Didn't say a word once we got in here, just sat there with her head down. There must be something about her, I suppose, to be a survivor. God knows best."

"She's a fucking freak if you ask me," Nathan said.

"Watch your language!" Jack's dad snapped. Jack covered his mouth with his hand and smiled. He'd seen people ripped apart by giant animals, exposed innards and blood spraying like tomato sauce across the tasteful tan carpet in the ferry's bar, and his dad was worried about him hearing the word fuck.

Nathan slunk out in a mood. "I'll try to find her," he said. "Don't want her wandering off and leaving a door open, or starting a fire, or anything."

Once he'd gone Jack's dad stood there awkwardly, watching

Elizabeth unpack and glancing at Peter on the bed. After a minute or two of stilted conversation he nudged Peter's foot with his own and inclined his head slightly at the door. Peter looked up, nodded and stood.

"One more box," he said. "Left it at the top of the stairs." Elizabeth said nothing, but continued examining the obviously inferior foodstuffs.

Jack's dad glanced down at Jack and frowned, trying to convey stay put. Jack smiled. His dad left.

Elizabeth carried on unpacking, ignoring him.

Lucy.

She was walking around the ferry somewhere, or hiding, or perhaps she had already left. Whatever, she had something to say to him, of that he was sure.

Jack sat back on the bed, tapping his head softly against the wall.

"So what's God got planned for me?" he asked.

"I beg your pardon?" Elizabeth looked at him as if he'd broken wind.

"If He saved us all, and we're like Noah and his animals on the boat, he must have a plan. Why me? Why me and my dad?" It had started as a throwaway remark, something to get some conversation going with this vaguely frightening, sour old woman. But now that he'd asked, Jack began to wonder. Why him? Why him and his dad? Who chose survivors in a case such as this?

Surely it was not all down to luck.

"It's not for us to know His work," Elizabeth said. Her eyes looked deep and full of tears. There could have been endless sorrow in there, had she the confidence to display it. She went back to stacking cans in the small wardrobe as if Jack had never even spoken.

Convenient, he thought as he slid off the bed. At the door he grabbed the jamb on either side and leaned out. He could hear his dad and Peter talking in subdued tones from one direction, hidden by a kink in the corridor where the stairwell rose and fell. His dad was doing most of the talking, although Jack could not make out the words. They were grim, he knew. They must be. Life or death words, used all the time now, words that should never have been spoken on a ferry designed for taking holidaymakers away, and certainly nothing his dad should have ever had cause to say. He sounded like a poet composing in a well; the words had a sad rhythm.

Jack looked the other way down the long corridor. All of its doors were shut. He guessed that Nathan had gone that way after Lucy.

And he heard her again, an unknown word whispering along the corridor and losing meaning with every door it passed, each empty room filled with memories of dead people draining its sense. Again, she sounded like Mandy. Mandy had been wise and good, and she'd been his best friend in a strange, antagonistic sort of way, they'd fought like cat and dog until the day she ran away from home, and they'd loved each other ever since.

Ever since.

Even when she was dead.

Jack glanced back at Elizabeth—she was still unpacking, tutting, stacking—and then started down the corridor. He went quickly, not quite running, not quite walking, glancing back, expecting his dad to call after him.

He didn't want to worry his father. But Lucy was lost somewhere. And Jack was sure that were he to find her, he would learn some things.

Some awful, irresistible truths.

❖

Lucy was on deck.

After the previous night Jack did not think it was a safe place to be. Yet as he stepped outside and felt the sun on his face and the soft sea breeze in his hair, he was unafraid. He was searching for Lucy, and he had yet to turn the wrong way. It was more like simply strolling to where he knew she would be. Perhaps she had told him where she was going, either in the way she'd looked at him or in what she'd said. Jack tried not to think about it too much. He found it disturbing.

So he walked along the ferry on an upper level on the seaward side, looking out to sea and wondering what was there beneath the waves. He paused halfway and leaned out over the railing, but there was a canopy overhang that prevented him from seeing the smashed bar window. There was nothing to hint at the previous night's events.

Lucy was at the stern where he knew she would be, leaning on the railing and looking down the beach at the breaking surf, as if gazing at a journey long past.

"Hello," Jack said.

"Hello squirt."

"I'm twelve years old."

"Yeah?" Lucy raised her eyebrows as if surprised. "Old enough to squirt then, squirt."

Jack looked away and felt his face flushing. He'd heard about that. He'd thought about it.

"I'm sorry," Lucy said. "Unfair of me. Hey, I'm seventeen. Pleased to meet you."

They shook hands. Strange, Jack thought, using ages as an introduction. Especially as he felt a lot older than twelve right now. Right now he felt like an adult, someone whose childhood was a blur in time. He could remember climbing trees and scrumping apples and playing knock-a-ginger in Tall Stennington, but that all seemed so far away, so brief, so innocent.

"You're freaking people out," Jack said.

"I'm freaking people out? As if they need something more to worry about after last night."

Jack shrugged and leaned on the railing next to Lucy. He was almost as tall as her, almost, and it made him feel her equal.

"You've got secrets," he said.

"Yes, but they're all dead."

"What?"

Lucy looked at him with that apologetic smile once again. She shook her head. Touched the back of his neck and squeezed, a sisterly contact rather than anything else.

"Have you ever thought of this as a clean slate?" she asked.

"What, everything that's happened? All the dead people?"

"Yeah."

Jack thought for a moment. "No. My sister's dead, and my Mum's dead. I can't start again."

"You're only twelve, yeah?"

"Yes."

"You're old for a twelve year old."

Jack smiled, hoping it aped her own knowing expression. "I've grown up quickly."

They were silent for a comfortable couple of minutes. He saw a single seagull in the distance, rooting in the sand for an elusive morsel, and he pointed it out to Lucy. She said nothing.

Jack wondered whether his dad had missed him yet. He felt guilty for running off like this, but he'd needed to find Lucy, ask her some things. He thought his dad would forgive him.

"Can you believe any of this?" Jack asked.

"Nope. Four weeks ago I was doing homework for my A-levels, choosing a dress for my sister's summer ball in college, worrying about whether that Parsons kid fancied me. Now..." She trailed off and looked down at the sand. Far below them, in the shadow of the ferry, seaweed had washed in and tangled itself around the propeller. The seaweed was dead.

"Do you believe in God?"

Lucy shrugged. "I believe in him as much as any of this. So yes, I know he's there."

Jack frowned. "What do you mean?"

"God's beyond belief. That's why believing in him is so... special." She smiled at Jack and ruffled his hair. Somehow it was not condescending. "Besides, I have proof. In this, not in God. Although maybe it's all one and the same."

"Huh?"

Lucy lifted the hem of her T-shirt to reveal her stomach. "I've always thought that people who demand proof of God's existence are blind to their own." She lifted higher until the underside of her bare breasts were revealed.

"Holy shit." Jack stepped back from her, his trainers squeaking on the shiny deck. "Holy shit, holy..."

The skin of Lucy's stomach had a fine brown sheen. She turned slightly and Jack saw colours there, like oil on the surface of a puddle. There was a patch directly beneath her left breast, about the size of his fist, which looked different from the rest of her, alien, as if he was seeing through her skin to another truth. He could not help moving closer. Reaching out, his hand seemingly a mile from his face, his fingertips brushed her there, and Lucy leaned forward to let him. He could see her nipple, pink and soft as a marshmallow, but not even that held his attention because he was touching her, touching, and her skin was hot and ridged with knotted skin, raised with points trying to break through.

When he looked up at her face her eyes were wide, pupils deep and black as the sea at night, her lips pressed together as she pushed forward at his hand. Jack had never had anything so sexual happen to him, but he was sure she'd only wanted him to feel, to see that she was different. Her keenness was for acceptance and a form of understanding, not for sex.

"You're..." he said, but he could not finish.

"What?" she asked. She lifted her T-shirt slightly higher until her whole left breast was revealed. Jack looked, amazed, but his eyes were still drawn down to the spread of weird skin just below. "Different?"

"You're one of them," he said. He stepped back and nudged against the railing. The beach was a three second fall behind him. The sand looked soft from up here, but he knew just how solid it would be should he fall.

Lucy frowned, dropped her T-shirt and turned away. "I'm sorry," she said. "I didn't think it would scare you. I thought you might understand. I thought you could."

"What do you mean? I don't know what to think. Why didn't you... why did you stay you last night?"

Lucy turned back to him and she was crying. Jack wanted to hold her, but it all felt so awkward. She'd just shown him her tit. She didn't feel like a sister anymore.

"I'm not sure," she said. "I don't know. Maybe because I'm fighting it. I don't know anything, Jack, that's why I don't say much. Everything's so frightening." Her tears were flowing now, her voice low and soft so that it did not break when she spoke. Still Jack could not hold her. That skin, that roughness... like spines below the surface. Or the roots of feathers.

"How long...?"

She shrugged. "Just the last couple of days. Jack, I can believe it. I can. See, my mum wasn't living dead. My dad was. Yes, he was." She looked past him over his shoulder, whole stories, whole unspoken terrors in her gaze. Jack felt frozen to the spot by her silent recollections. He thought about telling her to name what scared her, but that was a secret thing that Mandy had shared, precious to him. And Lucy was not his sister.

"Same with me," he said instead. "Except it was my mum who... well, it was the other way around."

"So maybe you're like me!" She seemed suddenly animated, different again from the old Lucy they had known up until now. "Did you feel anything last night? When they were after us, trying to get in? Any... drawing? Temptation? An affinity?"

"A what?"

"A closeness. Did you feel close to those things? Did you pity them?"

"No," Jack said, but there was a sick taste of untruths in his mouth, even though he could not actually place them. "I don't think so. But I heard someone talking to me, last night and today. Whispering, like they were in the next room, but I couldn't understand the words. I think it was you."

Lucy shook her head. "That's not me." But she avoided Jack's eyes now, and he wondered just how deep the lie went.

"Jack!" His father appeared from the other side of the boat. "Jack, where the fuck have you been?"

"Dad?" Jack's voice was quiet with fear, guilt, and a terrible shame at the tears he had brought to his father's eyes.

Lucy slipped away and ran along the deck, but Jack's dad did not seem to notice. He only had eyes for his son.

"Don't you ever, ever disappear like that again. You got that? You got that?" He was shouting, kneeling, and then crying as he took his son in his arms, pulled him tight. "After everything, Jack, just don't do that to me. Promise? Promise me, you'll never just go like that again?"

"Dad, I'm sorry, I promise."

His father held him at arm's length and looked him over, as if checking him for wounds. "Jack," he whispered, "you're all I've got left."

They hugged again. Jack began to cry. It was guilt and shame, but also an unwanted understanding that the same went both ways.

They were all that was left of a family.

❖

Jack, his father and Nathan shared one room, while Lucy slept with Elizabeth and Peter. Nathan had to crash on a pile of blankets on the floor but for once he did not bitch and moan. They were exhausted from transporting supplies to the rooms, but Jack wondered whether they had the same trouble sleeping as him. He lay in bed with his eyes wide open that night, staring at the ceiling, glancing out the window at the smudge where the moon hid behind clouds, wondering if it was still full, waiting for the sounds from outside, the slap of wings at the air, the splash of unbelievable fish, the scrape of claws on the hull, the clomp of webbed and taloned feet along corridors as things crawled around the ferry searching for them.

And he waited for the screams from next door.

Nothing happened. His mind was silent—no uninvited

whisperer now—and the only noise from outside was the soporific shush of the sea against the beached hull.

His father snored gently beside him. Maybe Peter was snoring too, next door. That afternoon the two men had buried Steve and Oscar. Janine had vanished; all that remained was bloody smears along the corridor walls. They had talked little about it upon their return.

They had also cleared the attackers' corpses. Disposed of them, his dad said. Jack guessed it was out through the smashed window and into the sea.

So he lay there in the dark, aware that Nathan was awake too but not wanting to talk. He should have told someone about Lucy—his dad, at least—but he was afraid of what they'd do. Nathan seemed not to like her anyway, and he would need no excuse to turn that dislike into some unpleasant actions. There was no law any more. No one to make sure things were right.

Jack wondered whether anyone else he knew had survived the past few weeks. He had uncles and aunties and cousins in Devon, more in the North of England, and his mother's mother lived in North Wales. But if his mother had succumbed, perhaps that meant that the rest of her bloodline was susceptible too.

What did that mean for Jack?

He hadn't noticed any changes. After his conversation with Lucy he'd gone to the bathroom and scanned his body, looking everywhere, trying to see any discolouration of the skin that might indicate something going on beneath. A change. He felt different, in ways that were too deep and unexpected to discern fully, but he put that down to everything he'd gone through, the grief he felt and the tears he cried every night for his mum and sister. A part of him had died with them.

He prayed it would not rise again.

But his skin was clear, and any aches and pains could be attributed to the day's labour and the chaos of the previous night.

He listened; heard nothing.

Perhaps the were-creatures learned. After that first attack, maybe they'd regrouped and planned a more covert assault for tonight, although they had seemed so vicious, so animal that Jack doubted that. No, maybe the planning and scheming would come when they were human again, for a time. Perhaps now.

Safe is what you make it, Jack thought. Even for them. But he could not remember where he had heard that first.

Whatever town they had come from—a safe seaside town with a pier and tea shops and amusement arcades—they would be back there now, licking wounds. A tattooed raven-man, tending the shotgun blast in his thigh. A blonde moth-woman, stitching a slash to her side put there by broken glass.

Lucy had that roughness on her stomach, like the skin of a plucked chicken, part of her and yet as separate as can be.

Jack's dad had become their leader. He cried, he had lost his wife and his daughter, and they looked up to him to lead and protect and make decisions, however grudgingly Nathan did so, however much Peter and Elizabeth believed themselves too fine to be involved. Jack was stupidly proud. Lucy had blemishes. She whispered. His dad was crying, shaking him, telling him to never, ever run off like that again, and as he did so feathers sprouted from his temples, his neck, his eyes, and his voice changed from a human cry to avian.

Dreaming and nightmaring, sweating and twisting next to his father in bed, Jack found a troubled sleep.

◈

In the morning when the tide went out there were footprints in the sand. They were human, some wearing shoes, some not. No one on the ferry claimed them, they'd all stayed in their rooms that night, sleeping and dreaming bad dreams. But as they stood on the foredeck of the beached vessel, Jack glanced across at Lucy and saw a faint smile half-hidden by her long hair.

As ever, she knew more than the rest of them.

"Ten of them, it looks like. Maybe a few more," Jack's dad said. "Weird that they walked so close to the sea. Would have been easier going up by the dunes."

"Maybe they thought their prints would be washed away by morning," said Peter.

"Maybe they wanted to leave them for us to see," Nathan said. "Dry sand wouldn't hold prints."

"Who are they?" Elizabeth pressed herself into Peter's embrace.

The footprints separated a hundred feet from the ferry and spread out, fanning around the bow. There were definite prints in the opposite direction too, so at least they had gone away again. One set had kicked through a slew of dead seaweed, and it clung to the trail like the fragments of a shadow.

"It's them," Lucy said. "They won't give in." And for some reason, she had the final word.

❖

Later that day, after Jack had wandered the boat looking for Lucy but not found her, they had the old discussion again.

Nathan was all for leaving. Peter and Elizabeth wanted to stay; Jack thought it was because they just weren't used to walking long distances. And Jack's dad could argue both ways. There were merits in staying, he said, because the boat was relatively safe—although the attack had gone a long way to disabuse them of notion—and if help ever came if would surely home in on the ferry. But they could go as well, walk along the coast to see if there were any more survivors, larger communities or even official help.

"What's official?" Nathan said. "The government who are to blame for all this in the first place?"

"You're blaming politicians for a plague of walking dead zombies and werewolves," Jack's dad asked.

Nathan nodded, not reading the sarcasm.

"I heard it was something a long way away," Elizabeth said. "Wasn't it honey? Something on the radio?"

Peter merely shrugged. "Panic gives everyone a theory."

"Safe is what you make it," Jack said. He thought of remaining barricaded in instead of traipsing across open countryside. And then he thought of escaping before the next full moon. Either way, everyone ignored him.

He left them talking and went to the stern. His dad had made him promise that he'd stay on the boat, and he had. But he also knew that if he saw Lucy in the sand dunes he'd go to her, talk to her, ask her what she knew. That silence, that quiet smile, hid far more than she had let on. And Jack was hearing the whispers again, a voice that sounded like Lucy calling him, speaking to him in a tongue he could not quiet understand. He had to ask her about that. Because although she had said it was not her, Jack was sure.

There was something else. She'd shown him her chest, stood there in daylight and lifted her T-shirt for him to view her tinted skin, and her nipple had stood out pink and soft. He wanted to see that again.

Standing at the railing, looking along the beach away from where the were-creatures had come from, Jack wondered if safety lay that way. The safety he envisaged as a twelve year old was a big city filled with army and medical personnel, quarantine sections, antidotes to the strange illnesses afflicting the population ... ideas straight out of Hollywood. But he had grown up a lot, quickly, and he knew that even if there was help, it would be something less organised, more chaotic. A town of survivors perhaps, struggling to defend themselves, welcoming more survivors simply because they were added manpower to increase their defences.

He turned the other way, looked past the ship and around the wide curve of the beach. There was a little seaside town along there peopled with were-creature. Right now, though, they were people, probably hurt, definitely suffering. Normal people, like him or Lucy.

And people could be talked to

Jack wandered the decks, thinking just how this could happen and what it would achieve, and when he finally found Lucy he was no longer searching for her.

"Hey squirt," she said.

Jack stopped and looked around. He couldn't see her anywhere. She'd spoken for sure, it wasn't just in his head. She said that voice wasn't hers anyway, although he didn't really believe it.

"Where are you?"

"Over here." Jack caught movement from the corner of his eye, and Lucy sat up in one of the lifeboats. She smiled that knowing, confident smile, beckoned him over. He remembered how her nipple had looked so soft in the sun, softer still contrasted against the spread of rough skin below it. Jack walked to the lifeboat, climbed the arm holding it in place and dropped in next to Lucy.

"What are you doing in here?"

"Hiding."

"Why?"

"I'm different and no one likes me. You've seen this." She touched her chest and stomach.

"That's not true." As he spoke Jack realised that it was true. Even his father seemed dismissive of her. It was almost as if they knew she was different, one of them, the were-things. If she was.

"I'm going back," Lucy said. "I'm leaving in a minute, I'm going to where they are. They'll be able to talk to me now, for a while at least. And maybe I'll find out what I'm becoming."

"Has it spread?" Jack asked. Lucy lifted her T-shirt and showed him her stomach. Normal skin. No sign of anything strange, no blemishes at all.

"Moon's waning," she said. "I'm going back to normal, if you can believe that. But what else is there?"

I'm going back, she'd said. Back to the village... back to normal. And then he was back with Mandy in their cottage as she confided in him, told him she was running away from home, and maybe if he'd told his parents instead of keeping his promise of silence they would have prevented her from fleeing, held the family together. Who knew how that may have changed things?

But Lucy was not his sister.

"Why were you—?"

"I wanted to see you first."

A thrill shimmered through Jack. Lucy was smiling again, hair dropped over her face, eyes deep and dark and promising. There was something sexy about it, alluring, like those naked womens' faces in the magazines Tommy Bullock had brought to school. That 'fuck me' look, Tommy had said.

Lucy shuffled forward on her rump until her face was inches away from Jack's. He hadn't cleaned his teeth that morning, so he held his breath. What if she wants to kiss me?

"Lots of things are changing, squirt," she said. "I'm changing. I can feel it inside, even though I'm back to normal out here." She tapped her chest. "And it doesn't... well, it feels good. Not bad, not monstrous. Good."

"So why did you wait to see me?"

"You can sense it, feel it. And you hear it. I just wanted to say, when the time comes don't be afraid to make your own choice. Safe is what you make it, after all."

Did I hear it from her? Jack thought. *Or did she say that because she's heard me saying it?*

"Did you come from where they are?" Jack asked. "You did, didn't you. You knew that woman who was a fox, you said something about her while she was dying on the floor."

Lucy's smiled dropped and she suddenly seemed very old, very adult. She looked away from Jack, kneeling so that she could see from the lifeboat and out to sea.

"Mrs Jackson," she said. "She owned a trashy tourist shop down by the pier. Sold seals made of shells, polished stones from the beach, old wine bottles coated in shells and turned into a lamp, all that sort of shit. I stole a fiver from her when I was thirteen. Just strolled in, reached over the counter and plucked it from the till. She shouted while I was running out, but she never followed me, never called the police. Maybe she would have if I'd done it again." Lucy smiled.

"When did you run away?"

"She liked her men, did Mrs Jackson," Lucy continued, appearing to not hear what Jack had said. "Never tourists, though. Always guys from the town. She was a real heartbreaker, my mum said."

"She was a fox," Jack said.

"Yeah." Lucy frowned. "Strange. I don't think there's rhyme or reason. I've never even touched a bird."

They chatted some more, swapping weird, unbelievable stories about the last few weeks. Each successive expression of disbelief from Lucy made Jack believe her more; and really, he suspected that she was even more clued up than she seemed. She'd lost her family. Her mother was still alive, somewhere, so she said. But to Jack, she was someone so alone.

Lucy gave him a kiss before she left. She must have intended it as sisterly, but afterwards Jack sat back breathless and shocked. He'd never felt anything like that before. He could smell her, a sweet staleness that hinted at many hidden things. And below that, faint and distant, the wild scent of the air.

Jack knelt and looked out to sea as Lucy clambered back onto deck. He felt as if something important was being left unsaid, like a film finishing without the final reel. But Lucy did not even look back.

She's going to the town, he thought, where all the were-creatures are. He wondered where she really belonged—where any of them belonged. And the more he wondered the more confused he became, until it seemed that it just didn't matter. People into animals, animals into people. Either way it was something extraordinary.

He imagined Lucy gliding above the clouds, a wondrous bird, hair wafting by her shoulders, wings spread wide. He felt himself growing hard down there and tried to divert his thoughts.

What would he become, were he to change?

Jack jumped from the lifeboat and went to find his father. Just as he passed inside he heard a voice again; or rather a gaggle of voices, like a roomful of people talking at the same time. They were all telling him something slightly different, but it built into a cacophony he could read, messages relayed through feeling rather than hearing. He felt the tug that Lucy had mentioned, the drawing and temptation, and the more he thought of her the more it manifested in his mind. The voices grew fainter, yet more insistent.

She would be off the boat by now, heading for the dunes.

Jack leaned against the wall and closed his eyes, and eventually the voices all merged into one: Lucy. She repeated her words from earlier, but Jack was sure that they were spoken afresh. *When the time comes don't be afraid to make your own choice. Safe is what you make it, after all.*

Maybe Jack could talk to them, touch them, make things safe. For him, for his father and everyone else. Lucy came from there, she knew those people...

And after all, his mother had always told him that communication was more powerful than violence.

He left the ferry to follow Lucy away.

❖

Even then, he wasn't sure what he would do. When he arrived at the town they would see that he was different. The big question was, would they care? Would they, in the time that they were human, look upon him the same way as when they were changed?

As meat.

He thought not. Lucy was different but good, he was convinced of that deep down. She was strange, secretive and seductive, and she annoyed the hell out of the others, but she was good. Somebody bad could not have made him feel like he did now, even though he could not quite explain it. There was an attraction, a sexual urge that his young body and mind were trying to come to terms with, but also a deeper feeling, an understanding.

She's not my sister, Jack thought. But he wondered just how well he'd really known Mandy. Perhaps living in the same house, sharing the same parents had discouraged any desires to really understand each other.

He ran from the beached ferry straight into the dunes, moving quickly and enjoying the exertion, the breeze in his hair and the sense of doing something for himself. He'd had to grow up a lot over the past few weeks, although sometimes it felt as if the change was only skin-deep, forced through necessity, incomplete. But now Jack felt the thrill of making his own choice, taking his own lead. His neck prickled at the thought of people watching from the ferry. His ears burned in readiness for the call to return. But none came.

His father was back there, unprepared for the worry and terror he would feel when he found out Jack was missing. That almost halted Jack in his tracks. The guilt was a rich, heavy thing, compressing his chest and burning his throat and eyes. His dad had suffered enough, he deserved no more, and here was Jack leaving him again...

But it could turn out for the best in the long-run. Jack had some ideas that he could help. And as he ran through the dunes, up and down, the sand slowing his progress, he happily used this to excuse what he was really doing.

He was listening to that mysterious voice in his head, trying to track it down.

Jack headed inland, hoping that there would be a coastal road leading to the town—he and his father had walked onto the beach from the opposite direction, and this was all new ground. He had no idea how near the town was. It could be one mile away, or ten, but that did not concern him. Jack would get there.

The dunes sprouted dead rushes like hair on giant boils. Here and there a blade of green peered through a curtain of brown, valiant life fighting off widespread death. These occasional green grasses were like the wrens he'd seen, or indeed the people on the boat: survivors. There was no telling whether they would continue to survive—that had been a topic of conversation on the ferry ever since their arrival—but this had seemed to be a concern for other people. Those in charge, Oscar had kept saying. Those in charge. It was only a phrase, but it had not taken long for Jack to come to think of it as being essential to Oscar's mental equilibrium, just as God was to Elizabeth's.

Those in charge.

Jack thought that those in charge were gone. Maybe the town he was heading for, the strange people he was going to see... maybe they were now in charge.

He ran, not tiring, exhilarated by the sense of freedom. With each step the tension left his body and guilt fell away. He wanted to keep the guilt, he felt bad as it lessened, but the sheer joy of being alive brought a grin to Jack's face. He would have shouted, were he not still within earshot of the ferry.

He had not left the boat since they had arrived. Three weeks ago, tired, terrified, drained, the ferry had seemed like a haven for his father and him. There had been a doctor there then—he'd left soon after, said he had to go back to his home and bury his family now that the living-dead blight seemed to have ended—and he had given both his father and Jack something to help them sleep. It had been a deep, dark sleep for Jack, filled with dreams where he knew too much for a twelve year old boy, went places he had never been, talked with people he had never known. When he eventually surfaced it felt as if he'd been asleep for days, although it had been only twelve hours. Refreshed, yes, but perturbed as well. Even the ambiguous landscapes of sleep had been changed by whatever had happened to the world.

The survivors on the ferry had quickly settled into a strange day-to-day existence, never really planning ahead, too afraid to do anything other than find food, comfort each other, share stories and wait for help. A small group had left at the end of the first week, tired of waiting for help to come to them. They had not returned. The others... for them, hope soon became a constant, the god they lived their days for. And in a way their existence had become timeless. Jack wondered if they'd still be there in a year, still hoping, still doing nothing but waiting.

Over the last dune, in a roadside ditch, he found some bodies. He slid to a halt on the dune's slope, sending small waves of sand out toward the huddled corpses. His cry scared nothing into the air. The landscape was motionless. It was only as he stopped running, held his breath and sat back that he recognised this total silence, a stillness to things that had not been apparent when his footfalls thudded into the sand, the breeze rushing past his ears filled his head with movement and life. Now it was blood hissing in his ears as his heart stuttered in shock. The landscape seemed to draw in, compact down to him, the bodies and the spread of sand between them. He gasped, instantly fearful that the sound would wake them up.

They'd been there for a long time. Jack had seen plenty of recently-dead, weeks ago when he and his family were fleeing across the countryside, and two nights before, Oscar and Steve and Janine, the blood and the smell of recent wounds. But these bodies were different, less recognisably human. There was a car on the road, Jack registered that at last, with its doors open and its insides as torn and ruptured as those of its apparent owners'. It was bright yellow. Never lose that in a car park, his mum would have said.

There were four bodies, parents and two kids. Jack was too far away to be able to see any detail, but they were piled in the ditch together, their skin a uniform colour of wet ash, and here and there he could make out the white glint of bone.

He crawled slowly sideways like a crab, edging from the ugly scene but not turning his face away. It was horrible but fascinating, and for some reason Jack knew that he had to keep his eyes on the corpses until they were out of sight. A childlike disgust, perhaps. Or maybe he'd seen too many dead people walking to turn away right now.

It took a couple of minutes' crawling until he could stand and step onto the road out of sight of the bodies. Something called out, startling Jack. He looked up and shielded his eyes from the sun. Circling high on invisible thermals, a raptor stared back down.

Jack ran along the road. It was a single lane, the tarmac old and crumbling away at the edges where no proper kerbs had been set. As he headed slightly away from the dunes, hedges sprang up on either side. They were strange conglomerations of living and dead plants, and he was comforted to see that the greenery here seemed to have the upper hand. Death faded, life grew, and it would not long before the hedges were back to their former glory. That at least gave comfort.

He wondered where Lucy was and whether she had come this way. If she had then she was running too, otherwise he would have caught up to her by now. She was out here somewhere, another splash of life in a landscape so denuded, and he thought again of the knots of skin across her chest, the soft pink nipple she must have know she was showing him. He ran faster.

His trainers slapped on the road surface. The road twisted ahead of him, disappearing around a bend and leading to who-knew-where? He was free of the ferry, and the danger that must be out here added a frisson of fear, something that he should not enjoy but did. He was running, not walking into whatever lay ahead. He felt in control.

His father fading into the background with every step he took, Jack raced toward yet another changing point in his life.

❖

Just past midday he crested a rise and saw the town spread across the hillside before him, halted by the sea in the distance.

Jack stopped to catch his breath. He'd been trotting, walking, sprinting, walking again, looking around all the time but always keen to reach his objective. And now, here it was. A seaside town, a place he'd never been but one which he recognised from a dozen family trips over the years: the long straight road along the front; the golden gleam of the sandy beach; slated roofs speckled with seagull crap; houses laid out in regular rows or curves. Further in there would be streets and streets of bed and breakfast accommodation, self catering flats, hotels and, eventually, beach huts, paint peeling and windows smashed by the local youths.

Lucy must be there already.

A sudden sense of import hit Jack, the realisation that whatever choice he made now could cloud his future forever. If he turned and went back along the coast to the ferry, back to his father who was probably already beside himself with worry, then he would be acting safe, chasing a feigned security. But if he ventured down into the town, safe may be whatever he made it. He could be welcomed down there. He could be killed.

Maybe, just maybe, he'd find the place deserted.

Were-creatures, he thought, not vampires, they won't all be asleep in their basements, they'll be... But he did not know what the inhabitants of the town would be doing. What does a werebat do when there's no full moon? Normal things? Eat and worry and go to the toilet and drink and throw stones into the sea, seeing how many times he or she can skim? Does it worry about where its next meal will be found, come next full moon?

Does it even know?

Jack moved off the road and sat in a field overlooking the town, staying in the shadow of the hedge. Now that he'd stopped running he realised that he could hear the sea again, whispering onto the beach and breaking against the struts of the small pier jutting out from the sands. There were seagulls drifting above the town, but only a couple. Normally there would be hundreds, Jack guessed, screaming and dipping and diving and fighting over discarded fast-food or broken crabs from the rock pools at the ends of the beach. Now, the two birds were silent, and they kept a distance between them. Perhaps even they could not trust any more.

Jack's father would never trust him again. That was the truth. Even if he went back now and apologised, said he was trying to make things safe, trying to talk to these people...

And that thought brought the present, the here and now smashing back. What was he to do? What could he do?

He looked carefully down into the town. There were no signs of movement other than the lonely seagulls, some washing fluttering in the breeze, litter rolling along the long front. He was amazed at how much of this he could actually hear; the sheets snapped at the air, discarded chip wrappers scratched at the concrete. With loud noises no longer present—there were no vehicles moving anywhere, and the raucous shouts of holidaymakers were a thing of the old world—the smaller sounds found their voice.

Footsteps, somewhere. Jack could not see where.

A window opening and closing.

A door slamming shut.

He saw no movement but the people were there, and he had come this far to talk to them.

Slowly, feeling terribly exposed, realising also that he could be doing a very stupid thing, Jack stood and walked down the hill towards the outskirts of the town.

There was a footpath worn into the hillside. It ran adjacent to the road for a while, then veered off and took him down beside the first few houses on the town's outskirts. These were big bungalows, well maintained and with a pleasant lived-in look that several weeks of Armageddon had yet to erode away. The path turned into a pocked tarmac road and Jack passed the houses, glancing left and right, constantly expecting to find someone watching him from a garden or behind a net curtain. A seagull called out, and when he looked up there was only one left in the sky.

The whole landscape was manmade—houses, fences, roads, garages, sheds, pavements, telegraph poles, even the gardens were designed, shaped and planted, not left as nature intended. The silence was strange here, it did not belong to a place so regimented, and Jack thought that chaos could ensue at any minute. The potential for it was thick in the air. The attack on the ferry was fresh in his mind, and he suddenly realised that he had no idea at all whether these people, these were-creatures, would be changed back to normal. There was no way he could know, no rules to state what should be happening. He was trusting Lucy, he supposed.... But no, not even her. He was trusting books, films and the media, everything he'd ever seen and read about werewolves and how they only appear at full moon.

How, really, could he possibly know the truth?

The air was heavy around him, a breath held before a scream in his ear.

Every door was about to open, each corner about to reveal a man, a woman, a monster.

A tree swayed slightly in the breeze and rubbed its branches and twigs together. He looked up and some of the bark appeared fleshy, pale pink and sprouted with fistfuls of twigs. Were-tree, Jack thought, and why not? Bats and fox and weasel... why not tree?

He stared at the trunk but could not make out a face.

The road stopped at a junction and Jack turned left, heading down a slope and into the town. Still there were no people, no signs of movement, although he had the unsettling impression that there was movement everywhere but where he could see. He wished Lucy had waited for him. She'd known that he was going to follow her, after all. She must have. Perhaps she'd led him on for some unknown reason...

"Wait!" a voice said.

Jack spun around. An old woman had emerged from one of the terraced houses lining the new street. She looked around fearfully, her eyes never actually alighting on him. "Wait!" she said again, still not catching his eye.

"I've come to speak—" Jack began, but she was not listening.

"Not safe here!" she said. "There were things in the street. Things. Running and crawling and flying. Tried to get at me, but they know an old fighter when they see one, they know."

"Where are they now?" Jack asked. He actually backed a couple of steps away from the old woman, moving blindly, subconsciously preferring an unknown danger behind him to this sudden stranger. He did not think about that at the time—the fact that she'd really scared him—but later he would. Later, he would wish that he'd thought long and hard about what happened next.

It might well have saved him.

"Don't know," the old woman said. She had hair so white it was almost blue, like glacier ice. Her eyes were as cold. "That's what makes it worse." Still she looked around, eyes darting here and there as if chasing a burned-out shadow.

"Well, I came here to talk..." Jack began. And then he wondered just who or what this woman was. Human, yes, afraid, yes... but had she been human two nights before?

"They'll eat you if they catch you!" she said. The fear seemed genuine. "Inside. We can talk in here. Come on! I'm not waiting out here forever. Make your mind up, in or out, come on, come on!"

"Okay!" Jack said. The front of her house was as loud as her voice had become, a collage of colours and textures designed specifically to attract attention: rounded red door jamb; bright green window frames; painted shells pressed into yellow render like hundreds and thousands. It looked like an explosion in a sweet shop. Strange that she was trying to hide in there.

She stepped aside to let him in. She had an old-woman smell about her stale yet sweet, something he remembered from his grandmother and when she touched his back to guide him in her nails scratched through his tee-shirt. She had an old woman's hands, not claws but clawed. Her nails were long. Not too long, but long enough to notice.

She shut the door, threw the bolt, leaned back, closed her eyes and sighed. The relief seemed great, far too rich for the

Changing of Faces

short time she had been out in the street. Jack had the unpleasant idea that she had been trying to get someone like him in here for ages... and now she had. Company, he thought, maybe she's been alone here, surviving, for weeks. He smiled at her when she opened her eyes and she smiled back.

"Good lad," she said. "Good lad. What's your name?"

"Jack Haines."

"Jack. You be calm now, Jack, and Eve will look after you."

And she did. Jack had not realised how hungry he was until Eve sat him down in her dining room and went about preparing some food. The kitchen opened onto the room and he watched her cooking, bustling, chopping and cutting, mixing and frying. The smells were so succulent and mouth-watering that he felt faint. On the ferry they'd been eating prepared foods from the kitchen store, tinned beans and sausages and vegetables heated over carefully-shielded fires in one of the cabins. They were hardly feasts. Here, now, Jack was sent back in time—mere weeks, but it felt like lifetimes—to when his mother had used to cook them a huge meal on a Sunday, and not always a roast. Mexican, Italian, Chinese, the table would groan beneath the results of his mother's labours in the kitchen, and his dad always rounded the meal off with one of his own specially prepared sweets; apple pie or hot chocolate cake.

Jack closed his eyes and the smells took him away, and when he opened them again he found that he was crying. For an instant he was back in the cottage and it was his mother standing in the kitchen, not this strange old woman called Eve. And if he turned around Mandy would be sitting behind him, pulling faces or reading or sulking, depending on how her mood was that day.

"Hungry?" Eve asked, but she already knew the answer. She brought the first laden plate to the table—a dark meat, coated with a thick pepper sauce, mixed with fried potatoes and onion—and Jack was digging in almost before she'd put it down.

The tastes made him sigh. He smiled at Eve and she smiled back, and he saw that she was a kindly old woman. She was probably terrified by everything that had happened, a survivor living in a town of freaks, frightened now by the people who had been her friends and neighbours. He wondered how many times they'd changed—maybe only once, if this had all started after the living dead stopped walking and died again—and what a shock that must have been for Eve.

Yet she had survived.

"You're not eating?" Jack asked.

Eve shook her head. "I ate earlier. I'm not that hungry, young Jack, since..."

Since I changed, she was going to say, and Jack stopped chewing, the gob of meat and potato ready to slip back and choke him.

"...well...since everyone I've ever known went odd."

"Odd is the word," Jack said, scooping more food into his mouth. Eve stood and fed more wood to the big stove. Lucky she'd held back, Jack thought, not gone electric or gas with her cooking. Good job she'd shunned that sort of technology. Maybe the world was going to be ruled by old people, for the time they had left.

"So where did you come from? Are you on your own?" Jack could see the other, unspoken question in her eyes: Are your parents dead? And for some reason, he did not want to tell her the whole truth. There was something about her face when she'd closed the front door, that emphatic sigh of relief, which made the truth seem somehow more precious. I need to keep my secrets, Jack thought, and it sounded like something Mandy would say.

"My family are dead," he said. The grief, the tears were not false.

"So why here? Don't tell me you've been wandering ever since the dead stood up at last."

"At last?" Jack asked.

Eve brought more food. "God's will," she said. "He decided none of us are worthy of the eternity he promises. I suppose this is the alternative."

Another Elizabeth, Jack thought, but he was too busy eating to worry about that.

More fried meats, homemade burger and chips, and by then he was full. He leaned his chair back onto its hind legs, then remembered how his father had used to tell him off for doing that.

Eve smiled. "Full, or can I get you some more?"

"I'm full," Jack said, and he was. In fact he didn't think he could move, not for now, and the idea of sitting here and letting the huge meal go down was fine. He needed to talk to people in the town, had to find Lucy, had to try to make it safe for all of them, his dad in the ferry and Nathan and... but sitting here right now, warmed by the stove and comforted by this old lady's familiar presence, actually cosseted by her fear, things just did not seem so urgent. The room felt smaller than it had before. Eve was larger. Jack's skin was cool and his eyelids drooped. He'd eaten too much, that was for sure.

"I'm here to talk to Lucy," he said, and his mouth sounded very far away from his ears. "She lives here. And the others, the other people... were-folk... talk to them... make things safe for, for..."

"Nothing's safe with them around," a voice said, and although it must have been Eve she sounded younger, more vital, like a collage of voices whispering to him from a distance, revealing the truths he had come here to uncover. She used few words but they were hypnotic, and Jack wanted her to speak again because it made him feel so calm, sleepy, protected.

He opened his mouth and nothing came out, although he thought something went in. His mouth was a very long way away now, further than the ferry, further than home, but still he tasted blood as his tongue was grabbed and pinched.

Testing ripe fruit, he thought. And then he felt himself going away.

❖

When Jack awoke it was dark. The day had passed. He was lying on a bed, and there was a rooflight in the sloping ceiling above him, giving him a clear view of the stars. He looked around for his dad, listened for the hush of the sea against the stranded ferry's hull, wondered just why the porthole had changed from round to square... and then he remembered.

"Eve." Even the whisper sent his head ringing with a terrible headache. His mouth was dry, his stomach aching and he badly needed to visit the toilet badly. He'd eaten so much and then fallen asleep, not realising how tired he was, perhaps catching the best sleep he'd had in ages in this strange woman's stranger house.

He was in the roof. The sloping ceiling showed that, the rooflight, and the room felt small and cramped. He could not recall walking upstairs. He was small and wiry, true, but Eve was a little old woman, tired and alone and afraid. Surely the last thing she'd have done would be to lift him from the chair—a dining chair, hardly the most comfortable of places to fall asleep in—and carry him up to her spare room. It was the last thing she could have done.

And it was dark!

Jack sat up and listened, trying to ignore the throbbing at his temples and the lethargy of his limbs. It was night time in the town of the were-creatures, and he could hear nothing. No howling, whining, screeching or the clacking of claws on concrete. He reached up and touched the window, pulling at the stiff catch until it turned slightly and let in the cool night air. His skin goosebumped and his bladder contracted even more. In the distance, faintly, he could hear the sea stroking the darkened beach, but other than that there was nothing, not even a breeze playing at the gables.

The first sound came from inside. A creak on the stairs beyond the door, another, and then a quiet and polite knock.

"Jack. Are you awake, lad?"

"Yes," Jack croaked, his throat sore and dry. He stood, swaying, the room feeling far too small to contain him. He closed his eyes to try to maintain his balance, but the whole world seemed to be tumbling with him as its focus. He sat back down on the bed.

Eve scratched at the door. It took her a few seconds to open it—

Locked, she had to unlock it.

—and then she came in carrying a tray.

"Hello lad," she said. "Brought you a midnight snack." She bent awkwardly and placed the tray on the bed next to Jack. It was weighed down with chocolate bars, cakes and cans of fizzy drink.

"Toilet," Jack said. "I need the loo." He needed more than that—answers to questions he was too afraid to ask—but for now the toilet was a priority.

"It's broken." Eve spoke quickly, trying to hide her lie. "You'll have to use the bucket there, at the bottom of the bed.

Jack saw the bucket, shook his head, felt his guts churning from all the food he'd had the night before.

"I can't," he said. "I have to go."

"There's some paper there too," she said. "And I won't be back for five minutes, so don't you worry. Here. Have a drink." She popped the tab on a can of cola and poured it into a plastic beaker. It frothed and fizzed. Jack took it from her and gulped greedily, relishing the harsh bubbles soothing his sore throat, feeling a burp building but enjoying it too much to pause. Eventually he spluttered and spilled the drink down his T-shirt.

"Why can't I go?" he said.

"What?" Eve looked genuinely aghast. "Lad, I'm only helping you! You can go whenever you want, but... it's dangerous out there. There are things. I don't know what they are, never seen anything like it before, but they're out there full moon or not. They walk the streets. I've seen one of them eating... eating a cat. My cat, old Whiskey. Just picked her up and tore her apart without breaking stride. I'm protecting you, Jack, not keeping you here. But... go! Leave!"

She stood aside and motioned Jack to the door. Things, she'd said. They walk the streets... full moon or not.

Jack stood, swayed, made it to the bottom of the bed and sat back down. The world was moving again, even though he was not. He wanted to use the bucket. He looked up and Eve had gone, shutting the door slowly behind her and scratching at it again, locking it. Jack managed to squat over the bucket, crawl back into bed and then he went away again.

Night flooded his mind, and the stars were in his dreams.

❖

Somebody was prodding him. He'd fallen into a ditch after the change, weakened by the exertions of something so unnatural and not meant to be. Weakened too by his night out there. On the prowl. Looking for food but going hungry, because most things still alive were just like him.

Had he the energy he would have snapped upright, slashed out at the abuser, opened them up to steam into the night. But as Jack opened his eyes he realised that he was back as his old self now, a pale weak shape resting on white sheets. He ran his hands down over his chest, stomach, groin, and a terrible sense of loss hauled him from the refuge of sleep.

Someone was still poking him. They were using a stick, scratching at the flesh over his ribs. He opened his eyes and it was Eve, kneeling at his bedside, and Jack realised that she was not using a stick at all. It was her finger. Long, bony and tipped with a grotesque curled nail. She had lifted the hem of his T-shirt and was digging her finger into the fleshy parts around his waist.

"What?" he asked.

Eve shuffled back, surprised.

"You're still with us!" she said, shock feigning relief. "Still in the land of the living! I had to wonder there for a minute, lad. You were breathing so quietly."

Then why the prodding? he wanted to ask, but it was still

Changing of Faces

dark, he was still tired, disorientated. He listened carefully but heard no sounds from outside. Perhaps that merely meant that they were very, very good at staying silent.

He wondered where Lucy was and hoped that she was okay.

"You settle back down," Eve said. "Poor lad. I'll cook a lovely big breakfast for you in the morning."

That sounded good. The room darkened even more as tiredness returned to claim Jack again. Yes, it sounded good. The breakfasts his mum had used to make on a Saturday were wondrously rich in his memory: sausages, bacon, hash browns, beans cooked in the frying pad, eggs poached to explode across his plate, racks of toast... his father eating with him, Mandy still in bed, sleep was a teen disease his dad said, and it was nice to have that time, familiar yet always fresh and fun...

As he drifted away his eyes opened one more time, an already-forgotten dream startling them wide. Eve remained in the room. She was little more than a shadow amongst shadows, standing silently in the corner, watching him. Perhaps even guarding him.

Maybe there really are things out there, Jack thought. But he had begun to wonder.

❖

In the morning Eve brought up a bowl of water and took his toilet bucket away, and while she was gone Jack washed and dressed. When she returned with breakfast he was awake and alert, although his heavy sleep had left him with a headache and a disturbing sense of bad dreams. Lying in a ditch. Someone poking at him. Someone watching.

"Why can't I leave?" he asked her. "Can't I come downstairs to eat?"

"Don't you like the room?"

Jack looked around the bedroom. It was nice, he supposed. Unlived in—the wallpaper was unmarked, the carpet fresh and as new, the units looked like something from a DIY store display—but nice.

"Yeah," he said, "but..."

"Sometimes they do house to house," Eve whispered, and Jack knew that she was lying. She did not look at him as she spoke, busying herself instead with arranging his breakfast tray on the bed. "Checking for anyone not like them."

"Why haven't they found you yet?"

She looked at him, and he remembered her poking him in the night. Like a joint of meat. She is like them, he thought, but somehow the idea did not fit quite right.

"I don't answer the door. I'm an old woman, not fresh meat, my smell puts them off. They hardly even know I'm here."

"You cooked me breakfast," Jack said. The spread on the tray was everything Jack had hoped for, and more. A fully cooked breakfast, toast, cereal, orange juice and even a couple of small homemade cakes to round it off.

"I did!" she said. "You need to build your strength. For when you have to get away from here. You'll need to run."

Why didn't they smell the cooking? Jack wanted to ask. Why don't they see or smell the smoke from your fire? But the questions were too dangerous because they were close to the threat he felt, too obvious. Jack knew that she could not have a satisfactory answer for them... and he was scared of the truth.

Safe's what you make it, he thought, fearing his ignorance and needing it as well. So he ate, and Eve's presence brought back memories of a sentinel shadow in the night.

When he looked up she had changed. Not physically—nothing so obvious—but her demeanour had altered, the way she held herself. Her eyes were wide, her face more alive than he had yet seen. She looked hungry.

After breakfast he drifted off to sleep once more, worried that he was becoming ill. Worried too that soon, he would find a patch of skin on his body changing colour and texture.

He wondered what he would be.

Changing of Faces

❖

It seemed like a single day and night, but it must have been many, all passing behind a locked door.

During the nights Jack slept, stirring sometimes to find Eve prodding his flesh, sometimes not. On occasion she was a shadow in the darkness, watching him sleep and wake and sleep again, her image bleeding into his dreams and existing there still when he awoke, surfaced from fantasies of being something else. A few times he woke up and Eve was not there, so he went to the window to look out. The town, bathed in starlight, looked very beautiful, and he could see the diamond glint of waves breaking along the beach. The town slept, but the sea never did. Perhaps Eve was old as the sea, always awake. The rooflight was very high up, the drop was sheer. No way out there.

Once, in the street below, he thought he saw something move. It was a shadow shifting deeper in the dark, but it may have been his own field of vision shifting as he turned his head. Still, he felt watched. He hoped that it was Lucy.

When daylight came Eve would come with his breakfast, a bowl of water and, once or twice, some new clothes. He wondered where she found these, but guessed they were from some of the shops in town. Which meant that she went out. Which in turn meant that everything she'd told him was false. He really knew that already, but to hear the lie from her mouth was something he wanted to avoid. At present she thought she was deceiving him. He supposed, even though he knew that she was less—or perhaps much more—than she claimed, he was actually deceiving himself.

Jack drank what she brought for him, ate and ate and ate... and slept. Sometimes he heard noises from outside but was too afraid to look. A couple of times he even heard voices, but to see them spoken by something inhuman would have been unbearable.

Sometimes Jack thought of his father, but the constant sleep seemed to relegate him to just another dream...or a fading memory.

Jack dreamed of being something different. Upon waking he could remember little, other than feeling as tired as that changed thing, running or flying or crawling toward food. And he would check his skin, concentrating on the fleshy bits around his waist, wondering if Eve could perceive a change he could not yet see. He found nothing, but that was little comfort. Inside, where he guessed it really mattered, he felt different.

Some nights he tried to see whether the moon was full again, but clouds hid it away.

At one point during that night of many nights, Eve began muttering to herself. In Jack's dream her voice was the whisper of wind past his ears as he ran or flew, but when he awoke he knew that the shadows were talking. He could not make out the words, but the tone went from pleading to aggressive and back again, seemingly all in one breath. It was not the voice he had been hearing back on the ferry, but it could have easily been a part of it. He had never really heard these words either, although their meaning seemed to be coming clear. Eve's own whisper never resolved itself into anything coherent, but still Jack thought he knew what she was saying and why...because he felt the drawing, stronger than ever, like a promise in the depths of night luring him, dragging him through sleep and dream and nightmare towards its own inevitable fulfilment.

A promise...or a threat. Eve's voice revealed neither.

He dreamed of his father, and running, and blood and screaming and pain, and in the ambiguous moments between sleeping and waking, crying and breathing, day and night, he could not make out whose voice spoke of agony.

He recognised it...but he did not wish to know.

❖

"You're getting better," Eve said.

"I didn't know I'd been ill."

She was standing by his bed, left hand resting on the mattress as her right hand squirmed beneath the sheets. Jack tried to shuffle away but he could not move. He felt her hand touch his hip, like a dried up spider taking its first tentative footsteps across his flesh. He winced, Eve smiled. The fingers closed together, pinching a wad of flesh.

Her mouth was watering. It stank. It stank of old death, the dried-up musk of a dog's corpse in a ditch three months after it had been run over.

"Yes," she said. "Getting better." She stood, nodded down at the food and drink-laden tray she'd brought him and left the room.

Jack rolled over in the bed, sending the whole room spinning around the tip of his nose. He was hungry as hell, and the thick sausage-and-cheese sandwiches were begging to be gobbled up. His throat was so dry it felt like stone, his tongue was suddenly swollen with the promise of a drink, but he looked down at the glass of bubbling lemonade... thought of Eve's stinking grin, his tiredness, her prodding fingers, his skewed perception of night and day and sleep and dream and screaming, who was screaming?...and for the first time in that small attic room, he left himself thirsty.

It won't take long, he thought. Get whatever it is out of my system. Won't take long until I can try to escape, it mustn't take long. Because he was hearing things in the night now, and whereas before they could have been voices, now they were definitely not.

It couldn't take long. Because it would not be long before Eve came to eat him.

He slipped into a troubled sleep, and the dreams were there again. His father. The blood. The pain, and the scream he wished he did not recognise.

❖

Something howled.

Jack sat upright in bed, staring into the dark. Silence hung in the air like a dead echo. He listened, cursing his breath and thumping heart and the blood coursing through his ears. Maybe I dreamed—he thought, but the idea was cut short by that sound again, something outside and a long way off, but talking directly to him.

A howl, a scream and a shout all rolled into one. It faded away and then came back, echoing from mountains that were not there.

Jack closed his eyes and it grew darker. God, his head hurt! When he was a young kid he'd gone climbing in the woods with a couple of mates from school. They'd been goading each other higher and higher into the old oak that stood at the wood's perimeter, and Jack had taken the final dare to try to reach the top. He would have climbed down safely, too, if it hadn't been for his friends' heckling. Jealousy, he had thought at the time, they're jealous because I got to the top. Then his hands had slipped and that impossible moment—no, no, can't be happening to me, not now, this is unreal, this is a dream and I look so stupid—merged into his long, painful fall.

He must have hit every branch on the way down, and somehow broke nothing.

The next morning, his headache had been bad enough for his parents to call the doctor.

This was worse. It felt like someone had placed sharp sticks in his head and set them on fire. He'd seen his dad hungover sometimes, and he imagined that this was how it felt, and he could not for the life of him understand why someone would ever do that on purpose.

Other noises sprang up outside, and Jack stood for a peek from the window. That was when he realised he was his own person again.

He could walk, without wobbling and swaying on his feet. He was thinking clearly and cleanly, the throbbing of his head keen. The tray of food and lemonade remained untouched by his bed. Food and lemonade ... and something else.

Changing of Faces

"Fucking old witch," he muttered, enjoying the venting of his thoughts, relishing the freedom he had found again.

Relative freedom, at least. Because the door was still locked, and outside... the things were abroad.

He moved the curtains aside and moonlight flooded in. The clouds had cleared away, as if afraid of what they would face this night, and the moon hung fat, heavy and full out over the sea. The little town looked as if the moonlight had drowned it, a liquid flood that had brought on the sounds he heard now. And in the distance he could see things happening, movement in shadows, shapes running through the streets, hulking on rooftops or hovering above them. He moved forward slightly and looked down into the street... and saw the dog. It was the biggest dog he had ever seen. It crawled along the gutter as if stalking something, sniffing at the ground, its massive hind legs bunched knots of muscle gliding it forward. In the moonlight it looked as if it should be a rich golden colour. On its back it wore the shredded remains of a Motörhead tour T-shirt: Born to Lose, Live to Win. He watched it go and then glanced up as something big rolled through the night air, turning and spinning, falling and climbing as if flight were a totally new concept. Jack tried to make it out but it disappeared over the rooftops and inland. In a way he was glad. Bird or bat, it had started out as neither. Down nearer the sea there was more movement. It was too far away to make out properly, but Jack was sure he could see shadows squirming and flipping across the beach, the silvery splash of water marking where they met the waves. They left trails across the sand that glowed in the moonlight.

Something fell off the small pier and splashed into the sea.

There was a pain in his stomach and Jack leaned over quickly, groaning and grimacing. Poisoned me, he thought, but he instantly dismissed that notion. Why poison her own food?

The other idea that came to him was too awful to bear, but the fear gave it certainty. He ran his hand under his T-shirt. His skin was smooth and slick with sweat. Nothing sprouting there, no spines or feather or fur.

Not yet.

He glanced back outside, fascinated and disgusted and terrified all at the same time. Across the narrow street there was movement on the ground floor window sills. Most of the flowers in the window boxes were dead, but a couple of them were twisting and gyrating their way upright, like blind snakes responding to the moon's charm. Flowers? thought Jack. Not just people changing... flowers too?. And he thought of the living dead ants and cows and fox, the birds and beetles and trees, and he wondered what the fields and hedgerows and gardens would give birth to tonight.

In the distance, on the hillside he had come down from an unknown number of days earlier, a copse of trees shivered in the night. They reflected starlight, the obsidian black of huge beetles still rooted in the earth.

Something else drifted across the sky but this thing had control, it was graceful and strong. It was so high and fast that it was barely a shadow, cruising the town in its inevitable search for food. And back down in the street, in a souvenir shop doorway a few doors along, something twisted and turned in the shadows, enlarging, shrinking, as if it constantly flipping inside out with indecision.

That must hurt, Jack thought, and the pain in his stomach bit in again. He groaned but remained standing.

He felt so alone here, so scared, and he wanted his dad. He also had the unsettling sense of being left behind by events. Things were changing. Things were changing, and like a discarded friend he was being ignored. He felt like the last boy picked for the football team. Out in the night evolution was happening. He'd learned about evolution in school, and although the very idea of survival of the fittest and progress through mutation thrilled and excited Jack, now it felt as though he—everyone, his dad, the survivors on the ferry— were being shunned by time. He could not help but imagine them all as fossils, strange two-armed, two-legged creatures that had ruled the world once, for a time, only to be cast aside and defeated by... by...

And then he wondered where Eve was.

He spun around, certain that she was standing behind him, so certain that he felt her clawed hands scratching at his back and pinching the new flabbiness around his waist. He saw her by the door and tried to step back, but the back of his head hit the sloping ceiling, and there was nowhere else to go.

It was only a shadow. Eve had not crept into the room while he was watching the changes outside. But he knew that she was somewhere close by. And then he heard something bumping around downstairs, banging against walls and scraping across the floor, knocking over furniture, crashing through doors... coming for him. Eve, ready to eat at last.

Up the first staircase. The footsteps were fast and furious, the smashing as something crashed along the walls indicating that it was big, angry, hungry.

"Oh shit!" Jack hissed, and the pain exploded in his guts again. Not like this, he thought. He'd been trapped here for days, maybe weeks, drugged and cowed down, and now that his mind was finally his own again he wanted out, escape, and... not like this. The pain brought tears to his eyes but he wiped them roughly away. He would not allow his vision to be clouded again.

There was only one way out, and that was through the window.

More crashing from down below as the thing reached the first floor, and then it started up the smaller staircase that led directly to the bedroom door. Only seconds now, maybe five seconds before the door burst open and he got to see what Eve had always been destined to become.

The window jammed. Swollen in its frame? Or perhaps Eve had secured it, nailed it while he slept, readying herself for this night.

There was an old Ottoman at the foot of his bed. He lifted it, thanking fate that it was not loaded down with blankets, and heaved it at the window, pushing with both hands. He feared what was outside—the walls of the room closed him in and hid and protected him—but he feared what Eve had become much, much more.

The glass shattered, the old timber framing gave way and splintered out into the moonlight. Jack shoved again, and the Ottoman's momentum carried it through the window, the ragged edges of smashed glass searing its sides and drawing acid lines across Jack's forearms.

The door opened behind him. Something screamed out, a ragged, pained cry that could rise from no human throat. Claws ripped across the plastered walls and teeth snapped at dark air. Something wet hit the back of Jack's neck. Spit, he hoped, but it seemed to linger there like a tongue tasting his fear.

The pain still throbbed in his guts, like an engine turning over.

He did not turn to look. If he had done that Eve or whatever she had become would have had him. Instead he launched himself up out of the window head first, gashing his hands on the broken glass, the blood making his grip slick and painful.

Jack's emergence into the open was almost shocking. The room had been dark and dingy, and out in the moonlight he could see so much more, feel more of what was happening around him in the little seaside town, hear the cries and whispers and growls. He tipped forward and landed face-first on the pitched roof, grinding his cheek into the moss and seagull shit-encrusted slates. As his body pivoted and his legs kicked upward behind him, his heels struck something hard. Eve. Beneath the chin. Whatever she had become, he had kicked her in the face upon leaving.

As Jack began to slide down toward the gutter and the sheer drop beyond, he realised that the danger he was facing could only be much, much worse than that which he was leaving behind.

He tried to glance behind him at the smashed window. The

action turned him onto his back and his belt caught on a nail. Slates cracked beneath him.

Another scream in the night, too far away to be Eve but definitely approaching at speed.

The nail snapped or popped out and he slid again. However much he tried to dig in his fingers he kept moving... and now there was only air beneath his shoulders, he was tipping back, feet lifting from the roof—

Another scream, so close that he felt the warm breath of whatever uttered it, and as he fell he saw a brief glimpse of Eve at the dormer window. She was monstrous, a huge bird with few feathers, her skin wrinkled and pitted and seemingly wrapped around a frame much, much too small. She had changed, the moon had sung her its own song and made her whatever she was. But she was still old.

Too old to hunt, for sure. Too decrepit to run.

But still hungry.

Jack spun, his senses in freefall, and he realised that he was going to die. He'd known this for a few years, of course—it had been a great fear of his, along with the potential deaths of his family—and he had often sung himself to sleep at night by naming his fears, exploring and exposing them, confronting what must come instead of letting the truth of things hide and fester and rot in his soul.

In his final moments, Jack thought of his dad. How frantic he must be, how distraught. And he realised how selfish he'd been running away like that, following some fanciful notion of adventure, letting weird, poor Lucy lead him away from the only place he could possibly be safe.

His stomach still hurt.

Jack wondered what he would have become.

And then something hit him from above. Here comes the pain, he thought, here comes the impact as my head hits the ground

...but...

He was flying.

His feet and shins suddenly burst into pain. It felt as though knives were being driven in there, piercing skin and flesh and grating on bone, and Jack could not help but cry out. His head dropped back naturally and above him—below him really—he saw rooftops and roads and open spaces passing by, dark dashing shapes picked out clearly in the moonlight. Warmth flowed from his feet, over his knees and to his thighs, and he knew that he was bleeding badly. Whatever had plucked him from mid-air—and he was going to look up soon, he really was—had made sure its hold upon him was unbreakable.

He was rising, the thing carrying him turning in a slow circle above the town, and Jack could see the true nature of this strange place's population. Creatures roamed the streets, the back gardens, small parks, the beach, the pier and the hills leading out of town. In fact these hillsides were alive with black shapes, all flowing in one direction, their minds apparently set on one thing.

The ferry. They were going to attack again, and this time they'd know the strengths and weaknesses of those inside.

Don't be there, Jack thought, please don't be there, Dad. Please be gone. Tears dropped from his eyes onto the town below, not all from pain.

He looked up between his feet and saw the huge bird of prey that had taken him for its own. Its body was sleek and covered with a healthy sheen of feathers. Wings beat heavily at the air, fast and furious as it struggled to maintain its own weight as well as his. He could not see the thing's head, its eyes, and he was glad. He wondered where it would land so that it could begin to eat him.

Jack glanced quickly at where the bird's talons dug into his feet and shins, not wanting to see too much because he knew from the pain that it must be bad. He looked away because his blood was black in the moonlight, and there was a lot of black soaking into his jeans, more dripping away all the time and speckling his tee-shirt and the underside of his chin—

And then he looked back.

Changing of Faces

The bird's legs above the claws were thick, wider than his wrist, and on its left leg it wore a silver ankle bracelet.

"Lucy," Jack said.

The bird called out, its voice full of violence and hunger.

"Lucy, it's me, Jack, please Lucy you can't..." He realised then that if this was Lucy—and now he was sure—then she must know who she had. She'd been hanging around outside the house, gaining an occasional glimpse of him at the dormer window of old Eve's house, and now that the change had come over the town she'd come to pluck him from danger at the last possible moment.

He did not want to think about why she had taken him. A sharp image flashed across his mind, memorised from a David Attenborough natural history programme he'd seen when he was about seven: a bird of prey, mouse clasped in its claws, head dipping down and up, down and up, shreds of glistening red flesh and gristle and fluids lifting away from the mouse, its struggles, its tail waving as the bird ate it alive.

"Lucy, please!" he said. Maybe she'd lured him here, her intentions clear to herself all the time. A victim...young, impressionable, fresh, separated from the safety of the ferry so that she'd never have to take part in the second attack.

Maybe she'd never been his friend at all.

She screeched, and something responded from elsewhere. Jack was swung around as the massive bird dipped in a tight circle, its claws biting into his legs even more. The other voice was joined by two more, and then Jack and Lucy were being buffeted from all sides. The other birds were only slightly smaller—crows, perhaps—but there were three of them, and their claws and beaks were aimed at the bird of prey's prey...not the bird itself.

Lucy tried to avoid the attacks, but the crows came in from all angles. Jack closed his eyes and puked as he was flipped around like a dead rabbit in a buzzard's grip. He thought his legs may rip and break off at any moment and he would fall, leaving Lucy circling higher and higher with his bloodied lower legs impaled on her talons. His puke coated his face and scalp, then splash across his stomach and groin as Lucy spun in the air. The crows came in again and again, claws lashing at his outstretched arms, beaks prodding at his hip, his thigh, his neck. Lucy was doing her best to save him—for herself, perhaps; for her own feast—but Jack was dying. He could feel open wounds kissed cold where the night air rushed across the fresh blood. He thought of his mother dying in her bed in that strange colourful house in the woods, and it was sad that he was dying so badly. Mum would have been so upset.

Lucy let go. He fell. He had no idea how high he was, how long it would take for him to reach the ground and put an end to this. He heard her screech and one of the crows cawed in pain, black wings beating at the sky as it fell, a flurrying mess, one broken wing whistling as air rushed through the gaping wound pecked through its surface.

Lucy's talons cut into Jack's legs again. He cried out and she cried with him, perhaps in sympathy.

The bird flew on. The remaining two crows continued their attack, most of their slashes and jabs missing, but the ones that connected hurt Jack less and less more. How much blood? Jack thought, is it eight pints or eleven? How much has gone, feels like about five, maybe six, maybe even nine...

The crows suddenly seemed to realise the easiest way to steal him from the big buzzard's grasp. Their attacks veered away from Jack and they concentrated on Lucy, slashing at her wings, her tail feathers, the back of her head. She screeched out again and again, and Jack could feel the vibration of her pain thrumming into his legs. She snapped left and right, and Jack felt the first waves of unconsciousness pulling sensation away from him. To pass out now, to go away from all of this, seemed Heavenly... but the idea that he would never wake up again kept him sharp and in pain. The cool night air whipped at his wounds, Lucy's talons met around the bones in his shins and knees, he cried tears and blood, the crows were relentless in

Changing of Faces

their attacks, coming in again and again and again until, eventually, Lucy began to weaken and lose altitude.

And then the crows veered away and disappeared into the distance.

"Lucy," Jack slurred through his pain, and her cry sounded just as weak. She flapped her wings and kept them airborne, but they were drifting lower and lower now, and as Jack's head tipped back he saw the pale bandage of a beach stretched out below them.

As they fell from the sky into the dunes, he saw a man-made blot on the coastal landscape: the ferry.

In its windows, lights blazed.

Attacking these windows were the crows, just two of many.

The final thing Jack heard before their terrible landing was the distant cough of a shotgun.

❖

Something was pressing him into the sand. Jack was torn and hurting, but the thing that concerned him most was the weight, a deadweight splayed across him like a blanket of warm stone.

He opened his eyes but could see nothing. They were filled with sticky blood.

But he could hear. The sounds of battle from beyond the dunes and along the beach. The screams and cries of the werecreatures as they ran or swam or crawled or flew, all of them intent on breaching the ferry's defences to reach the fresh meat inside. And once or twice, screams that may have been human.

"Dad!" Jack whispered, and a shotgun called out to him, and the weight above him shifted, and Jack could not fight the faint that took him away.

❖

In his unconsciousness, screams sounded. He recognised those screams because it was he who had so recently uttered them.

They would come again, he knew, when he awoke...as a human, as the boy Jack, because the voices had lied. They had not promised him, they had lured him, and his own dreamt-of scream mocked as he silently fought his pain.

❖

When he came to again the sounds were the same. It was still night. The shotgun blasts were more intermittent now, and Jack could hear a consistent thud, thud, thud as things bashed themselves against the stricken ferry.

The weight still wore him down but it seemed to have shifted, lifted imperceptibly. He turned his head one way to try to wipe his face and eyes on his shoulder. He blinked hard, squeezing his eyes shut, opening again, and he felt a crust of dried blood break and allow him sight.

Jack was looking into the giant buzzard's eye. His breath hitched in his throat and the huge eye blinked. He remembered the cynicism in Lucy's gaze, but this was purely animal, any personality stolen completely away by her change.

"Lucy," Jack said. "You're hurt. Let me up, let me out, I'll try to help." The bird turned its head slightly so that the cool beak rested across Jack's throat. He felt its sharp tip press into his shoulder. Lucy quivered, eyes blinking, and Jack felt the fight going on there, knowledge versus instinct as her avian heart told her to press in with the beak and pick out Jack's warm insides. Food, fresh food, would give her strength. That's why she had him, surely? He felt the fight inside her and apprec-iated it. He also realised that it could change at any instant.

"Let me up," he said again. And then he realised just why she was still lying across his prone body.

Something came at them through the dunes, a scuttling thing that clicked and clacked as it ran, puffing up tufts of sand like bullet impacts in a war movie. Its claws snapped at the air, its stemmed eyes catching a dozen moons. When small things got big you saw detail you could never make out before, and the terror was in the detail. Like its mouth...

Lucy pushed up and placed her taloned feet either side of Jack's waist. The crab came at them and she pecked at it, beak and claw clashing and scarring each other with silvery streaks. The crab backed away but quickly came in again, both claws cutting at the air. This time Lucy hunkered down and went for its segmented legs, screeching as one of her wings was sliced. The crab lost a leg, amputated a foot above the ground, and it scuttled back, standing on its remaining legs and swaying slightly like a drunk in a stand-off.

Jack was petrified. A giant buzzard and a giant crab were fighting over him, duelling to see who would get his tastiest morsels. He wanted his dad. He wanted his mum. He wanted to wake up, but the agony all across his body told him that he was already awake, especially the rich, keen pains in his legs, so intense that he could not tell where one leg began and the other ended. Maybe they'd gone. Perhaps both feet had been ripped off and he was feeling the ghost pains he'd read about. Fears and terrors too awful to begin to name.

Lucy relaxed herself onto his body again and rested her beak against his face. In the distance Jack could still hear the sounds of the attack on the ferry, but here something happened, a brief silence in which something seemed to be communicated between the two unnatural creatures. Mine, Lucy seemed to say, pressing her beak into his cheek so hard that Jack believe that she would go on pressing, slowly, casually, until the bones in his face broke and she drove onward into his brain.

But she stopped when the crab moved away, and lifted her head, and raised herself slightly from his tortured body. The fight still shook through her.

Jack tried to breathe normally but there were pains in his chest. He wondered why he had not changed—his stomach still hurt, his joints ached—but he guessed that he never would. Perhaps in his mind, deep down, he'd been wishing the change upon himself, but outside he was as normal as the people he'd left behind. As for the pains... Eve had been drugging him. The only real change was his newfound disregard for his father's feelings and wishes.

Jack felt wretched.

But to fly like a buzzard, to run like a fox, to swim like a seal...

So thinking he felt darkness pulling him down once again, and he gave in to it willingly. It would steal the pain for a while. And whatever her intentions, Lucy was watching over him.

✤

It was only when Jack surfaced again that he realised just how badly Lucy was hurt. She was still there, straddling him, wings splayed around him to hide him from view, and even though he heard and sensed things rushing around them they were left alone. He was hers. The other were-creatures obviously had their own meals to sate them that night... but that did not bear thinking about.

The shotgun blasts still came now and then, as did the screams and screeches, but Jack could not find that as comforting.

He could hear Lucy's breathing, shallow and fast. And he could feel it, each ragged gasp adding to its own pain. He was cut and gashed and almost sick and blind from the agony, but he thought Lucy was dying. If she did die, and changed back, and the other things saw her dead body trapping him here... there would be nothing to keep them away. There was no way he could fight them off. And it wasn't as if he could run.

Jack thought about shouting for his father, but the ferry was too far away. Besides, he'd brought this on himself. He'd been trying to make it safe, that's what he told himself, trying not to listen to the other, more painful truths: that he'd desired so much more.

How could he have been so wrong?

"Lucy, thank you," Jack gasped. "I followed you, you know,

because I wanted to be like you. Wanted to change. Something was telling me I could, and I'm still not sure who or what that was. Maybe it was you. Or maybe it was just me. So deep down I didn't recognise myself. My sister said we all have our dark side. She read horror, and stuff. And she became a zombie." He trailed off, thinking of Mandy and what she had been, what she had become. His mind always tried to skirt that last time he had seen her, casting it into the deepest part of the sea of memory, treading water in the shallows until he felt he could hold his breath long enough to relive it again. The fact of her fate was always with him, but the actual memory of it was too much.

"Stay with me," Jack said, and he was not entirely sure what he meant. Now? Forever? "Stay with me."

Lucy gave no sign of having heard, but when a twisted, sickly-looking weasel sniffed around a few minutes later she jerked to her feet, spread her wings and screeched. The were-weasel turned and fled, and Lucy dropped down again, her eyes wide and black and totally inhuman, breath clicking as if something inside had snapped.

Jack's night darkened, lightened, darkened again as he drifted in and out of consciousness. He saw and heard his father pursued through his dreams once again, but it was not Jack doing the chasing. Perhaps it was merely his own fears over what he thought he may have become. In the innocence of sleep he made this the reason he had fled, but the thought rang hollow, the idea was false.

Occasionally a shotgun blast echoed across the beach, telling him that things were not yet over.

❖

Jack saw the dawn. The eastern horizon was smudged pink, or maybe it was the blood in his eyes. The shotgun no longer fired, but neither could he hear the screams and growls of the attacking were-creatures. They would be back in their small town now, safe for another month, licking their wounds and picking the flesh from their paws, claws and teeth.

The were-buzzard was still weighing Jack down, but she no longer felt warm. Just before the sun came up to change her back, Lucy died.

Jack closed his eyes as he felt grotesque movement, heard the strained wet snapping sounds of her body reverting to its former self. In his mind's eye he remembered the strange girl who had bewitched him so, her attitude and outlook and that patch of tainted skin on her chest, enough to aggravate his own dreams of change. When he looked again it was Lucy lying atop him, pinning him to the ground with her deadweight. She was naked and pathetic in the dawn. Her wounds were terrible. How she could have survived for so long...

Jack eased her off him, trying not to let her face touch his, her hands, the hair clotted with blood and something worse. He averted his gaze from the worst of her wounds, but like the memory of his final time with Mandy they were merely sucked under and hidden deep. He would see them again, when he relived all bad things.

He did not look at his legs. He should have bled to death, but now his legs were burning with pain, heavier than they should have been, wholly human yet still changed, perhaps never to work properly again.

He wondered if there was anyone left alive in the ferry.

Jack dug his hands into the sand and hauled himself up the side of a dune. He hoped there was only one, prayed to a God he had never really believed in that he was near enough to the beach to be heard when he shouted, seen when he waved. The sand coated his bloody wetness and burned its way into the wounds, adding to the pain. He'd been crying in his sleep, and this had washed the blood from his eyes. He should be thankful for that misery at least, he supposed. He wiped at his eyes and blinked a few times, seeing clearly at last.

The sky was still pink. The colour of diluted blood.

He could hear the sea hushing onto the beach, unconcerned

at the trivialities of time. It did not care if his father was alive, it did not see Lucy lying dead because she had found it in herself to protect him, not to eat him. If there was one like her then there must be more, but then Jack remembered the kindly, helpful Eve, and he wondered.

He reached the top of the dune and saw the ferry three hundred yards along the beach, the sea swirling lazily around its beached hull. He could crawl there, he thought, but he was not sure he wanted to. Not through that.

Corpses lay strewn across the beach like pale mushrooms, spotted red. There must have been two dozen bodies, all reverted to their human selves in death, twisted and broken where they had fallen or been pushed. A few more floated in the sea around the bow of the ferry, nudging against the metal hull as if still trying to gain entry. The sea there was pink. More diluted blood.

Dad, Jack tried to shout, but his throat was dry and hoarse, and the effort drove spikes of pain into his chest. He could not stand, he could not crawl, he could barely even breathe.

Bracing himself on his left hand he raised his right arm and swung it back and forth, back and forth.

There was no sign of life on the ferry's deck. Perhaps it was a ship of dead people now, but Jack would not think that. If that were so, then he was dead too. There was no one to help him now, no one to save him.

Dad! He tried to shout again, but it was not even a whisper.

And then he saw movement. At first he thought it was another dead body bobbing from the seaward side of the ferry, but then the dingy floated into view, heading out over the small incoming waves, dipping and rising as it was lifted and dropped.

Someone sat in the bow, shotgun resting over their shoulder.

Someone else sat in the stern, steering the small outboard motor.

There was no one else. Or if there was then they were lying down out of sight, bleeding certainly, maybe even dying. More dilution. Their band of survivors, thinned out by death. And they were leaving.

"Dad!" Jack said, a whisper, even though from this distance it was impossible to identify the occupants of the boat. He wished it was his dad, he hoped, because anyone not in that dingy must be dead. They were escaping. Fleeing. Leaving him.

"Dad!" He could not manage more than a whisper. He waved frantically but he was weakening, a wound on his shoulder bleeding again and his legs begging for mercy.

The dingy seemed to find voice and roared away from the beach, bouncing from the larger waves, the outboard motor adding tune to the incessant rhythm of the sea.

Jack tried to stand, could not, crawled as quickly as he could down the beach. By the time he reached a man whose head had been blown off, the dingy motor was fading into the distance, lost to him just as surely as Mandy, and his mother, and Lucy.

He cried into the sand and the coolness of last night's tide soothed his cheek. His stomach did not hurt anymore, but everything else did. There were no more voices in his head, and at least now it would be four weeks until the next full moon. He had time on his side if nothing else.

Jack sincerely hoped that his father had gone. If not—if he found his dad's body inside the ferry if and when he managed to clamber up the steps—he would surely be alone in the world.

And Jack had never been alone before.

THE END

MAYBE ONE DAY I will walk again.

It's one of Jack's more lucid moments. He is counting the days not by day or night, nor by his watch, but by the shape of the moon. It has grown thin, sliver-like, and then edged towards whole again since he fell on the beach, legs torn and broken, bleeding into the sand. His pain has not been diluted. It is as rich as ever. When he is conscious it burns in his bones and he wishes for oblivion, and when he's delirious and swaying on his hands and knees, he sees dead things walking, and people turning into hungry animals, and he prays that he'll wake again.

He has been crawling for days, away from the sea and the ship, the bodies rotting into the sand and the things that might return there come full moon.

But why would they? he thinks. *Everyone is already dead.*

He knows that his wounds are infected. He feels the burn there, and sometimes he can smell them. He can't bring himself to touch the open cuts and gashes, and when he looks he feels sick.

You're never meant to see your own bones, he thinks. *I've got a skeleton inside me.* The idea scares him, but he can't run away from himself.

He can't even *crawl* away.

During the nights he covers himself with the heavy coat he found on the beach. He still gets cold and damp, and it's at these times that the wounds hurt least. Then he has to start crawling again.

He's worried that if he stops moving, he'll die. *Got to have an aim*, he tells himself. *I've got to keep going somewhere. That's why Dad and I came to the coast, to go somewhere, to have a destination in mind so that we wouldn't just . . .*

Jack thinks his father is probably dead.

He crawls. The road starts to slope up. His hands and knees are shredded, but the pain distracts from the agony of his torn calves, ankles and shins.

One more hill. He could find and house and stay there. He could keep going until he finds something else. One more hill and then—

There's a man watching him. He's silhouetted against the setting sun, up the road a hundred metres, paused with something slung across his shoulders. Jack slumps to the ground exhausted, turned onto his side so that he can watch. As the man starts walking downhill towards him, Jack sees that the thing across his shoulders is a shotgun.

The man pauses a dozen steps away. He doesn't say anything. But he kneels, props the gun against his shoulder, shrugs off his rucksack and undoes the straps. Inside he has a bottle of water and some food. He also pulls out a couple of rolled bandages and a bottle of whiskey.

"Who are you?" Jack asks.

The man comes closer, saying nothing. He looks around for some time, ensuring this is not some sort of a trap.

Jack starts to cry. The shudders wrack his body, bringing more pain, but he can't hold them back.

The man kneels beside him and twists the top from the whiskey bottle.

"What's your name?" Jack asks. He doesn't answer. Jack thinks he's going to sit and drink, but then the man tugs torn clothing away from Jack's wounds and leans in, examining the mess. He knows, then, what the whiskey is for.

"I'm Jack," he says, starting to talk faster. "We were on the beach in a ferry, there were things there, were-things that came to try and eat us, but they weren't all bad and—"

The man brings the bottle close to Jack's leg ready to tip it. He pauses, raises an eyebrow at Jack.

"I'll call you Old Man," Jack says.

Old Man nods, then pours.

SHIFTING OF VEILS

AS THE SUN ROSE on a world moving on, Jack saw a figure crossing the landscape below. It was too distant to tell whether it was a man or woman, alive or dead. It moved steadily, resolutely, and with an obvious destination in mind. It was coming to the church.

Jack kicked a bottle down inside the bell tower and heard it shatter on the stone floor. A couple of minutes later he was joined by someone else behind the broken grille.

"Walker?" Jack asked.

"Can't tell from this far out," Old Man said. He did not seem out of breath, despite having climbed forty-three steps. "You stay, keep watch, keep your head down. I'll get the gun."

Old Man descended again, leaving Jack on his own. Usually that was how he liked it; the others in the church were hardly sociable. That was why he was the most regular volunteer to come up here and keep watch, with only the silent bells for company. But sometimes, with possible danger approaching and change about to touch their regular, monotonous existence, he wished for some comfort. It was times like this when Jack missed his family most.

The figure was maybe a mile in the distance, walking along what had once been a lane linking the church to the nearest B-road. The lane had changed now, as had the main road; hedges crowded in, the narrow route reduced from a car's width to barely wide enough to walk along. The landscape of fields and grassland had spread, and humankind's mark on the land had almost been wiped away. Jack still walked that lane occasionally, and he knew that the tarmac surface was crumbled and holed from plants sprouting from its many cracks and potholes. Previously, the wheels of vehicles used to keep the plants down. Now with humanity dead and gone, they grew free.

Dandelions and bluebells, brambles and grasses, tree saplings and wild roses, he could not deny their beauty. But it still sometimes amazed him at how quickly nature was reclaiming the world.

Fields had gone wild, crops spreading and blooming in defiance of a harvest that would never come. Tree saplings grew in clumps. Swathes of the hillside below the church were purple with the bluebell spring, and the several buildings visible were slowly being subsumed. Even the windmill across the other side of the valley—over the river, and standing sentinel above a complex of business units hidden behind a small woodland—seemed to be falling to nature now that it was abandoned. Two years ago there had been an old woman and two young children living there, but they'd never wanted anything to do with the church. Jack had respected the old woman's independence, but it had also made him sad. One day they'd vanished. None of them knew how, why or to where, and in time, none of them cared.

Sometimes, Jack thought he saw the old woman standing in a field close to the windmill, motionless and alone.

He raised the small pair of child's binoculars that Lady Day had brought when she'd arrived a little over a year ago. They were plastic, bright green and blue, and the lenses were scratched and weak. But they brought the distance a little closer, and potential dangers nearer. Three times in the past year, the binoculars had given them time to prepare.

Now, he wasn't so sure. Seen closer, the figure seemed to be

Shifting of Veils

walking with a stick. Jack could relate to that. It carried a rucksack or a loaded carrier bag tied to its back, wore a long brown coat, and every movement struck him as wholly human. That was good. No one had seen a Furie for over four years, and even the occasional sighting of a were-creature had dwindled since Lady Day's arrival. Walkers were inevitably cranky and weird, but they were preferable to the alternative. Human, at least.

Jack could still not make out the figure's sex, but soon he would see. The person came ever closer. They must have already seen the church, perhaps spied the piled logs and drying lines that indicated it was settled. Not all Walkers sought company, and when they did Jack was always unsettled. Occasionally they remained silent, as if loneliness had stolen away their voice. Others spoke nonsensically. Some, the most troubling, brought news from places beyond, and all the news was bad.

He sighed and shifted position. His left leg was giving him grief today. The knotted scars of his calf and foot sometimes twisted into cramps, and he had to stamp down hard, stretch his toes, and wait for the pains to recede. He'd tried to perceive a pattern to the discomfort—cold weather, warm weather, dampness, the desolation of memory—but the agony seemed purely random and cruel. A sad reminder of the nature of his loss.

Lucy, the girl who had turned into a were-buzzard and saved his life, giving hers in the process. The beach strewn with bodies. The stranded ferry, more bodies inside. But not his father's. He had never found his father's corpse in those frantic few days when he had searched, in and out of delirium as infection took hold and blood loss made him weak, hobbling, crying, but refusing to die. In the five years since, he'd thought of that lifeboat and the two figures sitting upright as it sailed away. Whether his father really was alive or dead, Jack's loss was no less keen.

Old Man jogged up the stairs. "They still coming?" he asked.

"I said we should keep the drying lines down when we're not using them."

"Company won't harm us at all." Old Man leaned the shotgun

against the bell tower wall and smiled at Jack. He was a big man, strong rather than fat, and his beard made him seem even larger. He'd let his hair grow long and his beard spread untended, and he stared from the foliage with intelligence and wit. He was always quite cheery, despite their situation. He once told them that he'd always been forced to make the best of things. Jack thought maybe he'd suffered terribly back in his real life, so the end of the world was just something else to deal with.

"Pretty sure it's a Walker," Jack said. He held out the binoculars. Old Man took them and looked.

"Yep. Using a stick." He glanced at Jack. "Two cripples together."

"Charming."

"Want me to help you down the stairs?"

"Piss off."

Old Man chuckled, then grew serious again. "You wait here a bit longer, get what you can. I'll go down and prepare the others."

"Maybe Jean can cook a rabbit stew."

"Yeah, maybe. I'll leave you the gun for now." Old Man started descending the stairs again. He paused, looking back at Jack. "We'll be fine," he said awkwardly.

Jack nodded and turned his back as Old Man went down again. They were hardly a commune, just five people living together in the same place. Jack did his best to encourage them to help each other, muck in, be at peace, but he knew in truth they were all alone. One thing an occasional visitor did do was bring them closer together.

It was all about survival.

❖

His name was Cass. Whether that was the truth, or just a name he used sometimes, didn't concern Jack. The fact that he used a proper name at all was a good start.

Shifting of Veils

"I'm Lady Day," Lady Day said. She pointed. "That's Old Man."

Cass smirked as he looked around at the group. His gaze alighted on Jack.

"Skinny Runt?" he asked. "Field Stalker? One-Legged Sheep Humper?"

"I'm Jack." He couldn't hold back a smile, and it felt good. Jack stepped forward and held out his hand, and Cass's own smile faltered a little. "Dad always told me to be polite to strangers."

Cass glanced at Old Man.

"No," Jack said. "My dad's gone."

Cass shook Jack's hand.

"That's Bob, standing over by the door," Lady Day said, nodding towards the church porch. "Jean's inside. You'll meet her in a minute."

Cass nodded at them all.

Bob whined a little before disappearing inside and trying to heave the doors shut behind him. He was too weak, too small. Jack had guessed his age at anywhere between thirty and fifty, but the man had never spoken a word since they'd found him wandering the fields two years before. He was a good cook, though, and he seemed safe enough.

"Jean might cook you some rabbit stew," Jack said. "Maybe. If she feels happy to, I mean. And if you'd like some."

"Like some?" Cass said. But he didn't answer his own question, and the silence quickly became uncomfortable.

"Got anything to tell us?" Old Man asked. "Anything from..." He waved a hand vaguely away from the church.

"Bits and pieces," Cass said. "Stuff and nonsense."

"You're a Walker," Jack said. "How far have you been?"

"Been out there four years, give or take," Cass said. "I've been north as far as the Angel, and south to the coast." He suddenly looked grim, weathered.

He knows so much more than us, Jack thought, and that knowledge seemed dangerous. "I'd like to hear," he said softly.

Cass smiled. "Rabbit stew."

Inside the church, Cass started talking even while Jean was chopping vegetables and boiling water.

"Been to lots of churches since it happened. Lived in a village in South Wales, nice little place, my wife went to church there. After she died... after the zombies—"

"We call them Furies," Lady Day said.

"They were zombies. That's what. No denying that, no sugar-coating what we all know and all saw."

My sister, Mandy, Jack thought. Closing his eyes did not see away the memory of her lying on him, trying to scratch, trying to bite. And at the same time there was that sense of her that he'd been catching more and more recently while he slept—watching him, frowning, eyes wide and startled.

"After the zombies, and Claire's death, I went to the church in the village hoping to find..." Cass shrugged. "Never did believe in God before it happened, and even less so now, after. But I still went. Claire used to help out there sometimes, watering flowers on the graves to try to make them last longer. Cutting the grass. I went, but the church was empty. Door was open, but Father James... he wasn't Father James anymore. At least someone else had put him at peace. At least I didn't have to do it."

Cass sighed. No one said anything. His grief was his own.

"So I started walking. Across the countryside, from church to church. I dunno. Just... wandering, thinking that they're solid places, easy to defend. But I never found one I wanted to stay in." Jacked watched him look around at the inside of their church.

They'd made a sort of common area in the chancel, shoving the alter aside and pulling down some of the heavy curtains to sit on. Jack and Bob had broken some of the pews from their fixings, but though they'd been dragged up to the chancel, most people still chose to sit on the floor; for those occasions when they sat together, at least. Behind the chancel was a small

Shifting of Veils

kitchen area. They used the old Belfast sink for cooking fires, and Old Man had removed a flagstone and excavated to access the built-over crypt below. It had taken him seven days of constant work using a blunted pick. It was cool and dry down there, and dead rabbits, badgers, and the occasional duck or swan would keep for days.

They had each chosen their own place to sleep. Old Man had the vestry, Bob slept wrapped in a curtain in the Chancel, Lady Day had claimed the base of the tower. Jean sometimes slept in the kitchen, and sometimes disappeared for days on end. She said she spent time foraging and hunting. No one was really sure.

Jack slept in the north aisle, in a nook behind a heavy wooden cupboard. He didn't feel any more comfortable there than anywhere else, but he'd pulled in many of the pew cushions, and made it at least bearable.

Sometimes he heard Old Man and Jean having sex in the kitchen.

Bob often screamed as he dreamed.

Lady Day would sit for hours on end when everyone else was asleep, always in the same pew, staring into space. To begin with Jack had thought she was praying, but he'd started to doubt that. He wasn't sure exactly what she was doing.

"I don't want to stay in this one, either," Cass said.

"So what have you seen?" Old Man asked. "Apart from the churches. What's happening out there?"

"You all just stay here?" Cass asked. "You don't look around?"

"We're safe here," Jack said.

Cass snorted but said nothing. Something was wrong. He was on edge, and although he seemed eager and happy to talk, Jack could see that he was deeply troubled. His eyes were never still, as if trying to catch shadows that always moved just out of sight.

"How many other survivors are there?" Lady Day asked. She constantly stroked her long silver hair. She tried to be Jack's mother, but he refused to let her.

"Other small groups like yours, here and there. A few larger communes. And Walkers, like me."

"But in the towns, the cities?" she asked.

"I stay away from them," Cass said. "They're old places. They're the past, and they don't matter anymore."

"But you must be tempted to go into—" Jack began, but Cass cut him off.

"No! Not at all. I walk past them. I have ... " He opened the rucksack he'd set by his feet and pulled out a handful of Ordnance Survey maps, "These. Not for everywhere, but for some places. And a bigger map showing the whole country. I avoid any built up area." He looked around at them all. "Have you really not been anywhere else but here?"

"I got here over four years ago," Jack said. "I came inland from the coast, and Old Man found me. He helped me, I was injured." He nodded down at his legs stretched out before him. "We found this place together, and Jean was already here. I needed rest, and I'd taken on an infection. Jean had a stash of medicines back then, and she used a lot of them on me. Then we found Bob out in the fields, brought him here. Lady Day came later. And here we are." *A group*, Jack wanted to say, but they were less than that. They were a commune of convenience, and sometimes they didn't speak to each other for days.

"And haven't you seen the echoes?" Cass asked softly.

"What?" Jean snapped. She had emerged from the small kitchen, followed by the smells and sounds of cooking food, spitting fire, boiling water. Her voice faded around the church's interior.

"Echoes," Cass said again. "Those old places that don't matter anymore are full of them, and that's why I stay away."

Jack frowned, remembering those strange dreams from the moments between sleep and waking—his sister Mandy, confused and scared; his mother, standing alone and startled as if forgetting who and where she was.

And when he looked around at the others, he recognised his own confusion and fear in their eyes. He was surprised, but not too much. If they'd all been closer, if they'd found a common purpose, maybe they could have talked about such things.

Cass was watching them all. He ran his fingers through his long, knotted hair and sighed. "They even come to the Walkers."

"What do?" Jean asked. Her face was drawn and pale.

"And it's strange," Cass said, "I've seen other things out there, in the countryside. Like nothing that's come before. Shapes, hints. One of them was a bear, and I'm sure something else, something older."

"I don't know what you're talking about," Old Man said, and for the first time Jack realised that he'd kept the gun close.

Cass seemed about to say more, but then he smiled. It barely lit its way through the grime on his face and the scruffy grey beard, but it did touch his eyes. He reached into his rucksack again, rooted around inside, and then brought out a half-full bottle of whiskey.

Jack remembered Lucy on the stranded ferry, her drinking to deny what was happening, and he flinched back when Cass held the bottle out to him.

But Old Man took it, and Lady Day, and when Jean brought out bowls of food the atmosphere eased as they ate.

Later, they started talking about the people they had lost.

And later still, Jack's mother and sister came to him again.

◈

These are not just echoes, Jack thought. They had come before, fleeting things that he thought were dreams or, even more ethereal, memories. But perhaps hearing Cass talking had given Jack's own visions weight. Allowed him to see clearer.

He was suspended between sleep and wakefulness, conscious but so obviously dreaming, and yet the dreams were imbued with a reality, a sensory richness that he had never experienced before. He could smell the musty pew cushions beneath and around him, taste mould on the air, and reaching out he felt the cool, dry stone of the ancient church wall. Yet he was desperate to retain the dreamy sensation, just as when he experienced déjà vu he craved for the feeling to go on and on.

He knew the shapes and shadows so well, and he wanted to reach out to them.

Mandy sat to his left, his beautiful sister with whom he'd bickered and fought so much. It was a younger brother's job, he'd told her, repeating something their father used to say in response to Mandy's protestations. She had taught him that naming the parts of his fear could go some way to tackling it, and he had used her advice again and again. But now she looked confused and scared, as if she did not realise she was dead.

Mandy, dead, scared, but maybe not knowing. Naming those parts did little to change what he saw. This dream was more than a manifestation of his fears.

His mother stood just outside the nook he'd taken for his sleeping place. She was frowning, reaching, lost. His heart broke for her. *But she's dead*, Jack thought. *And Mandy, dead.* He tried to say those words to tell them the truth, but he could not speak. Perhaps this dream, this vision, did not allow it. He reached out instead, one hand to Mandy and the other to his sweet mother. But their echoes faded away, their wretched images imprinted onto his memory and existing, at last, only there.

※

It was nothing like an existence. It was barely even survival, if he was left with nothing to preserve. He was living, not existing, and Jack had known for a while that something had to change.

The others were decent enough. What little he knew of them. Old Man had been a bricklayer, he said, but he'd retired a few years before all the bad stuff happened. He was a widower. His daughter lived in France with her French husband and their three children. They came to visit every Easter, but were becoming strangers as the years went by. If anyone was leader

Shifting of Veils

of their strange group, it was Old Man. But could someone who never told his real name truly lead?

Jack had arrived with Old Man, and from that moment he'd hardly looked beyond their surroundings. Wounded physically, shattered emotionally, the church had become his world. His legs had slowly healed, the infection somehow fought off. The drugs Jean and Old Man had forced into him had left him in a permanent fugue for a long time, stealing the pain but making away with most of his faculties, too. He became a memory of who he had once been, his character and self always on the tip of his tongue, and his senses had shrivelled—the taste of root vegetables, the smell of mould and must in the church, the sound of disinterested voices and sadness. The sight of grief darkening the church. He'd seen it, he was sure, like a cloud forming from within and bleeding out. It stole colour and texture, and made the here and now a washed out, subdued version of what had once been.

His own grief, and that of the others. They all had stories, and over time they told them.

Apart from Bob. For the two years he'd been there, the bald, slight man had never spoken, not even in his sleep. He listened to them, Jack was certain, sometimes taking it all in, sometimes not. He even contributed to the church, gathering firewood from the fields and hedgerows and taking it upon himself to tidy the building's insides and cook. But Bob was as far from them as everyone else. He might as well have been dead.

Sometimes Jack thought that about himself. Once or twice he'd actually thought it was the case, especially recently, waking into confusion and seeing and sensing traces of his dead mother and sister.

But he'd had a wonderful childhood. Whatever life had become, his family had given him a love of it. Though long ago in time, and even longer in memory, that went some way to keeping his desire to survive aflame.

That, and the idea that somewhere out there his father was still alive.

What he had never expected was to find him again.

❖

"Strange that we're all known as Walkers, almost everywhere," Cass said.

"Why strange?" Jack asked. They were having a breakfast of potatoes and vegetables, mashed and fried into pancakes. Surprisingly tasty.

"Because if it weren't for Walkers, people like you wouldn't know anything beyond these walls." He nodded around them at the church's interior. Dawn sunlight was flooding through the stained glass windows on the eastern wall, painting the air with haphazard rainbows.

Jack liked the dawn. Its colours washed away the disturbing visions of sleep.

"Walkers hold the world together. We're the connections. And we're known for it."

"You're like storytellers of old," Old Man said. "You know, hundreds of years ago."

"That's me," Cass said. "I tell stories."

"So are there lots of Walkers?" Jack asked. "I mean, we've seen people passing by from time to time. Sometimes they stop to talk to us, if they see we're here."

"Or if we choose to let them know we're here," Lady Day said.

"Yeah. But we don't see *that* many," Old Man said. "And we speak to even less."

"We tend to cross paths," Cass said, "walk the same routes, as far from the old places as we can. I've met thirteen others over the past year or two. Thirteen that I can remember, though I've seen twice that number. Up near York, I found three hanging from various trees, hands tied behind their backs. Their legs and genitals were mutilated with sharpened sticks. Something was waiting for us there. Hunting us. I ran for a whole day, never looked back. Spent some time in the Lake District after that, and there I had a . . . companion, for a while. Ashleigh. She died."

Shifting of Veils

He took more food from the central plate, aware that they were silently watching.

"So the thirteen you've met," Jack said, "what were they like?"

"Like?" Cass frowned, ate, chewing the question over. "Well... one woman ran everywhere. Never walked. We spoke for a minute, then she was too far away to hear my shouts. One man was looking for his missing dog. He'd walked down from Scotland, I met him south of Oxford. Otis."

"The man?" Jean asked.

"The dog. Never asked the guy's name. Then there was the Indian woman, Rohana, who'd sewn her eyelids open. A man called Angus who was so drunk he could hardly walk. Another one, he was... quite mad. I spent some time with him. He's quite the legend, that one. Two other Walkers I met knew of him, talked about him, and a couple of the little communities too. Washed in from the sea, it's said, and he's never stopped walking, not once, looking for his son. He told me his boy had run away but never been lost. Graham."

"Graham?" Jack asked.

Old Man sighed and reached for Jack, not quite touching his shoulder. "Come on, now, boy, you know—"

"What did he look like?"

Cass shrugged. "Like all of us."

"Tall?" Jack asked. "Thin?"

"Yeah."

"Glasses?"

"No."

"Broken nose? Blue eyes?"

"I don't remember things like that," Cass said.

"He never calls himself Graham," Jack said.

Cass paused with a chunk of food close to his mouth. "No. Gray."

"My father," Jack breathed, and the church started to spin around him. He closed his eyes and his legs hurt again, the pain crashing in as a manifestation of guilt, a memory of betrayal. He'd left his father on that ferry without telling him where he was going, or why. *And now he's telling people I've run away but never been lost, because he's looking so hard.*

"It won't be him," Old Man said, glaring at Cass.

"That's what he called himself," Cass said. "Gray. Not as if I can make it up."

"Where did you see him?" Jack asked. "When?"

"Maybe six months ago. East of here, thirty miles inland from the coast. North of Peterborough."

Jack was shaking. It was the need to do something, and the terror at the idea of leaving. *I've been here far too long*, he thought, looking around at the familiar strangers. None of them spoke.

"Six months," Lady Day said. "Long time. He could be anywhere now. He could be dead."

"He was going in circles," Cass said. "Big circles, wider and wider."

"You didn't ask what his son looked like?" Old Man asked.

"No!" Cass snorted a sour laugh.

"Why not?" Jack asked.

"None of my business. And don't you think I lost people too?"

Jack shrugged, expecting to be told. But Cass said nothing.

"You can't just..." Jean said. She sounded bereft.

But Jack decided that he *could* just leave. He could pack a bag with food and set off east, search for his father, the one living person who pinned him to the past and might let him move into whatever future any of them had. Here, he was frozen.

❖

It was a hot, sunny day. The sort of day that might once have inspired his mother and father to announce a trip to the coast, or perhaps a hike up one of the local hills to picnic on the summit. Jack would be excited, jumping around like any little boy anticipating a forthcoming adventure. Mandy might be quietly disapproving, or maybe silently looking forward to the day as well. She had never been a bad sister or daughter—not that Jack could remember—but at times she had borne the stereotype of a teenager proudly.

Jack's walk today would be much longer. It was daunting, and almost beyond his comprehension. The landscape had become so strange, and after four years of barely going more than a couple of miles from the church, the idea of anything beyond was almost alien. Anything further than what he could see from the church existed only in dreams of the past. It would start with a single step. But even before that, he feared he might hold back.

The air was still, the heat almost a solid thing, sweat gritty on his back and face. He couldn't remember a summer like it. Maybe it was the world trying to burn away whatever was left of humanity's scourge. Old Man had talked about that, suggesting that everything that had happened was some sort of defence mechanism thrown out by nature itself, a purging of its systems.

It's a detox, and we're the poison.

Lady Day said that was bullshit, but the idea had caused Jack many sleepless nights, musing on the idea of the world around them striving to finish them off. Jean said that everything was more beautiful than ever before—the clear skies, the gorgeous landscape, the wild woodlands and rampant fields. Jack grasped onto that idea. It was much easier to take than believing everything was out to kill them.

"What are you looking for?" Jean asked him. She might have been a kindly, mother-like figure in any other time.

"A bag. I've got to take stuff, but I don't know..." He was walking around the outside of the church, past the log piles, under the few scraps of clothing and blankets hanging to dry on the line. He thought maybe he could tie the arms of a sweater together and use it as a rucksack. Or maybe one of the old hessian sacks in the church's outside store would do. But this simple task was troubling him so much that he was almost crying.

It's what comes next, he thought. *That's what's really worrying me.*

"Oh, come on now, Jack," Jean said. She grabbed his arm and held tight, waiting until he looked at her. "You really want to go?"

"I have to," he said. "If there's even a small chance that's my father, I have to go."

"But we're all right here, aren't we?" she asked, a hint of desperation there, her own need to be told that yes, everything was fine. She was afraid of their loose group changing. Moving on, as the world had moved on.

"No," Jack said. He shook his head. "No, we're not. We're counting the days, the weeks, the months. Nothing gets better. It's about more than that, even now, even after everything. And there are changes."

"Changes?" Jean asked. She let go of him, one hand going to her throat.

"You know," Jack said. "Cass called them echoes. They're not just dreams, Jean."

For a moment he thought Jean was going to shout at him, or perhaps hit him. He was still, silent, a held breath. But then she turned and walked back into the church. Though he could not see, he knew she carried her ghosts with her.

Jack pulled one of his tatty jumpers from the line and knotted the end of each arm. Then he cut a small length of clothesline and fed it in and out through the woollen waist, drawing it tight. It would have to do.

Bob was watching. Jack saw him as he approached the small garden area they tended between the graves, and he wondered whether the quiet man had seen and heard his exchange with Jean. Probably. He was starting to think that Bob saw and heard more than all of them.

Jack lifted a tarpaulin and picked up a handful of potatoes, a swede, a nest of carrots. He wished they had some fruit, but the few raspberries and loganberries they'd managed to grow belonged to the others. He had to be fair in this. He was the one making the decision to leave.

"I'm doing the right thing, Bob," he said. No one knew the

Shifting of Veils

man's real name. "You'd do the same, wouldn't you?" Bob blinked at Jack then knelt between gravestones again, plucking weeds out from between lines of bright green shoots. It had felt strange to Jack when they started growing things between, and sometimes over, the old graves. He'd imagined roots growing down deep, seeking sustenance through rotted wooden coffins, and perhaps touching buried things that rolled and shifted once again beneath centuries of weight. But the newest grave was at least a hundred-and-fifty years old, and Old Man had persuaded him that this place was long in the past.

"You'll be fine," Jack said to Bob's back. "You'll be safe." He was really talking to himself.

Back inside the church, Jack glanced over to Cass and Old Man. They were sitting on two pews, speaking quietly, their voices escaping to the rafters as wordless whispers. He wondered what they were talking about. Maybe Old Man was trying to persuade Cass to tell Jack he'd been mistaken, the man hadn't called himself Gray at all, and it couldn't possibly be Jack's father. But it was too late for that now. Nervous, scared, Jack was also determined. And soon he would speak to Cass alone.

He dropped his make-do rucksack close to his sleeping space, folded a blanket and put it inside. Then he gathered up his few items of clothing and forced them in as well, the sweater already bulging.

He'd need water, and some way to carry it. A knife. Some matches to start a fire, if the others didn't mind him taking a box from their dwindling supplies. Perhaps one of the waterproof coats they tended to share, hung in the stone porch outside the church's main door. He only had one pair of trainers. The stick he sometimes used to walk was fashioned from an oaken branch, something Old Man had made for him over the space of a few weeks three years before. He would take that, too, and if he encountered danger it would double as a weapon, something that—

Panic was crowding him. At first he thought it was those echoes again, pressing in against his senses, his mother and sister whispering and frowning and pleading with him for something he could not give. But his breathing grew faster, his chest heavier. He walked to the front of the church and started climbing the tower, and it wasn't until he was at the top and looking out over the landscape that the pressure started to lift.

"I'm scared," Jack said to no one. He took out one of the grilles so that he had an unimpeded view, and welcomed the hot sun against his face and neck. He had never looked upon the church as home, but now that he meant to leave it was the one safe place. "Dad, I'm scared." Across the valley stood the windmill, abandoned now but for the birds that had made it their home. And beyond that, hillsides rose towards a ridge that had been the extreme of Jack's environment for too long. That way was east. That way might be his father, and perhaps one day he might actually be able to speak with him again.

His hot neck bristled. He glanced around, but those echoes remained just out of sight, behind him, but watching. He did not fear the memories of his mother and sister; his great dread was that they feared him.

That look in their eyes when he saw them—shock, confusion—made him sadder than he thought possible. Perhaps finding his father would be the first step to laying them to rest.

Jack sat there for a while, and it was his way of saying goodbye. This familiar place was already taking on the tone of past times, as if he had already left and returned to visit. And soon the time would come to say farewell to those he had lived with for four years. Friends? He wasn't quite sure about that. But they were companions, and in their own vague ways they had helped each other to survive.

❖

Later, around midday, he went back down. And Cass had already gone.

"What?"

"I persuaded him," Old Man said, shrugging. "In truth he

Shifting of Veils

didn't need much convincing. I don't think he stays anywhere more than a night, and—"

"But he was going to help me!"

"Don't think so, Jack," Lady Day said.

"Well, he said he wouldn't, but..." Jack was angry and scared. "But I was going to talk to him. Convince him. He's a Walker. He's experienced, he knows what's out there, and I thought he might help me find my Dad."

Old Man shook his head sadly. Lady Day sighed and turned away. She'd never had much patience with any of them, and Jack didn't think she was a very nice person. She'd told him that she had been a teacher, but she'd told Old Man she was a painter. No one knew the truth.

"Which way did he go?" Jack asked. *Not east. I'd have seen him if he'd gone east.*

"I don't think Walkers have a way," Old Man said, and his eyes went wide, mouth dropped open, as Jack shoved him back against the old stone wall.

"Tell me!" Jack shouted. His voice rang in the rafters. Something took flight up there in the shadows, startled. How many prayers had these old stone walls absorbed and ignored?

Old Man pushed back, but Jack was young, and fear fed his strength; fear that his one chance had just walked away. "*Tell me!*"

"We don't want you to go," Old Man whispered. He wasn't old, really, only in his fifties, and he'd given himself that name. But right then he looked ancient.

"I don't care," Jack said. "I'm sorry. But I don't. I just need to..." He eased back from Old Man. The brief potential of violence had shocked him. "I need to help my family. *All* of them."

No one responded to that. Not Lady Day, who stood with her back to the men looking towards the old altar. And not Old Man, in whose eyes Jack saw understanding and, finally, acceptance.

"North," Old Man said. "Not long ago. But Jack—"

"I'm not staying!"

"I know," Old Man said. "I was going to say, just be careful. I don't think Cass is as safe as you might think."

"Is anyone?" Jack asked. He went to his sleeping place where he would never sleep again, picked up his make-do backpack, and left the cool embrace of the old church.

They all watched him go. He felt their eyes on him, and the places they had all touched for the final time seemed to burn. Jean's cheek against his and her arms tight around him; Lady Day's surprising, soft kiss against his forehead; Old Man's hand clasped in his. Bob, that silent man, had hugged him hard.

Reaching the end of the overgrown lane and standing in the middle of the B-road, Jack looked back at last. The church was over half a mile away now, shimmering in heat haze. It looked so much smaller from this far away, the square bell tower barely reaching higher than the ancient oak tree in the graveyard, the silhouettes of gravestones like children hunched down in the sun. But he could still see the others there, watching. He raised his stick in the air and waved it back and forth three times, saw their arms repeating the gesture, like the shadows of distant wind-swept trees.

The road wound north, roughly following the course of the river that flowed out of sight beyond the wild fields to his right. He'd been down to that river many times since arriving at the church. For the first few times, when his wounds healed enough for him to walk that distance, he and Jean had tried to fish. But everything they caught had looked strange. Jack wasn't sure whether it was simply because he'd never fished before, and the fish he'd eaten had always been cleaned, gutted, and prepared for human consumption before passing through the supermarkets. But Jean said that some of the creatures they hooked were wrong, and she threw them back in.

After that, Jack had sometimes come down on his own. He liked the sound of the river. It flowed slow and wide here, and provided a constant background *shushing* to his thoughts. He liked to watch as well He'd come to regard the river as nature's

Shifting of Veils

clock, marking the passing of time in a more noticeable way than the shifting of seasons, and in a more tactile manner than the passage of the sun across the sky. Sometimes, it also bore time's evidence. He'd seen a bicycle tangled with an uprooted bush floating by. There had been a broken door, a dead sheep, and a long slick of oil that seemed to stretch out for hours, miles. And once, a hump of material that might or might not have contained a body.

As he walked he listened, and if he breathed softly through his mouth he could still hear the river.

"It'll keep me company," he said aloud, looking ahead. Cass had at least an hour's head start. He would have to move.

Jack was not used to walking quickly. He was lean, and Jean said they'd probably been eating better for the past few years than ever before. Berries and root vegetables, other veg from the small garden she tended, occasional meat riches—rabbits and squirrels, feral dogs, and once a wild pony had broken its leg in a field south of the church. Old Man had shot it in the head. Jack had baulked at eating horsemeat, but Lady Day had laughed and asked what he thought was in the cheap supermarket burgers he'd used to eat.

But he soon discovered that he was not very fit.

His leg started hurting as soon as he tried to speed up. He used the stick Old Man had carved for him to support his weight and grimaced against the pain. It was lucky he could walk at all—Lucy's giant bird-claws had penetrated his shins and heels to the bone, and Old Man had thought the bones themselves were cracked. Now, the sound of the stick striking the ground was almost hypnotic, offering a regular beat to his movement.

He had to catch up with Cass. Now wasn't the time to think about why the Walker had left without saying goodbye, nor his assertion that he had no reason to help Jack find his father. Jack would catch him, ask again, plead. Hopefully by showing that he'd left the relative safety of the church, he would demonstrate his determination and seriousness.

Perhaps Cass still wouldn't give a shit.

But Jack had to try. And if Cass still said no—if he shoved Jack aside, pushed him away, punched him to the ground—then Jack would stand again and go on his own. East, towards the sea and perhaps towards his father. He'd done nothing for long enough.

Jack had a sudden, powerful sense that he was no longer alone. He paused, but only for an instant, then carried on walking, thudding the stick down on the cracked road surface, using its impacts to measure the distance travelled, and guess at that yet to come. The sense of his mother and sister following him, their echoes silent on the landscape yet rich and whole in his mind, was strangely comforting.

I don't know if they're there. I don't know if they're in my mind and so in my eyes, or in my mind and nowhere else. I don't know if it's them or my memory of them, or perhaps just their own memory of what they once were. I don't know. But right now, that doesn't matter.

He didn't not turn around because he was scared. He kept staring forward because he knew that if he saw their familiar fear and confusion, that comfort would evaporate. Was it selfish to deny ghosts the attention they perhaps sought? Jack didn't know. But right then he had no wish to be alone.

❖

Later that afternoon the echoes had vanished, and he saw movement up ahead.

He'd caught sight of his mother and sister, now and then. Fleeting movement out of the corner of his eye, a sense of warmth and thereness behind his shoulder, just out of sight. He'd taken comfort from that. And with them accompanying him, several miles had fallen between him and the church. They were long miles, and troubling. Although he saw little he did not expect, the landscape beyond the church—the safest of havens, though still under constant threat in this strange new world—had become unknown to him.

Shifting of Veils

Now he was alone again. And on a hillside to his left, close to what might have been a farm but which now was an overgrown ruin, something waited beneath the trees.

Jack paused by a rusted gate, trying to make out exactly what it was. He pressed back against the hedge, keen not to be seen, equally eager to know what was up there. He squinted, shielded his eyes with his hand, closed one eye. But nothing brought the distance in closer.

Near the farm, a couple of fields distant, there was a pile of cow carcases heaped against a fallen fence. Plants had grown around and between them, but the pile was so high that he could still make out the black and white hides. There would be little more left of them than skin and bones, he knew. He wondered how they had been piled there, who had done it, why.

The farmhouse roof had caved in, windows were broken, and creeping plants had climbed the walls, probing tendrils into every opening. It looked sad, because it was obvious that the building had once been grand. Three storeys high, surrounded by barns and other outbuildings, it had stood dominant against the hillside. Now it was merely another part of the landscape. Perhaps the people who'd lived there—

The shape beneath the trees moved again, pushing out from the shadows and into the sunlight. It was still too far away to make it out properly. Cass? Perhaps, though Jack was not sure. The size was about right. But the sun was bright and there seemed to be a haze in the air, blurring distance. That, or his eyes were tired. He wished he'd brought the plastic kids' binoculars they used back at the church. He almost moved out into the gateway to wave, but something held him back.

It was the way the shape moved. It wasn't like a person at all, but more like a staggered, staccato film of someone with every fourth frame removed. It flickered across the hillside from the farmstead, then back again towards the trees. As it entered the trees' shadows once more, Jack started climbing over the rusted gate.

The second bar broke. Rusted, flaking metal scraped at his

calf and Jack cried out, once, as he fell to the side. Only his hands clasping the gate's upper bar prevented him from hitting the ground, but even this span of metal bent beneath his grip. Pain spread from his wounded leg where it was injured afresh, and he winced. Jean had hammered home to them how essential it was to be careful now. Medicine was rare and difficult to find, unless they travelled far and went into the towns and cities. And none of them had wanted to do that. *Even a scratch from a rusty nail could kill you*, she'd said. *We remember phones, computers and chemists with all the medicine we need, but in reality we've regressed five hundred years.*

Jack was going to check how much damage he'd done—he could already feel the warm-then-cold dribble of blood down his leg—but then he saw the shape coming at him across he fields.

It was drifting with no real sign of any limbs moving. He blinked and rubbed his eyes, watery from the pain. But it made his vision no clearer.

All he knew was that this shape was wrong. It did not belong. Unwelcome memories of the zombies he'd seen when this all began came flooding back, and then images of those were-creatures attacking the beached ferry where he, his father and a few others had sought refuge. But this was nothing like that. They had been monsters but had moved according to rules of physics. The thing coming at him now seemed to mock the very nature that had done so much to wipe humanity from the land.

Jack stood and stared, realising that his vision was in fact completely clear. His surroundings were sharp and defined. It was the shape that confused.

A riot of limbs, flickering movement, a hint of a face that seemed at once agonised and furious, mouth open wide as if to eat the land, the sky, the sun itself.

And then came the screams.

Jack felt a deep, debilitating sickness hollow him out, and then with every ounce of strength he could muster he turned to run.

Shifting of Veils

"Jack!" a voice called.

"No, no, no, stay away from me, don't come—"

"Jack, it's me! To your left!"

Jack looked and Cass was there, crouched down beside the wild hedge maybe thirty feet away. His eyes were wide. Jack had never thought he would see a man like that afraid.

"To me!" Cass said. "And Jack...start thinking of your lost ones. Start allowing them in."

"What do you mean?" Jack asked. But as he hobbled along the rough road towards Cass, he saw...

...he saw the air around the man blurred, but there was nothing threatening there at all. Cass was adorned with sadness.

"Let them come, boy," Cass said. He was crying, although it had not touched his voice. Only his eyes. Tears smeared clean lines across his cheeks and disappeared into his beard.

"What *is* that thing?" Jack asked as he approached. The screaming continued, rising and falling, a song of hopelessness.

Cass held out one hand, waved his fingers, and Jack held his hand. The man squeezed, hurting.

"Your loved ones," Cass said, looking over Jack's shoulder. He seemed distracted, almost not there. "I know you've seen them. You're not stupid. Naive, yeah, maybe that. So let them come before the wraith gets here, and maybe we'll both be safe."

"I don't know—"

"Maybe," Cass said, staring into an impossible distance. He turned his head and smiled over his shoulder at the blurred air around him. *He can see them but I can't*, Jack thought, *because they're his lost ones, not mine. Mine are...*

"Mandy," he whispered. "Mum." There was no transition; one moment they were not there, the next he felt them with him, pressing in close even though he could not physically sense them, warming him and loving him even though, when he turned and looked into their misty eyes, he still saw only confusion and shock.

I almost forgot what they looked like, he thought, and that time back at the church before they had started visiting him in dreams, and sometimes not, felt suddenly like a barren, lonely time. *I forgot the colour of Mandy's eyes and the way Mum's brow creases when she's thinking.* There was still plenty he did not recall, and after four years they felt farther from him than ever. But he supposed it was a start.

He looked again and closed his eyes, because they seemed so lost.

But Cass squeezed his hand. The man was whispering something that Jack did not understand, but simply hearing his voice was a comfort.

The air grew cold. Birdsong stopped abruptly. Something was approaching.

"Keep them close," Cass whispered in Jack's ear.

Jack opened his eyes to see.

Mandy and his mother were still there, floating at his shoulder, in front of him, drifting, eyes wide and expressions pained, but there with him all the same. *I miss you both so much*, he thought, and was that the flicker of something familiar across their faces? The shadow of sibling mockery twitching the corner of Mandy's mouth, the sheen of love smoothing his mother's frown-lines?

He could not say. Perhaps seeing that was as much in his imagination as seeing these echoes, these remnants of his loved ones in the first place.

The thing from the farm came through the hedge.

It was a storm of images and sensations. Leaves and twigs burst from the hedge as if hit by a car, yet the shape that came through seemed hardly to touch anything. Jack saw arms waving, bodies twisting, mouths gaping, and even so he wasn't sure whether it was the violent echo of one or many. The screeches were horrible, grating on his inner ear. There was a terrible, deep fury that physical surroundings seemed almost to flinch from. He didn't know whether the distortion was real, or a withdrawing of reality as seen through the echo's influence. It was like heat-haze above a quiet, long road in summer, and—

He is walking with his parents and Mandy, past the woodland to the south of Tall Stennington and towards a local pub. It's one of the hottest summers on record. Grown-ups seem to complain about it, and Jack can't understand, because it has been a summer of shorts and garden sprinklers, browned lawns and water fights, ice cream melting down his hand and the prickle of sunburn as his mother rubs moisturiser across his shoulders and chest in the warm evenings, barbecue simmering, Mandy giggling, his parents drinking chilled wine and sunset scorching the horizon. Ahead of them the road seems to have melted away, and above it is another road, and another, shimmering in the blazing sun. These roads go everywhere, his father says, and it's one of those memories that comes back to Jack again and again, unbidden and from out of nowhere.

But right then the memory meant something more, and he wondered which roads these echoes were following.

"They're fading," Cass said. "Losing their anger. Soon they'll be gone."

The fury that set the air aflame was dissipating, allowing nature back in. Birds started singing again as if nothing had happened. Close to the broken gate where Jack had been only a couple of minutes before, the air twisted and flowed, slower, calmer, until there was nothing there at all.

The screaming faded to wherever dead sounds go.

"What...?" Jack asked. He was shocked and scared. The coolness lifted, and he felt the sweat of fear across his back and beneath his arms.

"Echoes," Cass said. "I told you things out here are changing. I told you not to come!"

"You can't tell me anything!" Jack said.

Cass smiled, surprised. The smile quickly faded. "Come on," he said. "We need to get away from here. Somewhere quieter. Less haunted."

"And then you'll tell me what that was?"

"That?" Cass said, looking along towards the gate. The gap in the hedge already seemed to have been filled. He turned and walked back the way he'd come, saying over his shoulder, "You're not a stupid boy."

❖

For a while, Jack trailed behind. Seeing Cass just ahead of him made him feel safer. But there was still something between them that forced them apart, like two magnets repelling. All he could see of Cass's echoes were shimmers in the air, but Jack's own lost loved ones remained with him in a strong, vibrant way. They drifted behind him, following his movements, having no real relationship with the surroundings at all.

He almost spoke to them, but that was still a step further than he wanted to take. He was afraid that they would answer back.

Into the afternoon, his echoes seemed to vanish. He was not aware of them leaving, but between one moment and the next he became aware of their absence. He felt a momentary stab of deep loss, almost as rich as when they had first died. Then he saw Cass waiting for him along the road, the man's expression mirroring his own.

"It's always like that," Cass said. "At first I thought it was a torture. Her torturing me because I didn't save her, couldn't stop her from ... " As Jack approached, Cass continued. "Then I came to realise it's me who's the strong one. She's drawn to me because she's troubled. Unsure. I *think* she knows who I am and why she's with me. I *think*."

"Have you tried asking?" Jack asked.

"Have you?"

Jack shook his head.

"No. I'm frightened I'll scare them away."

They started walking side by side, as if they always had.

"I'm going to find my father," Jack said.

"Good luck."

"I was hoping you'd come with me. Help."

"Why should I?"

"You're a Walker. Have you anywhere else in mind? Somewhere important to be?"

"You don't really know a thing about me," Cass said. "Don't know where I'm going, or what I'm looking for, or how dangerous I am. I have my own aims, you know? You don't even know my second name. Why do you think I'd help you?"

"Because I'm a walker too, now," Jack said. As he spoke the words, the realisation set in.

Cass laughed. "You think so?"

The road approached a small village. Jack might have come this way years before when he was fleeing inland, wounded and delirious with infection. But he could no longer remember. It was a small settlement, and from this far away there was little detail to be made out. There were houses on the outskirts, but beyond that it was difficult to see.

"This way." Cass pointed uphill away from the road, over fields and towards a tree line that hid swarms of shadows.

"Up there into the trees?" Jack asked.

"Safer than there." Cass nodded at the village.

"That thing back there at the farm," Jack said.

Cass raised an eyebrow.

"A mad echo?"

"Maybe they're all mad," Cass said. "Maybe we are, too. Mad for continuing."

"What's the alternative?" Jack asked, realising straight away how naive he sounded. But Cass did not berate him.

"You're strong," Cass said instead. "Me too. I think I am, anyway. Seen people hanging from trees, curled around guns, smashed at the bottom of a long drop, burned to piles of bone and ash. And I think I'm strong for not giving in to death. But sometimes I wonder if that actually makes me weak."

"Why are they mad?" Jack asked.

Again, Cass waited for him to answer his own question.

"They're alone," Jack said.

"Maybe. You have your own, and I have mine. But others..."

no one for them to echo back against. No one alive for them to... tag onto."

"So they rage?"

Jack actually saw him shiver. "Or something else. What if they're the echoes of those who became zombies? And those who were were-creatures, before dying out?" Cass shook his head. "Think about that. Think about what that would do to your soul."

"You believe in the soul?" Jack asked.

"You don't?"

Jack shrugged, confused, and he suddenly felt naked beneath Cass's glare. Like the man was seeing through his weak flesh and blood and bone, deep inside. Into his soul.

"What would have happened if it caught me?" Jack asked.

Cass was growing impatient. "Come on. Up there, into the trees, and—"

"Cass!"

Cass breathed heavily a few times as if preparing himself. He stared at Jack. His gaze was strong, haunting. "I saw a man and woman in a pub car park, down near Reading," he said. "Year ago, now. Watched from a hillside. They were trying to get into the pub, I think. The wraiths came from out of the building. Smothered and killed them. I don't know how, I didn't get any closer to see. I ran. But... it hurt. Their screams, Jack. Their cries." He closed his eyes.

"Sorry," Jack whispered.

"Up there!" Cass pointed towards the trees. "Perhaps we'll find somewhere to spend the night. Not that I want or need your company."

Jack followed Cass up the hillside towards the trees. At the junction of two fields they had to force their way through a hedge, and in its clutches they found several bodies, so tangled together that one bone belonged to the next. They had been dead for a long time, perhaps from the beginning. There were two adults and two children. Jack wondered at Cass's own story, but he was old and wise enough to know now wasn't the time to ask.

Shifting of Veils

Through the hedge, into the field beyond, and they walked side by side again, silently.

I'm a Walker now, too, Jack thought again. His leg was hurting, though he was trying not to rely on the stick too much. His limp was obvious. But determination saw him through, and soon he found a pace that was comfortable and which didn't pain him too much. He'd always believed that he could never walk far, but right then he thought he could go on forever. *I've suddenly become a Walker, and it's like I was never at the church.* He thought of those he'd left behind only hours before, and already he wondered at their willingness, even eagerness to do nothing. Hearing about the man who might be his father had wiped most of the last four years from existence. For the first time in that long, Jack had something to strive for.

"Just a minute," Cass said. They paused in the middle of the large, sloping field. Perhaps there had been crops there once, but now it was a wild meadow, beautiful, and filled with potential dangers.

"What?" Jack asked. He followed Cass's gaze to the line of trees that had once formed the upper edge of the field. Now there were saplings edging outward from the forest. At the trees' own timeless pace, they were marching downhill.

"Looks okay," Cass said.

"Why do they come and go?"

"What?"

Jack looked around at the empty air about him. No hints of anything there, no wisps of memory.

"I have no idea," Cass said dismissively. "Come on, follow me. We'll find somewhere sheltered and build a fire."

"Isn't that dangerous?"

"Less dangerous that not having one."

❖

Later, after the sun had set and as Jack imagined Old Man and the others closing the church doors and retreating to their places to sleep, Cass skinned, gutted and spitted a rabbit. He seemed to be proficient at snaring, and within half an hour of setting several traps in a certain area of woodland, he'd caught their dinner. One sharp punch to the back of the head and the rabbit was dead.

Jack had offered to gut and prepare the carcass, but Cass had declined. Maybe he had his own way of doing things.

As the delicious smell of cooking meat filled the air, Jack held his hands out to the fire. He watched the flames flickering between his fingers. Fire was hypnotising, and sometimes it took him away from everything else.

"There are dangers," Cass said.

"Where?" Jack snapped alert, but the man's manner didn't indicate any threat.

"Everywhere. All over. You've been back in that church for a long time, but even there I'll bet you've been visited by them. Seen them, heard of them."

"Yeah," Jack said. There had been moments.

"But sitting there waiting for dangers to come to you is nothing like walking out amongst them. Out in the wild it's like you're inviting them to take a run at you."

"You can't persuade me to turn back."

"Not trying to." Cass turned the spit, and fat dripped onto the fire, flaring and spitting. "Just offering advice."

"Thanks," Jack said, but he was sad inside. He'd hoped Cass would go with him.

"The zombies died out pretty quick, mostly. Dunno why. Do any of us know the whys and wherefores of any of this? I saw something down near the south coast a few months after it happened, might have been a small herd of zombies moving through the city. Might have been something else. Didn't hang around long enough to find out. And two, two-and-a-half years ago, up near the Peak District, met a Walker who claimed there were zombies still alive up in the hills. Don't know how. Far as I can make out they need food, and the more zombies they made, the more food they denied themselves." He ripped a rabbit leg off and took a bite. "So," he said through a mouthful, "stay away from the Peak District. Good advice. I'm full of it." He nodded at the rabbit and Jack smiled, pulling off the other hind leg and blowing on it to cool it down. It smelled wonderful. He bit, and the taste of cooked meat and hot fat, flooded his mouth.

Chewing, Jack asked, "So what about the other things? Those were-creatures?" He thought of his friend Lucy the buzzard. Sometimes he dreamed about her. The idea that she was now one of those raging wraiths was almost unbearable.

"That was something different. Not many of them left, but they are still around. I've seen a few from a distance, although around full moon I'm usually shut away somewhere."

"Us too," Jack said, remembering those long days in the church, doors locked, fires and candles unlit, existing in silence and alone. Closed in with the others was when he'd felt loneliest.

"They're worse than the zombies. Always were, 'cos they're human too. They can plan and scheme. And they've changed over time, become more animal even when they're not changed. You'll know them if you see them. The way they move, way they look at you. Like prey. You can see it in their eyes. Haven't been up close to one for years, but I heard their eyes don't change back so much anymore. So a bird thing will keep a bird's eyes, even when it's back to human."

"We haven't seen anything like that," Jack said.

"Then you've been lucky." Cass chewed some more. "Other things, too."

"What other things?" Jack tried to imagine what could be worse. He couldn't.

"Packs of wild dogs. They've reverted to wolf status, mostly, and they'll rarely number more than a dozen or so in each pack. But they're vicious, and they don't mind what they eat. Wild boar. Real animals, not those were-things, but some are just as dangerous." He chewed thoughtfully. "And echoes of other things. I'm sure I've seen... animals." He threw a bone into the fire, sniffed, and stared at Jack. "You believe animals can be ghosts? Have souls?"

Jack shrugged. "I've never thought about it. I'm not sure there *are* ghosts, really."

Cass stroked his beard with his greasy fingertips.

"I mean, the echoes are *something*." Jack said. "But ghosts?"

"That's exactly what they are," Cass said quietly. "Don't ever doubt it. Your own echoes won't thank you if you do. Start thinking they're projected by you—your guilt, your grief—and you'll not pay them the attention they crave." He sighed heavily. "So, the animals. I've seen echoes of bears, deer, other things. Maybe even wolves. From years or centuries ago, I guess."

"Why are they coming back?"

Cass did not answer the question. He was staring into the fire. "I used to believe we were God's children. Animals didn't have souls. Now, I think we're all hollow, alive or dead. All of us. Just hollow and waiting to be filled with pain."

Without another word Cass lay down on his side facing away from Jack, and a few moments later Jack heard long, gentle breathing.

He looked around at the woodland they had camped in for the night. It was not yet fully dark—the sky up through the canopy was still light, and he could see the spaces between the trees—but the fire made the surroundings seem darker than they were. Perhaps like the echoes it was just another trick of the light.

"Mum?" he breathed. "Mandy?" No one answered. Cass shifted but said nothing. Maybe he'd heard, but it didn't matter.

Jack ate some more rabbit, then pulled the carcass from the spit and buried it. He didn't want the smell drawing in any night animals; dogs, boar, were-things. He suddenly missed the solidity of old walls and the coolness of that place built for worship by God's children. Jack didn't believe in God, but he did believe in the safety he'd left behind.

He sat closer to Cass as the night drew in.

Shifting of Veils

❖

He's in the garden of that strange house they had found, the house where his mother will die. The amazingly colourful, lush, fake plants and grass and fruit trees hang heavy, and all those false plastic fruits are dripping blood. But it's normal. It's accepted. As is his father, skin shining with a plastic sheen, as he chops at his mother's legs with an axe. She seems to not care. She smiles at Jack as he pushes the garden gate open, waving him over even as her left leg cracks into shards and splinters of fibreglass. *Everything you know is wrong*, his mother says, and he feels a lump in his throat, because he has forgotten the sound of her voice. He sobs, and the sound is rich and more real than anything here.

Mandy is there too, his older sister with whom he'd fought and argued, but whom he loved. She is sitting in a rocking chair across the other side of the garden, tipping gently back and forth as she tries to replace her eyes. In her hands are plastic eyeballs, and they seem to blink as she pushes them against her round, dry sockets. In her lap are her real eyes. They're bloody and messy, the strings of optic nerves splayed across her knees, and in this faux place they look distasteful and crass. *Name your fears*, Mandy says, *and when you can't do that anymore, they've got the better of you.*

Jack sobs again—his crying is louder and more rounded than anything he's seeing or experiencing here, and seems to originate elsewhere—because he has forgotten Mandy as well. Her true voice, the way she squints when she's angry. Being suddenly reminded again, the loss feels greater than ever.

His father throws the axe into the bushes and turns away from Jack. He walks quickly across the garden and through the fence, which crumbles easily before him. He does not once look back, and Jack reaches for him, begging him to turn, speak, do anything but leave him here.

Jack opens his mouth to shout, but the voice he hears is not his own.

"Can't stop, can't stop them... they contort... Rose, I can't stop them and..."

Jack snapped awake in the darkness and for a few moments, disorientated, he was consumed by the most terrible panic. *Where's the church, who took the roof, where's everyone gone?* But then he remembered where he was and who he was with, and Cass cried out again.

"I can't hold them back, *I'm trying but I can't!*" He was shouting, and in the dark his voice seemed so much louder.

"Cass!" Jack hissed. He threw his thin blanket aside and crawled across to the man, yelping as his hand brushed across still-hot embers from the dead fire. "Cass, you're dreaming, wake up!"

"We're not dreaming!" Cass shouted. "Rose, turn away and don't look!"

Jack looked around, though the night was heavy and thick beneath the trees. If they were being watched, he could not tell. He reached Cass, shook him, grabbing his arm and holding tight as he shoved him back and forth.

"Cass! Don't make so much noise."

Cass coughed and panted, groaning a few times as he pulled away from Jack and sat up. Jack could see his eyes glittering with borrowed moonlight, and could just make out his shape against the background. He was breathing heavily.

"Cass? Are you awake?"

"Yeah."

"You're sure? You're not going to shout again?"

For a moment Cass didn't speak. Jack sensed him freezing, tensing, and he prepared for the man to shout once more, terrified at what those cries might attract. But instead, Cass started to cry.

Jack had heard a lot of crying back at the church. Usually it was Bob, sobbing himself to sleep and always alone, because none of them really knew how to reach him. And sometimes he thought he'd heard Old Man crying quietly in Jean's arms after having sex in the church's confined kitchen.

But it had never been like this. Never so close that he could smell Cass's breath as he cried, and never so intense and wretched. Maybe he was trying to hold back the sobs, but that only made his tears flow harder. It was horrible, shocking, and Jack could only do what instinct told him to do. He crawled forward and threw his arms around the man.

Cass held on tight, burying his face against Jack's neck. More tears. His fists clenched in Jack's jacket, pulling him close.

"Don't worry," Jack said, "Shh, shh," and he felt vaguely ridiculous trying to comfort someone at the end of the world. He was the kid, wasn't he? He was the weak one who'd spent four years hidden away in a church. The tears should all have been his.

"Her name ... Rose," Cass said. "My little girl. My little Rose."

"Okay," Jack said.

Cass said no more, and that was fine. Jack wasn't sure he wanted to hear. Instead, the man and the boy held on for a while longer, sharing warmth and comfort in a cool darkness that might have been hiding anything.

A few minutes later Cass pulled away and stood up. He looked around. Sniffed at the air. "Dawn soon," he said. "It's going to rain today. Did you bring anything waterproof?"

"Yeah," Jack said, although he honestly couldn't remember.

Darkness had been retreating without Jack realising, and he saw Cass nod as he stretched and looked around again. "We're okay here for a while," he said. "Til full light."

"Then what?" Jack asked.

Cass had his back to him. He was shrugging off his jacket, scratching himself beneath his shirt. "I need a piss," he said. He walked off into the bushes, and Jack was left on his own with the remains of his own strange dream and Cass's tears drying against his neck.

❖

"I'll help you find your father," Cass said. He knelt by his rucksack and started rooting inside, tugging out a light waterproof jacket and a sweatshirt.

"You will?"

Cass nodded, then pulled the sweatshirt over his head. He slipped the jacket on and zipped it up.

"I thought you had somewhere to go?" Jack asked.

"No." He stared at Jack. "Not me. I'm walking with nowhere in mind. Every Walker I've met is the same, now. A long time's passed, and we've all reached wherever it was we were going. I found nothing there, so I..." He rubbed his eyes, sighed. "I keep on walking. But not everyone has to be alone, even now. And if there's even a chance of you finding him again... Well, it'll be nice."

"*Is* there a chance?"

"Maybe. I remember roughly where I met him. And it wasn't so long ago."

"You said other Walkers knew about him."

"Yeah. But it's a big country, Jack, and it's got even bigger since the end. The world's got wider."

"Thank you," Jack said. He thought he should say something more. Something about what had happened that night, the dreams, the screaming, and whoever Rose was or had been. But for some reason it was Jack's dream that came to mind and confused anything he might have said. His own dream, with his parents and sister in that strange garden, and those false plants that had been so laden with blood. Some of them had been roses.

"We'd best get moving," Cass said. He seemed different. His voice was somehow lighter, as if yesterday he'd been guarding against being too familiar with Jack. Perhaps in darkness and on the other side of dreams, they'd both made a friend.

It turned into another glorious, sunny day. Around midmorning they approached a tiny hamlet of four houses, holding back for some time to check for movement. There were dozens of birds flitting around the buildings, into and out of gardens, and through broken windows, and Cass said that birds were pretty good indicators of whether anything was amiss. These seemed carefree and chirpy.

"Might be food down there," he said.

"After so long?"

"Some tinned stuff will be all right for another year or two."

Jack didn't want to ask what would happen after that. Staying in one place, farming, was a good way to eat relatively well, and he'd discovered that at the church. He guessed that being a Walker was something else entirely, and he would have to learn about that, too.

They waited for another half an hour, watching. There was an economy to Cass's movements, and now he sat still and silent observing the houses. Jack guessed that a knowledgeable Walker never wasted energy unnecessarily.

When he finally deemed it safe, they went down towards the buildings. One of the houses seemed to have been completely ransacked, with windows and doors smashed open and furniture strewn across the overgrown gardens and the narrow lane in front. But the others seemed relatively intact. Cass chose a house close to the lane in case they had to make a rapid escape.

"What if someone's there?" Jack asked, and Cass looked at him wide-eyed.

"There's no one there," he said. "There's no one anywhere. Have you any idea how few people there are left?"

"Well..." Jack said.

"Later. We'll talk about it later. Right now just stick close to me." Cass pulled a big carving knife from an outside pocket of his rucksack and moved towards the house.

They paused briefly outside the closed front door. Jack bit back a smile. Old habits died hard, and he almost expected Cass to lift a fist and knock. But the man tried the handle, then wedged the knife in between the door and frame. A few tugs and wood splintered, metal whined as the locking mechanism was wrenched outwards, and he nudged the door with his knee.

It opened with a creak. Birds chirruped nearby. Cass paused, head on one side, then glanced back at Jack.

"Bodies," he whispered, then he entered the house.

The first thing Jack noticed was the smell. It was familiar—they'd ventured out from the church over the years, exploring abandoned farmhouses and country homes, and some that had not been abandoned—and he knew that this was an old smell, musty and dry, the scent of death gone by and time moved on. He hoped that the bodies were hidden away upstairs, but saw them as soon as they entered the living area. The skeletons of two adults and a child sat huddled at one end of the sofa, clothed now only in denim, cotton, and scraps of skin and hair. They were hugging. Jack recognised suicide, because he had seen others. He only hoped that they had found peace.

Cass barely spared the family a glance as he passed through the room and entered the kitchen. In a large walk-in larder they found a decent supply of tinned food, labels faded though mostly still attached. They selected something for lunch, then left the way they'd entered. Jack could not help looking at the smaller skeleton, wondering how old he or she had been, how scared. Yet he was jealous of its parents' embrace. Their hands were locked around the child, and however they had died, at least they had been together.

He breathed deeply and looked around, wondering whether sadness or grief would call his own family's echoes to him. But the air around him was still, his memories quiet. Perhaps they would choose their own time.

Outside, Jack closed the door behind him and pulled several times, trying to get the latch to work. Cass was staring at him. The man shook his head and walked away, and Jack hid his annoyance.

They left the hamlet and sat under a copse of trees on a small hill to eat. Chopped tomatoes with garlic, baked beans, and then a tin of peaches each. The peaches were tasteless, the syrup harsh and bitter instead of sweet. But Cass said they were still edible.

"Who was Rose?" Jack asked at last. The name had felt like a weight between them since dawn.

"My daughter," Cass said. "But she's dead now, so you don't need to know anymore. Come on. We can make ten miles today if we walk hard." He glanced at Jack's leg and the stick Old Man had fashioned for him, but said nothing.

They kept to minor roads for a while, sometimes pushing through the clasping branches of hedges that had bulged outward to fill the untended routes. They crossed a stone bridge over the river and passed a pub that stood next to it, terraced decking leading down to the river now home to spreads of dried mud from flooding that previous winter. The pub had burned. Its sign still hung on an archway leading into the car park, and it showed a military officer and a young woman. Jack wondered at the story behind the sign and realised that he would never know. When he used to ask his mum obscure questions she'd say, *Come on and we can find out together!* Then she'd usher her into the small office in their home and urge him to sit beside her on the chair while she accessed the internet.

He could barely remember the sense of her sitting beside him. He tried, concentrating hard as they passed a road junction and found themselves on a dual carriageway. He could remember his mother's laugh but not her voice. The way she stretched before standing from the sofa, but not how she would greet him in the mornings when he woke up. Did she come into his room, or wait until he went downstairs? Did she make his breakfast, or was that usually his father? So much intimate detail had slipped away without him even realising. He'd thought that he was keeping the memory of his mother and sister close, but in truth he had been existing from day to day while they slipped farther and farther behind. He'd let them go without even realising.

His dad, too. But his father was far from lost.

"We'll go north a little from here," Cass said, standing in the middle of the road and looking that way. "The going's easier, and to the east there's a big town we need to . . . " He drifted off when he glanced at Jack, looked at his feet.

"What?" Jack asked. But he could feel them with him again, his mother and sister. Behind him, always behind, and when he looked back he saw those heart-wrenching expressions of confusion and loss on their nebulous faces. "I remember you," he said, loud, wanting Cass to hear. But the echoes he carried with him did not react. He turned back to Cass, his living friend, and asked, "What do I do? How can I bring them closer?" Tears blurred his vision, but they made nothing clearer.

"I'll walk ahead," Cass said softly. "It's a private thing, Jack. And in truth I can hardly see them."

❖

"Why do you keep walking? I mean, if you reached where you were going and . . . "

"Why would I want to sit still?"

"I did."

"Did that make you happy?"

Jack didn't answer that, and his silence was enough. They were walking across a huge, rolling field of long grasses, and here and there were swathes where it had been chewed close to the ground. Cass pointed out white shapes in the distance, close to the wild hedge that separated this field from the next. Sheep, going about their daily routines seemingly without a care.

"Old Man called you a mythical figure."

"Huh?"

"Not just you. Walkers. He said that it was a new world, and that Walkers were the ones who'd adapted, survived and moved on. He said you were like wandering priests, or storytellers spreading their own word."

"Maybe some," Cass said. "But not me. And how can Old Man pretend to know anything other than those church walls?"

Shifting of Veils

"Then what *about* you?" Jack asked.

They passed a dead sheep, months old. It had been torn up and spread about. Jack saw a brief hazing of air close by, and remembered what Cass had said about seeing a bear, other things. The question of whether animals had souls had rarely bothered him, and it still did not now. He'd never been close to any idea of God, and how could a god have allowed all this?

"I started moving as soon as the zombies came," Cass said, surprising Jack with his sudden change of tone. He almost sounded eager to talk. "I was separated from my wife, Lou. Had been for a couple of years. She lived in a little place in Devon, Ottery St Mary, with our daughter Rose. I lived a few miles away and saw Rose almost every day—picked her up from school, had dinner with her and Lou, and most weekends she stayed at my place for at least one night. We had a good relationship, all of us. Lou and I . . . I was wondering what might happen.

"Then they came. I was working down in Exeter, and that night when it all began, I'd been with a woman I'd known for a little while. A strange thing. You ever hear the phrase fuck buddies?"

Jack shook his head. He'd had no one to speak to about sex, no peers, no parents. His innocence troubled him, but he could never tell Cass that.

"She was a nice girl, worked at the university. Had her clit pierced. Anyway, if I hadn't been walking back from her place at two in the morning, I'd never have survived. It hit hard and quick, the chaos. Shouts, then screaming, fires and sirens, fighting and people on the streets. Crowds running. People dying, walking again, eating. And my first and only thought was Rose and Lou.

"That's when I started moving. I stole a car I found idling in the street and drove as fast as I could to Ottery. The house was locked up safe, and I found them inside. But . . . it spread so quickly. Or maybe it hit everywhere at once. They took Lou while she was waiting out by the car, and from then on it was just me and Rose."

He fell silent, and although Jack knew that was nowhere near the end of the story, he didn't prompt Cass for more. He knew the end; he'd heard it in Cass's nightmares.

They reached the edge of the field, the silence between them growing heavier. There was a wide gateway that had not been overgrown, and in the road beyond a tangle of burned vehicles bore testament to another forgotten story of grief and pain. They eased past the wrecks and started walking along the middle of the road, treading on soft grasses and weeds growing up through the tarmac.

"After Rose died I continued moving, walking to forget," Cass said suddenly. "Not to find something, but to lose it."

"And did you?" Jack asked.

"I haven't stayed still long enough to find out."

"And now they're..." Jack started saying, but he caught a glimmer of tears on Cass's cheek, and the older man's face was creased and tensed. *Now they're walking with you,* Jack was going to say. He wondered whether Cass was pleased that his dead family had returned to him.

And thinking of the visions of his own startled, terrified mother and sister, he wondered just what Cass saw.

❖

Within two days, the church seemed a lifetime away.

Their journey revealed so many new sights, sounds and experiences that those years spent at the church faded in Jack's memory, taking on hues vaguer even than his dead family. Memory seemed to play tricks with time. There was his life as a child, the ruin that had befallen the world, and then the now, his journey with Cass to try to salvage something from whatever remained. That long time spent with Old Man and the others was a mere fragment, condensed in his memory to little more than a short series of almost identical days. And that was mainly what they had been. Their survival at the church had been little more than a living death.

Now, Jack was starting to feel alive once more. Destiny, fate, both might still be beyond his grasp. But at least he was doing something than just moving. He was seeking, both his lost father who might yet live, and the truth of his dead mother and sister. By the end of this part of his future, there was no guarantee he'd find anyone alive. But he vowed that he would do everything he could to understand the dead.

He judged progress by time, not distance. Two days after leaving the church Cass took them across a motorway bridge. The road below them was jammed in one direction with cars, vans, coaches and lorries parked bumper to bumper. The other direction was all but clear of vehicles; two police cars and a single, sad pushbike were all he could see. Towards the end, Cass said, they'd tried to evacuate the cities. From the bridge they could see at least a mile in each direction, and the band of colour was strangely beautiful. If they moved or looked closer, the beauty would be replaced by yet more horror. But he would take what he could get.

"That's not what I wanted to show you," Cass said. "Come on. This way. Not far now."

"You've been here before?"

"I've been walking for four years. I've seen a lot." He led Jack across the bridge and down a slip-road into an industrial estate. There were a few vehicles here too, some with doors still open where their occupants had fled. *What* they'd fled, Jack could guess. He could also surmise that they didn't get very far.

They found a stack of corpses against the low wall of a warehouse car park. There were hundreds of people there, maybe more. A bulldozer sat yellow and rusting, its scoop still lowered into the scars it had scratched into the concrete surface, the metal scoop filled with the dead. They didn't go closer to investigate. The remains were mostly skeletons now, staring starkly from shredded clothing and with knotted hair still shifting in the gentle breeze. Countless stories that would remain forever untold.

"Just around here," Cass said. "I'll warn you, it's a bit . . . weird."

Jack followed Cass around the corner of a large manufacturing unit, and he could only gasp at what he saw.

He'd never been this close to a Jumbo jet. He'd flown to France with his family when he was eight, but he could hardly remember that, and the aircraft had been much smaller. Confronted with the nose section of the jet now came as quite a shock—its sheer size, its incongruousness. Behind the tall front section was a long path of destruction where it had come down, a swathe of ruined and burned-out buildings, aircraft parts, scattered vehicles, and a wide wound in the land that had sprouted grass and shrubs in the years since the crash. One broken wing was visible leaning against the remains of an office building in the distance. Further away, several large industrial units had burned to the ground. A huge engine sat on its own in a wide, empty car park. A row of seats was upended against a soft-top sports car. Jack could see something in the seats, but he didn't look too closely.

"Wow," he said.

"Yeah," Cass agreed. "When I found it I climbed inside. The front third of the plane's intact, I thought there might be food or other useful stuff."

"Did you find anything?"

"Not much. Bodies. But not enough."

"Not enough?"

"Lots of the seatbelts had been bitten through. They must have crashed, died, then come back."

Jack could barely comprehend the sight. He turned his back on it and looked across a road at a small woodland instead, watching birds flitter from branch to branch. Nature always made sense, even if it was slowly wiping out everything humankind had been. Perhaps that was the greatest sense of all.

He suddenly remembered something his mother had said. *They say we're destroying the Earth, but really we're just destroying ourselves.* He heard her voice, rich as sunlight, and saw the way she tilted her head when she spoke, the look in her eyes, the invitation to his father to dare argue with her, and it was the first time in a long while a memory of his mother had been so clear.

Jack smiled. Something whispered over his shoulder, and it was not Cass.

A day later they came to a large road junction with traffic lights, a flyover, and slip-roads. A body dangled from every streetlamp along the roads. Jack stopped counting after he reached fifty. They were not recent—many had fallen away as they decayed, flesh rotting, bones breaking—and there was no way of telling whether they'd been dead or undead when they were strung up.

That same afternoon they passed a village with a deep defensive trench dug around its perimeter. There were piles of furniture at regular intervals along the trench, vehicles pushed onto their sides, and stacks of building materials, all serving as lookout posts and firing stations. Outside the village lay piles of dead on roads and heaped against wildly overgrown hedgerows. The battle was long since over.

"Do you think...?" Jack began, but Cass shook his head.

"No. Look." He pointed at one stretch of trench that crossed a field, and Jack could see the familiar, depressing tangle of bones and rotting clothing in a pile across the trench. "It's too quiet, anyway," Cass said. "If there was still someone there they'd be looking. They'd have seen us by now."

"Maybe they're hiding," Jack suggested.

They waited for a while, but just before dusk a noise rose from the village, an ululating song like tone-deaf children singing an unknown rhyme. The hairs rose on Jack's neck and arms. His stomach was filled with ice.

"Let's move on," Cass said quietly, and Jack had to run to catch up.

That night they slept in an old caravan parked by the side of a road. There was no car attached, and Cass said it had probably been abandoned at the start of the ruin. Cass fell asleep straight away, sobbing softly as the air shifted and pulsed around his head. Jack lay facing away from the older man, but that night his own echoes stayed away.

The following morning, someone knocked at the caravan door.

❖

"I live here," the woman said from the open doorwayShe had the darkest eyes Jack had ever seen, huge pupils, soft brown irises, and he found himself falling into them, swimming, frantically treading water as she stepped up into the caravan. She pointed at things. "This...and this...and this, all mine."

"Sorry," Jack said. "We didn't touch anything, we're only—"

"Don't talk to her." Cass was on his feet, knife in his hand. The woman glanced at him and the knife, then immediately dismissed him and focussed on Jack again. Her eyes were dreamy. She wore a loose shirt and shapeless jeans, but Jack could see from the way she held herself that she was lithe and athletic. Not thin from hunger, and weak. Strong.

Well-fed.

"Jack, we're leaving," Cass said.

"Oh, I don't mind visitors," the woman said. She was still standing in the open doorway, her stance unthreatening, yet blocking their exit nonetheless.

"No, that's fine." Cass held the knife down by his side, hesitant. He glanced at Jack, who raised an eyebrow. "We have places to go," Cass said.

"Really?" the woman asked. She wore a gentle smile that Jack could not imagine her without. Maybe it was mocking, or maybe it was simply contentment.

"You really live here?" he asked.

"Yes," she said. "And why not? It's comfortable. My body heat warms it quickly enough." . *Taller than she looks*, Jack thought, *wider*. She exuded something he hadn't known since Lucy, back on the grounded ferry. He felt a hot flush of blood, a dizziness of lust, animal magnetism. The woman's smile widened a little more.

"We don't want trouble," Cass said.

"Who does?" she said. "There's been plenty of that." But still she didn't move. She was looking Jack up and down, a frank appraisal that seemed to take in every part of him. He knew he had an erection, but trying to hide it would be so obvious. His innocence felt branded on his face, an unmistakeable part of him.

The woman's gaze invited so much. He smelled her musk, and it was nothing human. He wasn't sure if she was breathing quickly, or whether her nostrils were flaring as she took in deep breaths of his scent. He was confused, scared, lustful. Suddenly Jack didn't like what was happening to him, and when he glanced to Cass he wasn't sure what that man was feeling. A Walker, he knew far more of what was out here.

Jack could see Cass's hand clasped tight around the knife, his knuckles white.

"We do have to go," Jack said. "I'm looking for my father."

The woman did not reply.

"Move aside," Cass said.

She was staring at Jack. She was beautiful and dreadful.

"Fox?" Jack asked. "Weasel? Something strong and vicious, anyway."

Cass drew in a sharp breath. The woman smiled.

"I knew a girl who became buzzard. She was my friend, and she was changing. It frightened her. She ran away because she didn't want to hurt me, but I followed her. Then she changed and saved my life. You're not all monsters."

"There's nothing monstrous about us at all," the woman said. "It's really rather beautiful."

"But you're still planning to eat us," Cass said. It should have sounded ridiculous, here in this old caravan in which families had holidayed, kids watching TV or playing board games while adults drank wine and fell asleep on uncomfortable furniture. But the words almost made Jack pass out with terror.

"Oh, no," she said. "Only the boy."

Cass moved forward, knife raised, but Jack quickly stepped between him and the woman. One hand flat against Cass's chest, he could smell the woman's breath and feel the heat radiating from her body. He stood so close that some of her unkempt hair touched his cheek. Her eyes went wider, nostrils flaring.

"Mmm," she said, "I know that smell."

"What?"

"Your scent. I've smelled it before. Some scents are familial, you know."

"She's fucking with us," Cass said, pushing against Jack's hand. "You have no idea, Jack!"

"I know I don't want anyone to die here," Jack said, without turning. He couldn't look away from her. Perhaps he was hypnotised, like a rodent before a snake, but he thought not. It was more like fascination.

"That madman's your father?" she laughed softly.

"You've seen him?" And suddenly Jack was afraid that she'd done more than seen him. Perhaps it was more than the smell of him that would seem familiar, and that's why she wanted to eat him. Perhaps it was the taste, as well.

"You were human once," Cass said. He eased back from Jack, lowered the knife. "So help the boy."

"I could keep you here," she said.

"I'm sure you prefer the hunt," Cass said.

The woman laughed softly, and for the first time she seemed almost human. She even brushed one hand through her hair, a delicate gesture that belied the brutality alive in her eyes.

"Ten days ago," she said. "Fifteen miles east, closer to the city. But not *too* close." She faked a shiver of fear, still smiling.

"Thanks," Jack said. For the first time the woman's smile slipped along with her complete control of the moment. Was that a spark of memory Jack saw? An instant of doubt? He quickly swallowed down his surprise and pushed gently past her, moving her arm aside, marvelling at the heat pulsing

Shifting of Veils

beneath her skin. She felt like she was on fire. She turned, forcing him to pass her face to face. He felt his erection pressing against the tops of her thighs, but when he looked up she had pushed her face in close, sniffing, inhaling his scent. He saw something pass across her eyes—a milky film, a second, translucent eyelid—and he stumbled down the caravan steps, barely remaining on his feet as they met the ground.

Cass was behind him, knife still clasped down by his side.

"Walk," Cass said.

"I left my pack—"

"Fucking *walk*!" He shoved Jack in the back, pushing him onward, and they walked along the road.

Jack looked back at the woman watching from the caravan doorway. *She has my scent*, he thought, and he wondered what the next full moon might bring. But this far away she was simply a human form in shapeless clothing. She could have been anyone.

❖

"Do you think she was telling the truth?"

"I don't care," Cass said.

"Why?"

"Just not right now. Come on. We're still too close."

"We've been walking for three hours. My leg hurts. I need a break, a drink."

"Don't you have *any idea* what she was?" the man asked. He was still holding the knife, and he'd barely slowed their pace since leaving the caravan.

"No," Jack said. "But she let us go."

Cass stopped walking. They were closing on a larger main road again, and they'd been passing more and more abandoned vehicles. Tyres were flat, bodywork starting to rust, and many of the windows were obscured with growth on the inside—algae, or moss, or something else fed by whatever rotted in the vehicles' seats. Sometimes the doors were open, showing what was or wasn't inside.

Whenever he wondered at all those lost stories, he tried to remember his sister's voice, a mannerism, an aspect of her personality. He did his best to recall the way his mother walked, or spoke, or random things she'd said that should have stayed with him forever. He'd kidded himself that he was starting to remember; their confused, scared faces—in his mind's eye, or perhaps in the air beside or behind him—said otherwise.

"We're getting closer to the city," Cass said. "I've never been further east than here." He tilted his head, listening. There was a soft breeze rustling leaves among the roadside hedgerows, and birdsong, but that was all.

"I can't stop if he might be ahead," Jack said.

"It's dangerous," Cass said. "The wraiths. And other things in the city, too, probably. I've heard of survivors banding together, protecting their communities."

"I can't stop," Jack insisted.

Cass nodded. "At least let's have a rest," he said. He clambered up onto a BMW's roof. As he looked around Jack caught his breath, allowing himself to feel out the pains coming from his leg. He'd been ignoring them for some time now, scared that to take notice would allow the pain to slow him, perhaps stop him from walking altogether. It felt like bad cramp. He stretched his calf and winced as the muscle rebelled. But the stick Old Man had fashioned for him was strong, and it took his weight. Even if he had to hop he'd never stop moving forward.

Charley horse, his mother says, *that's what the Americans call it.* She's sitting on his bed, pressing his foot back and gently rubbing his calf muscle. Her hair is awry from sleep, and the rest of the house is quiet. Jack can hear his dad snoring. His mother hasn't turned the light on, coming to see him in the darkness when she heard him crying out. *It's just your muscles twitching and knotting, that's all. Stretch it out. It'll be fine. Okay, my little Jackie? Mummy's here.* She sits with him for a while longer, and when he next wakes up it's dawn and his mother has returned to her bed. He feels an instant of loss. But his cramps are gone.

"Mum," Jack gasped, shocked at the clarity of the memory.

"Okay down there?" Cass asked.

"Yeah." Jack looked around. And for just a moment, so fleeting that it might only have been wishful thinking, he thought he caught a glimpse of his mother's fading face over his shoulder. Not quite smiling, but no longer lost, scared, confused. In his search for his father, perhaps he was finding the rest of his family as well.

"There's somewhere up there we can rest for a bit. And I'll catch some food." Cass jumped down beside Jack. "Sure you're okay?"

Jack nodded. He thought about saying something about the unbidden memory, the sight of his mother beside him, but it felt so personal.

"Have you seen them again?"

Jack nodded. A lump rose in his throat and tears burned behind his eyes.

"Come on." Cass took his hand. It was such an intimate, supportive gesture, and although it surprised Jack he did not pull away. It was nothing strange. Just one person supporting another.

They crossed a ditch and an overgrown field together, and when they reached the old hay barn, though they no longer held hands, Jack felt closer to Cass than he had to anyone since losing his family.

He was a Walker, he understood, and more than anything, he had made himself ready and willing to help.

The barn must have been dilapidated before the ruin had set in, and since then it had only degenerated more. Hay bales stacked in there by the farmer had long-since rotted away to almost nothing, and now it was taken mostly with brambles and nettles. An old tractor sat in one corner, rusting. Cass moved out of the sun and stood by an overturned water trough.

"Okay then. Food. I'll catch something to eat, you get a fire going."

"You can just go out and catch something any time you're hungry?"

"Lots of practice," Cass said. He pulled a handful of nets, metal pegs, and a catapult from his rucksack.

"Or maybe you're really a were-fox," Jack said. Cass raised an eyebrow, and Jack laughed to show he was joking.

He took several minutes to ignite a fire, careful first to shift away any clumps of hay still hidden beneath the brambles. It smoked for a while—he'd used some rotten timber piled beside the tractor for kindling, and it was damper than he'd thought—but then settled. By the time Cass returned with a rabbit, Jack had piled several crumbling bricks around the flames to concentrate the heat.

As he gutted and skinned the still-warm animal, Cass began to talk.

"I've been trying to remember her," he whispered. "My daughter. My Rose. Sometimes I think I'm almost there, and I look to see if she's not so frightened. But it never quite works. She's like . . . a memory just out of reach. My life with her, before all this, feels like a dream. You ever had a dream that carries forward into real life? Something you're not aware is a dream as soon as you wake up, or which you forget, but then later it intrudes, and you can't quite figure out how real it is?"

"Yeah," Jack said, though he could not think of anything specific. Maybe because a lot of the past few years had felt like a nightmare.

"That's how Rose feels to me. Some days, I wonder if I ever had a daughter at all. That maybe before all this I was on my own, not with an ex-wife and a beautiful little girl who I saw every weekend and twice in the week." He smiled sadly. "It's ironic that I remember my ex in pretty much every detail."

"Is she . . . ?" Jack asked.

Cass shook his head, knowing what he meant. "After Rose first appeared, I expected Lou. But she never came."

"Then maybe she's still alive?"

Cass's face dropped. He looked down at the animal he was still butchering, at the blood dripping between his feet.

"Cass?" Jack asked, cautiously. *I don't know him at all. Who he is, what he's done.*

"I didn't get there in time," he said. "Lou had been... they'd really torn her up. I wonder why I haven't seen her echo, and I think it's something about love. She no longer..." His tears were silent, falling like weightless diamonds. "Rose had only been bitten."

For a long time Cass was silent, attending to the animal. Jack did not prompt him. If he chose not to continue his story, that was just fine. Jack was pretty sure he knew how it ended.

"I think being remembered is what they want," Jack said. "Or need. I'm not sure the dead can want anything. My sister and my mother." Cass looked up, and Jack continued. "I think I'm getting there, slowly. Today I saw my mother almost smile." He sobbed, one wretched gasp that produced no tears but rang through his senses. He fisted his hands, then held them out open to the fire. It was still only afternoon, and the sun shone, but it was good to feel the heat on his palms.

"My mother used to say there was a veil between this world and whatever else there is," Cass said. "And that some people can lift it to look beyond. Maybe the confusion we see... Rose's face, her fear... is because of this shifted veil. We understand that it's moved, but maybe the dead don't."

"Remembering them gives them peace," Jack said.

"Yeah. Remembering them brings the veil down again."

"I'm doing my best," Jack said.

"Me too." But Cass's frown remained.

They ate the rabbit. Something about that time felt good, and so they sat there for a while afterwards, kicking out the fire and looking over the vast, silent landscape. There was something very wild about the view, and very tranquil.

It was not silent for long. Around mid-afternoon the breeze changed direction and brought with it a high, shifting sound.

Many voices, calling out together. Crying. Screaming.
The echoes of Peterborough were welcoming them in.

◈

"It's stupidly dangerous."
"I know. But I've got to go."
Silence for a while. Then, "I'll go with you."
"Thank you," Jack said.
Cass nodded. They walked together.
In the distance, the weight of the city seemed to clasp onto the sky.

◈

"How are we going to find him?" Jack asked. It was a very obvious question, but one that had until now only played at the fringes of his mind. The specifics of his search hadn't seemed to matter because in truth it was so wide. But now, approaching the city where his father might be, the scope of his quest seemed huge.

"Keep looking," Cass said. "Maybe ask any Walkers we come across, and anyone else."

"Anyone else? The only person we've seen in the past two days was that woman. Whatever she was."

"There are others. They're around. They just hide." Cass smiled at Jack. "You should remember that from the church."

Jack did. Several times he had hidden up in the bell tower and watched a person or a small group passing along the road in the distance. Sometimes they'd paused and looked up the hillside towards the church, but mostly they simply walked by, slow and aimless. The curious and perceptive sometimes came closer, and then they were welcomed. But watching people passing them by was when Jack had realised that they were hiding.

He and Cass moved across the countryside instead of

following roads; this close to the city Cass said that was safest. At around four p.m. they heard a terrible noise, and watched as a twisting, contorting mass of wraiths moved along a vehicle-strewn main road. Jack shivered with fear, closed his eyes, and then opened them again when he felt his lost family beside him.

Between blinks he saw Mandy's familiar, lost expression, and his heart broke for her.

But his mother had changed. Her sadness remained, but now she was looking at Jack. Staring directly at him, as if she could truly see. As she started moving, Jack gasped and reached for her.

"What?" Cass asked. His own echo shimmered beside him, ambiguous, yet the glitter of tears on his cheeks were clear to Jack.

"She's not behind me anymore," Jack whispered. "My mother. She's moving ahead, and—"

"Which way?"

Jack nodded. They were hiding behind a stone wall between two fields, shielding themselves from the distant mass of angry wraiths. His mother stood several yards away by a gate, and—

—she laughs as she climbs the gate, hitching her skirt up and carefully slinging one leg over. His father is already on the other side, and as Jack's mother slips, laughter taking on a note of startled hysteria, he steps forward and catches her. He's laughing too, now. They look at each other, kiss, and for a moment Jack is not there, and his parents are sharing that time purely with each other. Yet he is happy in their happiness.

His mother was looking at him wide-eyed, expectantly. She moved a little further, fading, shimmering.

"I think she wants us to follow," Jack said. He took a deep breath and looked back at Mandy. Still there, still wretchedly lost. But she remained almost solid, even when he reached out his hand. Even when he touched where she should be and felt nothing.

"So let's follow," Cass said.

The howling and screeching wraiths retreated along the road, and Jack took the lead, following his mother's echo down towards the city.

As they walked, something strange began to happen. A sense of peace settled over Jack. The wildness of their surroundings, the threat from once-human creatures, the screeching wraiths, the ebullience of nature in its suffocation of all that humankind had once made of it, these concerns were seen away by the act of following his dead mother. She moved strangely, flitting from place to place like a badly edited movie, yet his mind was flooded with memories of walking with her.

They are in the woods, just the two of them, and she is trying to name the species of trees. *Just because I love everything here doesn't mean I know what it's all called*, she says. *Besides, what's in a name?* To begin with she seems embarrassed that she can only name two tree types, but then she and Jack make up their own names. They laugh together, and the morning seems to go on forever.

He trails her through the supermarket, not wishing to be there. She seems to pore over items forever before placing them in the trolley. Yet the moment he loses sight of her he panics, and it's a few endless, eternal seconds before he sees her familiar shape perusing a display of biscuits.

She walks along a beach...

He follows her around their garden...

His mother strolls along the canal towpath and he is behind her, always trusting her sense of direction, never doubting for a moment that she knows where she is going.

"I see her," Cass said, his voice soft and strained with sorrow.

Jack frowned, because it felt like an intrusion. But then he realised Cass's meaning. He glanced back over his shoulder, catching sight of a shimmer in the air before Cass—his daughter, uncertain and ambiguous.

"It's like she's real," Cass said.

Jack smiled and walked on. Mandy had faded to less than a shimmer beside him, but he was still aware of her echo within

Shifting of Veils

him. And as he followed his mother, he tried to remember his sister as well.

She's talking to him in his room the night she ran away. She's telling him to name the parts of his fears. She's fighting with him, shoving him onto the sofa only half-playfully. Rowing with their parents, Jack watching, she's a fiery young woman. Always a little distant from Jack's life because of their age difference, she is also a friend to him when he needs it. Once, she even tells him—

"I love you, you little squirt of horse piss."

"Horse?"

"Yeah."

"Why not a dog? Or a platypus? Or a bison or a sabre-toothed tiger or—"

"Because a horse has got a big dick and pisses a lot, and you're a squirt of it."

"And you love me."

"Hey, you only get that once."

"Give me a cuddle, Mandy."

"Don't push it, piss-squirt."

They laugh together, and it is one of those moments that becomes timeless and retains its clarity in his memory, always.

Jack smiled and opened himself to more memories, welcoming them in, but at the same time trying not to force them. If he forced them, then his memories of his mother and sister might form as he thought they should be, not as they really were. He believed that was important. He thought perhaps his future might depend on the honesty of his memories.

"I love you, Mum," he whispered. "I love you, Mandy." There was no discernible difference. And yet as he followed his mother across the strange place the world was growing into, more memories came, clearer and more vital than ever before.

✧

The echo led, and they followed.

Jack could not be certain that they were moving closer to his father, but everything he believed told him that they were. And he started to wonder.

Was his father also haunted by his mother and sister? Could an echo be in two places at once? He thought so. He desperately wanted to believe that was the case, because their family had been so filled with love that any other possibility seemed awful. That they might have come to him *instead* of his father chilled him to the core.

The afternoon was drifting towards evening. Several times now Cass had suggested that they pause, rest, wait until morning. But while the memory of his mother led them on, Jack could only follow. He had no idea how strong the link was between them, nor how powerful her echo's drive. Maybe she'd never be able to do this again. He couldn't take that chance.

Around six p.m. they approached the first housing estate on Peterborough's outskirts. They followed his mother across several fields, wading through drainage ditches as her image drifted over them, and when they reached a main road she followed it towards the city. The houses were of a uniform colour, and hauntingly silent. One close to the road had been burned out, soot-smears across the brickwork like mascara running with tears.

The silence did not last. It was Cass who grabbed Jack's arm and squeezed, head to one side as he listened.

"You hear?"

Jack heard. Many voices in the distance, or perhaps one closer by, a wretched, soulful cry that rose and fell with the breeze.

"We'll be safe," Jack said.

Cass was afraid. The Walker didn't mind showing it, and Jack wondered at how much he'd changed just over the last couple of days. Maybe Walking had been his way of trying to escape the reality of things, and now Jack had slowed him down. Made him confront those things, those painful realities, head-on.

Jack looked over Cass's shoulder at the shimmer of his echo.

Shifting of Veils

"Concentrate," he said. "Remember her. Rose. Your little girl. Bring her with you, let her closer, and we'll both be fine." He turned and looked at his mother. She was waiting by a pedestrian pathway leading down from the road, looking back towards them. Jack smiled, but she did not smile back. He wasn't certain she even saw, not in any way that he could understand, and she looked like an image from an old film that had been played again and again. But when he edged forward, she moved again. Somewhere there was an awareness, and he wanted it to continue.

He felt Mandy with him, her presence stronger than ever before.

They walked in between looming hedges, pushing through clutching undergrowth where the path was all but overgrown. More wailing sounds came from close by, and then a series of loud, violent shrieks that were taken up from several different directions.

"Cass," Jack said softly, and then the Walker was beside him. They both took great comfort from being close to someone real.

"You said we'd be all right," Cass said. "I'm trusting you."

"Why?"

The Walker shrugged, as if he didn't really know. It was a surprising sign of weakness, and it scared Jack. He didn't know *anything* for sure.

They saw the first wraiths as they emerged from the mass of shrubbery into a children's play area. The shapes were swarming from between houses a hundred yards away, crossing a fenced-in ball play area, perhaps twenty of them contorting and thrashing as they screamed in torment.

Jack's back tingled and his body-hair bristled, and every instinct told him to turn and run.

His mother's image drew in closer than she had ever been. He felt Mandy just behind him, hand almost on his shoulder, and he sobbed at the sense of protection he suddenly felt. *I'm in their world now, and they're making sure I'm safe.*

Cass was breathing hard beside him.

"I told you we'd be okay," Jack whispered.

And yet though he had no doubts about that, what he saw was still terrifying. The wraiths set swings swinging and a roundabout slowly turning as they rushed towards them. He tried not to look, but to look away was even harder. He wasn't sure what was more dreadful—the danger he knew they presented to him, or the most wretched state of torture they portrayed. *Could have been me*, he thought, and it was a painful idea. *Could be Dad*. And that was even worse.

"Come on," he said, nodding to his mother's echo. "We're following. Come on."

They started walking and the wraiths drew closer, blots on reality. Screams did not quite match the fleeting images of opened mouths he saw. Limbs waved, striking the ground yet hardly making a noise. Voices rose and fell, wavering, songs of pain and torment. Yet Jack felt certain that they could not touch him. He remembered what Cass had told him about what he'd seen wraiths doing to the couple in the pub car park, but still he felt protected.

They crossed the play area, giving the wraiths a wide berth. The shapes flickered back and forth as if in indecision, then stormed away across the grass towards a high fence. They passed through the fence—it swayed, but did not break—and into a copse of trees. Still screaming, the tortured things disappeared from view.

Jack's mother led them on. They followed. Screeches surrounded them. It was a city of the dead, and perhaps they were the only living people here. *And Dad*, Jack thought. *He's here too, he has to be*. Mandy grew stronger, and yet her sadness remained, a stain he could not remove from her nebulous face, however good the memories he conjured. He thought he knew why. She had died a zombie, not a normal person. Perhaps she would carry that final, unbearable echo with her forever.

He wanted to know why his father had entered a city so filled with wraiths.

Looking at his mother inspired memories that he allowed himself to enter. Everything he saw of her was from some other time, glimpses of the past that strengthened the present.

She took them close to the cathedral, approaching a long, straight street. The cathedral stood on a hill, and from far away it looked untouched and unchanged. Perhaps when all these more modern buildings had been subsumed, it would be these old structures, steeped in history, that would survive into the future.

His mother's echo flickered and faded, then drew them away from the main street and into a narrow side-street. She paused outside a pub. It was called the Swan, and Jack had a sudden, intense flash of memory from a year before everything started to change.

His mother and father are drinking wine with their friends in their back garden. Jack is playing with their friends' son, Jeremy. He doesn't like him very much—he's younger than Jack, and spoilt, and he always wants to take control of their game— but it's a warm summer evening, and the adults are relaxed and smiling. Jack overhears a conversation. It's about where his parents met, and while Jeremy explains the convoluted rules of their next game of marbles, Jack listens wide-eyed. He's never imagined his parents not together, and to hear the tale of the first time they met is both scary and fascinating. That there was a time before they knew each other was incomprehensible to Jack.

"I was working at The Swan," his mother says, and there are a few incoherent comments from the others, intermingled with laughter. "Oh come on, it wasn't that bad. Anyway, one evening there was a bit of a punch-up in there, three young lads got thrown out."

"And you were one of the thugs?" the other woman asks, nudging Jack's dad with her foot.

He's not a thug, Jack thinks, *you are!* And he almost says it. But then his mother leans over and grabs his dad's leg, squeezing.

"No, he came to the bar to make sure I was all right. Glasses were flying, and...it was pretty unsettling, actually. And Graham made sure I was safe." She looks at him, and for a moment it is only the two of them in that garden.

Jeremy starts hollering, someone knocks over a wine glass, and the moment is ruined. But Jack always remembered that name: The Swan.

"In there?" Cass asked.

"Yeah," Jack said. "Yeah, if anywhere, my Dad's in there." He felt frozen to the spot. Four years. He hadn't seen his Dad in four years, and during that time the world had wound down, wraiths had risen, everything had changed so much. *Will he forgive me for running away? Will he even ... will he know me ... ?*

Jack looked to his mother's echo for comfort, but a strange expression had stolen over her face once again. For a second Jack panicked, thought that he was losing her. But then he realised it was not confusion and shock that he saw. It was nervousness.

As he reached for the door and pushed it open, he was aware of his mother's and sister's echoes fading from around him, and he felt them drawing him inside.

❖

"Dad," Jack said.

His father was sitting on a stool at the bar. He had a glass of whiskey in front of him, and a bottle stood on the bar's surface a couple of feet away. There wasn't much gone from the bottle, and the glass was still full. *Maybe it's gone bad,* Jack thought. *Or maybe...*

He saw movement behind the bar and tensed. But then he saw his mother and sister, standing there as if they had always belonged. They were even reflected in the big mirror hanging there, as if they were real.

"Dad," Jack said again.

His father's shoulders shook as he started to cry. He still didn't turn around, but he looked up at the echoes of his loved

Shifting of Veils   241

ones, perhaps expecting to see another. His eyes met Jack's in the mirror. *He's older, wilder, more scared, maybe mad, but that is still my dad*, Jack thought, and his vision blurred as tears burned in.

"I looked for you," his dad said. "A long, long time. Years. And I only stopped days, maybe weeks ago. I looked, Jackie, and I did my best." He started crying some more, his words slurred by tears. "I did ... my best, son!"

"I know, Dad."

His father still stared into the mirror. Jack started forward, and he saw his dad's drooped shoulders suddenly tense, heard his crying halt. The whole pub was a held breath.

"I'm not only in the mirror," Jack said. His father turned around.

"Jack."

Jack smiled through his own tears.

"This is your son," Cass said from behind him. "You've found him. He's found you." There was something wrong with his voice, but right then Jack only had eyes for his father.

He moved so close that they could smell each other's breath, and he saw every wrinkle and blemish and feature of his father's face, both those old ones that he recognised again right away, and new ones added more recently. There was a small, vivid scar on one cheek. *I'll ask about that*, Jack thought. He held up his arms.

As his father hugged him—hesitant, gentle, afraid that he would become whatever the rest of their family now was—the screaming began.

Outside, pressing against the windows and pub door, a swarm of wraiths had gathered.

"But..." Jack said, and he sensed for his mother and sister. They were there, and his dad smiled and nodded, acknowledging that he knew them as well.

"Rose..." Cass breathed. Then the Walker turned around and reached for the doors.

"No!" Jack shouted. He leapt across the bar, knocking a table and two chairs aside as he reached for Cass's coat. He grabbed and pulled, tripping over his own feet and hauling Cass down on top of him. The impact drove air from his lungs. Winded, he twisted and looked to his father for help, but he was already reaching down for Jack's shoulders, clasping, tugging as hard as he could.

"Cass!" Jack said. "She's with you, here and now, just remember her back and they'll leave you alone!"

"I try," he said. He stood, pulling away from Jack and backing towards the doors. Something was happening to them, and the wall surrounding them. Solidity was blurring. The wraiths were coming through. "I try but I can't remember, and I don't think she's not come back to be with me. She's haunting me because I couldn't save her. She's haunting me, and it's time to let everything go."

"It *can* be all right!" Jack shouted. "Dad, tell him it can be—"

"Not for me," Cass said. He closed his eyes, and just for a moment Jack caught a glimpse of a face over his shoulder. It was a little girl, and he had never seen anyone or anything looking so sad. It broke his heart, and knowing such fundamental, soul-deep sadness was possible, he would never be the same again.

"No, Cass," he tried to say, but his mouth was dry, and the sound of screaming stole his whisper away.

The wraiths came through. The pub's doors bulged open, but they forced through the wood of the doors as well, and the walls beside them, blurring reality and twisting, spinning, contorting as their screeches reached an awful, jubilant crescendo.

Whatever these wretched things wanted from the living, they snatched it from Cass.

Jack's dad grabbed him and heaved him up and over the bar, falling down behind it with him. Jack scrabbled to stand, but his father held him down.

"No! No, Jackie!"

"But he helped me, he's my friend!"

Shifting of Veils

"You can't." His father spoke softly. Jack knew the truth in it. Before he closed his eyes he saw those strange images of his mother and sister, squatted down beside them as if they were really there.

They were already beginning to fade.

The screaming was louder than Jack would have ever thought possible. Glasses rattled on shelves, bottles vibrated, and somewhere a sheet of glass cracked like a gunshot. Then Cass's own scream, so much more real, so human. It did not last for long. A wet thud, and then the writhing horde retreated back out of the pub, shrieks still echoing along the narrow street beyond.

With a terrible, dawning realisation, Jack realised that somewhere in that eternal cacophony was the tortured voice of the man who had helped him so much.

❖

Outside the city, they paused to look back.

Once, it would have been illuminated by streetlights, car headlamps, and the warm glow from houses, where families huddled against the dark safe in the knowledge that it could not harm them. Back then, everything had been safe. Now there was only danger.

But they were going home.

"How far is it?" Jack asked.

"Miles. Miles." His dad was changed. He hardly spoke, and sometimes he seemed to forget Jack was with him. He walked quickly, and Jack struggled to keep up. It was hard, because his legs were hurting. He still had the stick Old Man had made him, but the pain had settled into his bones now, deep inside from where he'd never be able to shake it. The pain was like a scar. It marked what he had done.

"I'm sorry, Dad," he said.

"Sorry?" His father didn't even turn around. "Come on. Out of the city."

"Why were you there?"

"Given up. I've given up."

"But not anymore?" Jack asked, pleading like a little boy.

His dad paused ahead of him, head tilted as if he was looking for something in the dusky light. He turned around, saw Jack, and his face broke into a grin. "Jack," he said, "I've found you."

"Yeah," Jack said. "Yeah."

❖

They spent that night in the same barn where Jack and Cass had rested and eaten earlier during the day. The remains of their fire was there, and Jack reignited it.

His father took over. Though he was quiet, Jack could see how experienced he was at surviving. He'd been out here on his own for years, looking for Jack, travelling, a Walker with a purpose that might have driven him mad. Jack wasn't sure about that yet. He wasn't certain quite what mad meant anymore.

Had Cass been mad to let himself go? Maybe. Or perhaps he had simply accepted the inevitable. Jack had heard a little about his lost daughter, Rose, but Cass hadn't opened up to him fully. Everyone had stories, most of those stories contained secrets, and he was sure there was plenty that Cass hadn't revealed. The truth had died with him. There were so many untold stories that would forever remain so, and that saddened Jack. Just another sign of how the world was moving on.

He watched his silent father preparing somewhere for them to sleep. He had a rucksack with him, and it seemed to contain far more than it should have. There were foil blankets, and a rolled up sweater to use as a pillow. He gave this to Jack.

He'd changed so much. Always slim, he was thinner than ever now, but also leaner, stronger than Jack had ever known. Where before his arms had been undefined, now they were knotted with muscle. He wore loose cargo trousers with many pockets, and a khaki t-shirt that did nothing to hide the strength he'd

Shifting of Veils 245

developed. *All that walking,* Jack thought. *All those miles travelled, looking for me.*

"You're looking well, Dad," he said.

He patted his stomach and smiled at his son, then rifled through his rucksack some more. He'd hardly spoken.

"I'm sorry," Jack said. "Dad, I'm sorry for leaving you on the ferry. Sorry I didn't tell you I was going. I followed Lucy, she was changing and I didn't want her to go, thought she could stay with us and we could look after her. Then this mad woman caught me, pretended she was looking after me when all the time she was... well, fattening me up. And when I finally got back to the beach I was hurt, and I was in time to see the end of the battle there. Were-things dead all across the sand. And some of those from the boat, too, I think. I was desperate. Wanting to find you. But I was bleeding so much, Lucy had saved me and died doing it, but I was hurt, so much blood, so much pain. And then I saw the boat."

His father pulled something from the bag and examined it. In the darkness Jack couldn't quite see what it was. Then he closed the bag, lay down close to the fire, and grew silent and still.

"Dad?" Jack asked. "Please?"

"Sleep," his dad said. "Long way to go. You need rest. Sleep." And he said no more.

Jack sat where he was for a while, aching to talk more with the father he had missed for so long. There was so much to say.

He thought he'd never sleep, but the exertions of the past days caught up with him. He dreamed of his mother and sister, so clearly that they might actually have been there. For the first time in his life he experienced a lucid dream, in which he knew he was dreaming and relished every moment. He spoke with his lost loved ones and shared his love with them. And when he next heard his father's voice and rose from his dream, it felt as if they were all together again.

"I never let myself believe you were dead," his dad said. He was sitting up next to Jack, one hand on his son's shoulder. It was still night, and the fire had burned down to glowing embers. Something cried out in the darkness, distant and haunting. "I couldn't. If I did, then there'd be nothing left, and I'd already lost everything else."

Jack sat up and huddled in to his father, sharing warmth. The man's hand clasped him close. Jack began to weep, the tears of a scared little boy being comforted, protected by his father. But he cried silently, because he didn't want to disturb whatever it was his dad had to say.

"When you left the ferry I was bereft. I wanted to go after you, but the others persuaded me to stay back. I so regret that now. I might have found you. But on the other hand, we might have both ended up dead. So I stayed, and when the attack came we thought we were prepared. But we were wrong, and most of the others died. When dawn came, only Elizabeth and I were still alive, and we took a boat and sailed away from the beach. But she soon left me alone. She was hiding an injury, and she died. I pushed her overboard. She floated with me for a while—a few hours, maybe—then I didn't see her again. I landed two days later, a long way north. And I started looking for you."

"We've wasted so much time," Jack said through his tears.

"Yes. No more time to waste. We're together again, now. All of us."

◈

Next morning, Jack told his father there was somewhere he had to go. As they walked he explained to him about the church and those people he'd lived with for so long. He felt he owed them the news that he'd found what he was looking for. "It'll give them hope," he said. "Because although they live day by day, their hope has long gone."

But when they reached the church again, hope was lost.

It was a blazing hot, still day. Buzzards circled high overhead, and an abundance of smaller birds drifted across the fields and

Shifting of Veils

sang from the undergrowth bordering the narrow lane. The church stood up on the hillside overlooking the landscape, and it looked like somewhere new. Although Jack had been there for years, right then he could conjure very few memories of the place. No washing hung out to dry, nothing moved. The gravestones cast short shadows. As they approached, Jack shielded his eyes and looked up to the bell tower. The grilles remained firmly fixed on the narrow windows up there, and he couldn't tell whether or not anyone was watching them.

"Old Man?" he shouted. "Jean?" No response.

"Old Man?" his dad said, chuckling softly.

"He isn't even that old," Jack said. They moved closer. Moments after he saw the first sign of movement up in the tower, the shotgun blasted out.

Jack fell to the left, his father to the right, burrowing into the hedges on either side of the road. They looked at each other wide-eyed, nodded that they were both all right. They were probably too far away for the shotgun to have any real effect, but it was still a shock. Jack had never been shot at before.

"It's me, Jack!" he shouted.

The shotgun fired again. Jack heard the patter and spit of pellets hammering down through the leaves and across the road surface, and several stung his arm and shoulder. There was no blood, but he knew he'd have bruises.

"Nice friends you have," his dad said.

Jack shook his head. What could have happened? He pushed from the hedge a little and sneaked a look. One of the grilles up in the tower had been pulled away now, and he saw movement in the opening. The sun was shining directly on that face of the tower, and Jack recognised Bob's bald pate.

"Bob! It's me, Jack!" He stood, arms held out by his sides, and started walking forward.

"Jack!" his dad said.

"It's okay, when he sees me he'll—"

Bob raised the gun again, and Jack leapt sideways. Another blast, and more pellets hammered down all around him.

"Bloody hell!" Jack shouted. "Old Man? Lady Day? Jean?" But there was only silence.

"Let's leave," his dad said.

"I want to know what's happened."

"For all you know he's gone mad and shot them all! Come on. Long way to go, Son."

Jack smiled and almost went. But he still needed to know. "You go back down the lane," he said. "I'm going to creep closer, see if I can see anything."

His dad sighed.

"Please, Dad?" It felt good using that word again.

When his father broke cover and ran back along the lane, Jack pushed carefully through the thick hedge, wincing as thorns stabbed through his clothing in many places. On the other side he kept low and close to the hedge and moved slowly forward. He was shielded from the bell tower here, just, but he didn't want to take any chances. The closer he went to the church, the more effective a shotgun blast could be.

Bob? Could he really have killed them? Jack couldn't see it. Silent and strange he might have been, but he'd never shown any signs of being violent. And Old Man could look after himself.

As Jack neared the low wall surrounding the graveyard, he saw the three new graves. They'd been dug close to the church. Each one had a wooden stake at its head, upon which had been fixed an item of the dead person's clothing—Old Man's hat, Jean's coat, one of Lady Day's boots.

"Oh, no," Jack said. He wanted to go closer, but at the same time he wanted to flee. He needed to know what had happened here, but he didn't want to risk everything now that he had found something worth living for again. Prevaricating over what to do, he only knew Bob was behind him when he heard the sound of metal on stone.

The silent man was leaning over the graveyard wall, shotgun propped on the stone and aiming down at Jack. His eyes were wide and red from crying. Jack could see blisters on his hands, probably from where he'd dug the graves.

"Bob," Jack said. His heart hammered, blood pulsed in his ears. The shotgun barrels looked very big and dark. "What happened?"

Bob's face tensed, his lips pressed together. His eyes began to water.

"What did you do?"

Bob took in a sharp breath, lifted the gun and pressed it to his shoulder. He waved it, indicating the fields and lane with a nod of his head.

"I can't just leave," Jack said.

Bob repeated the gesture. He shifted the aim of the shotgun from Jack's face to his leg, and somehow that made it seem more serious.

"Okay," Jack said, standing slowly and backing away. He looked from Bob to the fresh graves and back again, wondering at the work required to dig three person-sized holes. Bob's clothing was covered in mud. Tears streaked his grubby face.

"I found my father, and you could come with us," Jack said softly.

Bob opened his mouth and let out a tortured, grief-filled whine. Then he pulled the trigger.

Grass and mud kicked up several feet from Jack, and he turned and ran. At any moment he expected another shot and a thump in the back, but all he heard was Bob's strange, tortured cries.

He ran until he reached an easier way into the lane, and then he sprinted and met his father coming from the other direction.

"I'm okay," Jack said. "I'm fine. But..."

"We should go," his dad said. "We really should go home, Jackie."

"Home," Jack said. It was such a strange idea that he wasn't sure it would ever make sense.

◈

They found two bikes by the side of the road. Jack thought it was a bad idea, but his dad discovered a hand pump fixed to one of the bike's crossbars, and he pumped up the tyres. They stayed up. The brakes were seized and frames mostly rusted, but his dad giggled with delight as he wobbled along the bumpy road.

"Dad..." Jack said. They'd never be able to ride them for long. The roads were too broken up, hedges too overgrown in places. But he could not deny the joy on his dad's face.

"Jackie! Let's go for a ride!"

Jack smiled as the memory manifested. He and his dad used to do a lot of riding around Tall Stennington. Mandy had never been bothered with cycling, and his mum always used to say, *I'll leave it to you boys.* So it became their thing, him and his dad. Pack a rucksack with food and drinks, lather on the sun cream, check the tyres, and off they'd go, sometimes for several hours. They'd always come home hungry, and there would always been sore red patches on Jack's arms or legs which he'd missed with the sun cream. Later that night the stinging pain would be a sweet reminder of the great day they'd had. They found places on their bike rides that Jack never saw again, and as a kid he'd half-believed that bikes took you different places.

Every boy should ride a bike, his dad had said back then. And now Jack agreed with him.

He jumped onto the old bike leaning against the hedge, and after a few wobbly, hesitant turns of the pedal he was away.

"Come on, Jackie!" his dad called again. "Let's go for a ride!"

"Yeah!" Jack replied, whooping. Maybe they'd find somewhere unknown.

❖

As it turned out, the bikes were a pleasure, and the roads were easier going than Jack had thought. They were mountain bikes with decent gearing and chunky tyres, and they could manage most of what confronted them. Those times when the roads were too overgrown or broken, they carried the bikes across fields and through fledgling woodland, where saplings already

Shifting of Veils

reached their shoulders. His dad told him that much of Britain had once been woodland, and it seemed the trees were returning.

At night they made small fires, hunted, ate, and talked about their fears.

Jack was afraid that his leaving the church had been the catalyst for whatever had happened there. Perhaps it had been a change that no one he'd left behind could accept. Whether Bob had killed the others or not, Jack couldn't shake the idea that he had been the cause of those three fresh graves in that old churchyard.

Naming these fears helped him confront them, and talking them through with his father lessened some of the guilt.

"You can't blame yourself for someone else's actions," his dad said. "And whatever happened there, no one can use your leaving as a reason."

"But maybe I was the centre without even knowing it," Jack said. "Old Man was strong, but it was finding me that gave him reason to settle. Jean tried to mother me. Lady Day... I don't know about her. Maybe I kept things together, and my leaving caused it to all unravel."

"Maybe," his dad said, surprising Jack with the brutal honesty. "But if you hadn't left, maybe you'd be in grave number four. Ever thought of that?" His dad's eyes had watered at the thought. Jack imagined his father sitting in the Swan trying to recapture some precious moment from the past, looking up, and seeing the confused, frightened echo of his newly dead son.

"No," Jack said. "I hadn't thought of that."

"We're alive, together," his dad said. "It's sad that your friends died. But everything's sad, now. Everything."

The fire burned down, embers slowly dying out as night fell. As Jack watched them go, the heat of his guilt also cooled.

In those nights beneath the stars they also discussed their other fears. His dad told him of strange sights he had seen, and one time almost a year before when a group of people had followed him everywhere he went for several days, trying to worship him, creating in him someone on which to pin their hopes. "They were mad, and it made me sad," he said. "Sometimes I'm afraid they'll find me again."

Jack told the tale of the woman in the caravan. His dad frowned, shaking his head when Jack asked if he recognised the description. Jack worried that she would follow them, hunt them when full moon returned. She'd told him she had their scent.

The night listened to their fears. They helped each other face them. Knowing there was little they could do to counter them, sharing was the next best thing.

◈

Six days later they reached home. They had lived there as a family until a zombie had tried to break into their house, and then they'd left and had not returned since. Now they were back and the house was a ruin. There were signs that someone else had lived there for a while—some of their old furniture was piled outside, and there were two overgrown graves in the garden—but there had been a blaze, and half of the roof had collapsed down into the upstairs area. The windows were broken, downstairs rooms gutted by fire, and there was little there that might have brought comfort.

They dropped the bikes in the overgrown driveway. Jack's dad sat and cried for a little while, and Jack knelt and hugged him close. They were quiet tears, and never for a moment did he doubt his father's true strength.

Though the house was a ruin and the garden overgrown, floods of memories came to Jack. Most of them were good, and the ones that struck him the hardest were the very simplest recollections. His mother sitting in a garden chair over there, a cup of tea on the ground by her feet and a magazine in her lap. His sister lying on the lawn trying to get a tan. His dad painting the fence that bordered part of the garden, stripped to shorts in the sunlight and showing his hairy back. *You'll be like this one day*, his dad says as Jack teases him for looking like a bear.

His mother and sister no longer appeared to him, because they were already there. The more he remembered them in rich, vivid memories, the more they came to life again, and they were almost as together as they had ever been. Only almost. But it was close enough.

"We'll find somewhere else," Jack said, helping his dad to his feet.

"Yes," his dad said. "Somewhere new. But it doesn't matter. Home is where your family is, right Jackie?"

"Right," Jack said. He looked up at what was left of his childhood bedroom window, and remembered the moment when everything had changed and he'd started to grow up.

The night when something tried to break into the house.

THE END

TIM LEBBON is a New York Times-bestselling writer from South Wales. He's had over thirty novels published to date, as well as hundreds of novellas and short stories. His latest novel is the thriller *The Hunt*, and other recent releases include *The Silence* and *Alien: Out of the Shadows*. He has won four British Fantasy Awards, a Bram Stoker Award, and a Scribe Award, and has been a finalist for World Fantasy, International Horror Guild and Shirley Jackson Awards. Future books include *The Rage War* (an Alien/Predator trilogy), and the *Relics* trilogy from Titan.

The movie of his story *Pay the Ghost*, starring Nicolas Cage, is out now, and other projects in development include *Playtime* (an original script with Stephen Volk), spooky animated kids' film *My Haunted House*, *The Hunt*, *Exorcising Angels* (based on a novella with Simon Clark), and a TV Series proposal of *The Silence*.

Find out more about Tim at his website:

www.timlebbon.net